CALLIE ANDERSON

Copyright © 2017 Callie Anderson
All rights reserved.

No part of this book may reproduced or transmitted in any form or by any means, electronic or mechanical, including photocopying, recording, or by any information storage and retrieval system without the written permission of the author, except for the use of brief quotations in a book review.

This book is a work of fiction. Names, characters, places, and incidents are either the products of the author's imagination or are used fictitiously. Any resemblance to actual persons, living or dead, events, or locales is entirely coincidental.

To my brother and sister.
Thanks for always picking on me, jerks!

BE FEARLESS & BE EXTRAORDINARY

STAY CONNECTED

www.CallieAndersonAuthor.com
www.facebook.com/AuthorCallieAnderson
Twitter.com/AuthorCallieA
Instagram.com/AuthorCallieAnderson
Email: AuthorCallieAnderson@gmail.com

Chapter One

PAST

The thunder in the distance startled me out of my slumber, bellowing its loud rumble through my room. I wiped the sleep off my face and dragged myself out of bed. Padding my feet across the worn carpet, I made my way toward the window my mother had left cracked open. The afternoon had been muggy but the night skies held a crisp breeze.

I glanced up at the cloudless, star-scattered sky. It was beautiful, but it left the noise that woke me a mystery. It never thundered in Prescott. Well, not this time of year, at least.

My small hands pressed against the glass pane, pushing the window completely open. I stared up at the sky, mesmerized by the full moon and blinking stars. We didn't get many nights like these, so I soaked it in for a moment only to be startled by the sound of a door slamming. The offending racket pulled my gaze away from the night's beauty and to the back of the house next door.

I poked my head out the window to get a better look. Our neighbors had moved in three days ago but I had yet to meet anyone. My eyes followed a shadow from the back door to the edge of the deck. The moonlight illuminated a young man as he sat with his back against the railing, hugging his knees with his head rested on them. It looked as though his shoulders were shaking.

"That's it!" a deep voice roared from inside the house. "How many times do I have to fucking remind you!"

I squeezed my eyes shut and startled when the echo of a slap followed the man's bellow of rage. Inching over the windowsill, I spotted the man who was yelling in the hallway—a gentleman not much older than my father—berating a woman I assumed was his wife. My heart ached for her as she sobbed.

When the air went silent, I leaned even further out the window. I should have gone back to bed. I should have closed my windows. But instead, I found myself calling out to the boy on the porch.

"Psst," I whispered. The boy stopped shaking and looked back at his house. "Hey," I said a little louder. "Up here!" He looked up toward my window. "Are you okay?"

He wiped his hands across his face, and I knew he had been crying. "It's almost over," he said.

It took me a few seconds to understand what he meant. His sadness called to me, and I knew I needed to help him.

"Do you want to come up?" The words slipped out of my mouth. Never had I snuck a boy into my room. My mother would have punished me for the rest of my life. I didn't have friends; not for lack of trying, but my mother's constant need for perfection drove any kind of social life to the ground.

He was a potential friend.

A friend in need at that.

He rose to his feet and ran over to my house. He jumped up on the deck railing, climbed on the extending roof of the first floor and crawled over to my window. Startled by his climbing skills, I stepped back as he made his way into my room.

"Hi," he whispered.

Unable to form a sentence, I just stood there and stared at

him. It was dark but I could make out his dark hair and lanky body. He was taller than me by a few inches but he looked to be around my age.

"I'm Ethan," he continued.

"Leslie," I whispered as I shifted my weight from one foot to the other. Ethan scanned my room and I immediately felt self-conscious over all the girly things I had. The pink walls, the long mirrors my mother hung so I could scrutinize my every move as I rehearsed my routine. There were pictures of ballerinas scattered around the room and I had hung butterflies on the wall. I loved my overly girly room, but as he walked around examining everything, it all felt too childish. Too pink.

"Are you okay?" I asked again, looking back toward his house.

He sighed and bowed his head. "It's usually not this bad."

Crap. Was this something his father did most nights?

"I'm sorry." I didn't know what else to say. "Does he do it often?"

Ethan looked down to the floor and nodded. "Sometimes he drinks even more than usual and passes out before his anger kicks in." He shrugged and looked up at me. His eyes locked with mine and a shiver ran up my spine. Never had I seen my father intoxicated let alone abuse my mother.

I didn't know if it was the sadness I saw in his eyes or the fact I was desperate for a real friend, but I felt a need to protect Ethan. I walked over to my bed, grabbed my extra pillow and my throw blanket, and dropped them on the rug. "You can always stay here if you want."

"Thanks," he said, and for a split second, I saw a glimpse of gratitude in his light eyes. Ethan curled up on the rug and pulled the blanket over him.

I climbed back to my bed and slid under the covers.

"Goodnight, Ethan."

"Goodnight, Leslie."

I didn't know it then. But Ethan would be the first boy I ever loved and the first one to break my heart.

CALLIE ANDERSON

Chapter Two

PRESENT

My hands grasp the white tray and place it back on the cart as I make my way out of the TSA line. The officer gives me a kind smile as he hands me back my boarding pass and ID.

"Arizona. Beautiful state. Are you visiting for business or pleasure?"

"Neither," I reply as I collect my things.

"Well, have a nice trip. Merry Christmas." He waves me off and I'm more than happy to comply. I don't need his joyful holiday greeting. I'm too proud to accept it, really. There hasn't been anything joyful in my life for a few years now.

Shoving the papers back inside my purse, I slide my feet into my shoes and continue my walk through LAX. Oblivious to the world around me, I drag my feet toward my gate. Each step feels slower than the last but I know it's all in my head. It's the fear of going back home. The fear of seeing my mother again after so many years without contact. It's the uncertainty of the damage my father might have suffered from his heart attack.

It was odd to see my mother's name on the screen when she called. I thought she was calling to wish me a merry Christmas, but the notion of a joyful greeting was washed away when realization set in. She would never call to wish me anything. Not when I was such a disappointment to her.

The sea of people move past me, and I push the daunting thoughts out of my head. I promised my mother I would be on the first flight out. I figured no one would be traveling on Christmas Eve, but I was mistaken. The airport is flooded with bodies, everyone eager to reach their destination. Dragging my carry-on behind me, I reach my gate, doubting my decision to return home but knowing I really have no choice. With an hour to spare, I find an empty seat to wait and take out my headphones from my purse. It has been years since I've listened to anything classical. It's funny how everything can change in a split second.

I changed.

My taste in music, the life I live. It was never what my parents envisioned for me.

Most of my life, I was my mother's daughter.

A dancer.

She set a goal for me: Juilliard. They only took the best, and I was to study there, so I was taught to love ballet.

It didn't matter what I wanted. I was to eat, sleep, and breathe it.

It consumed my schedule. I spent twenty hours a week rehearsing, and by the age of twelve my toes were permanently taped together. I spent every season competing until my mother realized it was a waste of time to compete against people who weren't up to my caliber. It wasn't beneficial to drive around Arizona competing in local, regional, and national talent competitions.

My mother's dreams became my aspirations; I began to believe they were my dreams as well until Ethan moved in next door.

My ankle throbs at the mere thought of him, and I wiggle my foot, flexing the tight muscle. It's a dull pain that never goes away. Doctors tell me it's chronic pain, but I know it's a reminder of how falling in love destroyed me.

It has been eight years since the last time I saw him; for all I know he has moved on with his life. I know I have. Or tried my hardest to. I've learned to let go of the past and focus on the future. Life is precious; my best friend Emilia taught me that. There is no point in dwelling on the small stuff.

But Ethan wasn't small. Oh, God, not at all. He was the "what if" in my life.

What if it had worked out between us?

What if it he had followed me?

What if I never broke my ankle?

I told myself what we shared was a lie, a figment of my imagination.

But what I felt for him was an all-consuming, pure and innocent first love. The kind you never forget. The kind of love you store in a locked box, making sure you throw away the key and then toss into the deepest end of the ocean. It's a love that haunts you. It's what you compare everything too.

I inhale slowly and then let out a cool, calming breath, forcing myself once again to shut out thoughts of Ethan and the life that will never be. Nervously, I lace a tendril of hair around my fingers and twirl it. I sit for forty-three minutes completely lost in my thoughts as I listen to the playlist my mother made for me once upon a time. Her favorite Bach composition comes on and I'm transported to another time.

My mother.

I sigh and shake my head. She loves me, that much I know, but it never has been a traditional motherly love. It's been in her own Darlene way. She didn't kiss my boo-boos or make me soup when I was sick. No, not Darlene. She made me dance, rain or shine.

"Be better," she would say. "Be extraordinary. Prima ballerinas don't have the luxury of taking days off. Toughen up." If my toes weren't bleeding, it meant I wasn't pushing myself.

"Juilliard won't even consider you if your Allegro isn't perfect. Again!"

I wasn't allowed sick days because regardless of how I felt, I had to dance. I didn't have friends because I didn't have time for friendships. The girls at my school asked me over for a play date, but I had a regimen. After a while they stopped asking.

Ballet.

It was all I was. It was what my mother made me.

Until Ethan.

He was the boy who crawled through my window and captured my heart.

Anger and hatred boils through my veins as the hurt of his betrayal threatens to resurface. I ball my hands into fists and concentrate on the music blaring in my ears, inhaling and exhaling methodically until my heart rate is at a normal level. But I can't drown out the noise. Ethan and my mother are the only two on my mind.

I push off my chair and grasp the handle to my carry-on. "Screw it," I mutter. There's no way I can face her. Not when the sheer thought of her reminds me of my love for him. I maneuver around the aisle of connected chairs, apologizing as I hurry out of the sea of people waiting for their flight, when I hear the flight attendant make an announcement over the speaker.

"Good evening, ladies and gentlemen. We are now boarding Flight 437 to Phoenix, Arizona."

My feet stop short. I pull out my boarding pass.

Your mother can't control you anymore, and Ethan has moved on, so his father can't hurt you anymore, either.

The hour and twenty-minute plane ride from LAX to Phoenix consists of mild anxiety attacks and much-needed booze that costs me a small fortune. The intoxication I worked on vanishes the second our descent from the sky ends and our wheels touch the ground.

Inhaling all the air my lungs can take, I walk out of the plane with my heart racing in my chest. My feet push against the granite airport floors as I follow behind the eager passengers who make their way to baggage claim. Most passengers are greeted by family and friends and hugs and warm wishes are exchanged, but I don't bother to look for my mother. Picking someone up at the airport is beneath her.

I stroll over to the carousel to retrieve my lone bag from the conveyer belt and walk toward the taxi line. Within a short period of time I'm seated in the back of the car service I hired to drive me to Prescott. My head rests on the leather seat when my phone rings inside my purse. Pulling it out, Chloe's name appears on the display. Sliding my finger across the screen, I answer the call.

"Hello?"

"Merry Christmas, lover," Chloe sings, and even though she tries to hide it I can still hear the East Coast accent. She hates when people ask her where in Long Island she grew up in.

"Merry indeed," I joke, my eyes glued to the snowcapped peaks just visible in the distance. Chloe was the first friend I made when I moved to Chicago. We shared a cubicle at work, and hit it off right away. She was my tour guide as I familiarized myself with the city I now call home. She also helped me prepare for my first Midwestern winter. Never had I experienced frigid temperatures like that before. I grew up in Arizona. Prescott, to be exact. When it did snow, it was light, and quickly melted when the sun rose on the horizon. I wasn't prepared for the snow a blizzard could bring.

"How's LA? I can't believe you're making me go to Rae's Christmas Eve dinner today without you," she complains.

"Actually . . . I'm not in LA anymore." I shift my neck from side to side in an attempt to crack it. The non-stop traveling is catching up with my body not to mention I still have another hour on the road before I arrive at the hospital. "I'm in Arizona."

"Oh, fun! What for?"

"My father had a heart attack. My mother called me earlier to let me know, and I hopped on the first plane I could get."

Chloe gasps. "Oh, my God! I'm so sorry, Les. Is he okay?"

Closing my eyes, I pray for this to be some kind of a twisted life lesson in which I learn that I need to call my family more often and nothing more. "I don't know. I'm headed to the hospital now."

"Oh, sweetie, keep me posted, okay?"

"Of course."

"And if you need anything, please let me know."

"Thanks, Chloe. Merry Christmas."

I hang up the phone and slide it back into my purse. Glancing over at the rearview mirror, I spot the driver looking at me. His dark brown almond shaped eyes seem apologetic and I find solace in them.

Even if for a brief second.

Wheeling my luggage and carry-on behind me, I walk inside Freeman Hospital Center. My heart rate is humming in my ears but I keep my shoulders straight. I stop when I approach the receptionist and smile at her.

"Hi, I'm here to see my father, Lawrence Sutton."

She taps her manicured nails against the keyboard, humming to the Christmas music softly playing in the background. She pulls her gaze away from the screen and looks up at me. "He's in room 415." She hands me a visitor's pass. "The elevators are around the corner. You can leave your luggage here with me if you don't feel like carrying it around the hospital."

"Thank you," I say with relief and shove my suitcase behind her desk. I grasp the visitor's pass and make my way toward the elevator. The farther I walk inside the hospital, the more poignant the sterile scent is. My stomach churns and I grow nauseous. Simultaneously, my ankle begins to ache and I'm reminded of a different time in this exact hospital. A time when I was the patient, crying uncontrollably when the doctor informed me dancing was forever out of the picture.

My dreams shattered.

My destiny destroyed.

A cruel twist in my fate.

BROKEN DREAMS

I drill the button to the fourth floor repeatedly, willing the elevator to move faster. A panic attack is brewing inside me just as the doors slide open, and I gasp for air, my hands pressed to my chest as I try to calm myself. When the vertigo passes, I allow myself a few calming breaths before I walk into my father's room.

My mom sits with her back facing the door, and I take the moment to look at my dad. A tube is down his throat and he is connected to a few machines. He looks frail, nothing like the father I left behind.

I was always Daddy's little girl, or at least up until the accident. After that I didn't want to be anything. Afterward, it felt as if I didn't belong anymore; as though my parents were complete strangers. The pride and joy that shone through their eyes had vanished.

When I broke my ankle, all the years of training went down the drain, and my mother and I found ourselves with nothing in common. My whole life, my mother worked vigorously to make me a better dancer. To train harder, be better, then anyone else. A better version of her. She had me in the studio until dinnertime six days a week, and then all of a sudden that was not part of my life anymore. And once I was damaged goods, she was gone.

For years, all I had with my dad was one hour a day. One hour each day when it was just him and I, watching whatever game was on the television. I cherished those sixty minutes. Even he was lost after the accident. He tried to do what was right, but it only hurt our relationship more.

I was lost after I broke my ankle. For months I lay in the hospital bed depressed and alone. But he helped me find a way out. Recovery was grueling, but I learned not to quit, and started putting my broken pieces back together all alone. I enrolled in UCLA, moved out to Los Angeles, where I graduated college, accepted a job offer in Chicago and never looked back.

Tears well in my eyes and my vision blurs as the memories flow through my mind. I swallow every painful emotion and take a step through the door. Clearing my throat, I walk further into the room. My father's hand is ice cold when I grasp it, and a tear drops down my cheek as I close my eyes.

"I'm surprised you're here so soon." My mother's voice pierces the silence.

"Hello, Mother."

I find the courage to look over at her. Darlene is sitting in the recliner with a *Pointe* magazine resting on her lap. Her shoulders are back and as always, her posture is perfect. Her blonde hair is tied in a low bun like it had always been every day of her life. Without pulling her gaze away from the article, she speaks. "You've gained weight."

"It's been eight years, Mother. Of course, I've gained weight."

She slowly closes the magazine and looks up at me fully. Her green eyes are full of disproval when they meet mine. "It's sloppy weight, Leslie. You've let yourself go. Clearly."

"Mom." I pinch the bridge of my nose. "It's Christmas Eve. I've been traveling for what feels like a lifetime to get here. My father, *your husband*, is lying on a bed with tubes down his throat and the first thing out of your mouth is a snide remark about my weight?" I shake my head and run my hand through my long brown locks. "You haven't seen me in eight years and this is how you're going to greet me?"

"Don't cry, Leslie. It will give you wrinkles. Besides, you're the one who left and never looked back. After all my hard work the least you could have done was maintain an appropriate weight. Don't think a man is going to love the extra love handles."

"Mom." My voice is louder than acceptable for a hospital. "I'm not fat. I do spinning and yoga; I eat healthy and I stay active. Occasionally, I enjoy a bacon cheeseburger with fries, and tequila is my best friend. I also believe if I eat a pint of ice cream and no one is watching the calories don't exist. So please get off my back."

My mother is just being . . . Darlene. If I'm not rail thin with my ribcage visible, she considers me fat. This is how she shows she cares. Or at least that's what I tell myself.

"Don't you dare make this about you. Your father is lying there completely helpless." I sigh dramatically and grit my teeth so I don't lose it.

A nurse, no taller than five feet with jet-black hair walks in, her eyes scan the room. "Is everything okay?" she asks with a hint of concern in her voice. I know she overheard me and my mother.

I swallow back the anger toward my mother. *I never learn with her.* "I'm sorry. I'm his daughter. I just arrived. Do you have an update?"

She moves to my dad's bedside and peers up at the screens before checking his chart. "I'm sorry, unfortunately it will be best if you talk to one of his doctors so they can answer any questions you may have. I'll have a resident come in here and talk to you." She gives me a kind smile.

"Thank you." I glance down at my father and hold his hand tighter.

The nurse walks toward the door and stops. "Also," she adds and I look over at her, "we can only have one family member spend the night in the room."

"I understand," my mother replies.

When she is out of the room, I turn to face my mother. "After we speak to the doctor why don't you head home? I can stay here with him."

"You must have lost your mind." Her voice is condescending. "I'm not leaving his side. Besides, I don't drive anymore."

"Okay..." This is news to me. "How did you get here?"

"I came in the ambulance. I had Nora's youngest son drive the car over. It's in the garage."

Brushing my hand through my hair, I look back at my father. *How did this happen?* My hand remains gripping his until a doctor walks into the room. His dark blue scrubs are hidden under his white lab coat. He is younger than I would have expected. There is no peppering in his short brown hair. His smile is bright and wide when he approaches.

"Good evening, I'm Dr. Perkins. I understand you want an update on your father?"

I nod, unable to speak as the fear of what he is about to say consumes me.

"Your father suffered a STEMI heart attack, which means his carotid artery is completely blocked and a large part of his heart can't receive blood. At the moment he is stable and we have him on blood thinners. Tomorrow morning we will prep him for surgery. We'll know more then."

"Okay," I whisper. "Thank you."

I stare back at my father while my mother talks briefly to the doctor. My father is young, in his early fifties, and he's always been healthy and active. How did he get to this stage? I realize then that it must have been well over three months since I last spoke to him. A new wave of tears crash over me and I bite back a sob. I can't stay here. I can't watch him like this. Turning to my mother, I wipe the tears from my eyes.

"Since, only one of us can stay, I think it's best I head home. Can I have the keys, please?" My voice cracks.

Darlene digs in her purse and hands me the keys to the Volvo. "It's on level two in the parking deck," she says without looking at me.

"Please call me if you need anything or if his stats change." I walk out of the room before she has a chance to respond.

The drive home is painless, the noise of the rubber tires rolling against the asphalt is soothing. My tears have subsided but the ache in my chest has intensified. I can't help but think that if I had called my father more often he wouldn't be in this situation. I know my thinking is unreasonable but the guilt eats me up.

The highway is clear, so I make it to my old neighborhood within thirty minutes. Heavy clouds are high in the sky, making the moon less visible. Snow threatens to fall due to the higher elevation.

"A white Christmas," I mutter as I pull onto my street. The block is dark, and the lamppost lights are dim, not offering much visibility. A few houses are decorated with twinkly lights and all of them look just as I remember, three-bedroom, center hall colonial with a two-car garage. Gripping the wheel, I turn into my parents' driveway and open the garage door. My head remains facing forward and I force my eyes to look anywhere but toward Ethan's home. Quickly, I turn off the car, close the garage door, and head inside the house, hoping no one spots me.

Once inside, I take my time walking from room to room. Not a single thing has changed since the last time I was here. Pictures of me performing are still scattered throughout the house. My mother was once very proud of her legacy.

My ankle throbs as I stop at the framed acceptance letter from Julliard. My hands gently run along the glass as I read the letter. It was everything I ever wanted, my get out of Prescott ticket. Lifting the frame off the nail in the wall, I walk over to the kitchen and place it in the pantry. There is no need to showcase that anymore.

A migraine begins to form in the back of my neck and I close the pantry door behind me and go in search of some ibuprofen. I feel lost and alone. But most of all I feel helpless. I ran away from home. I ran away from a life I didn't want anymore. Being back here awakens so many emotions I can't deal with all at once.

Needing something stronger to knock some sense into me, I head over to the wet bar adjacent to the kitchen and find a bottle of tequila. With eager hands I twist off the top and chug on the light amber liquid.

The warmth of the agave alcohol swims through my body. I make my way up the stairs toward my bedroom. My hand laces around the bottle, giving me the courage I lack to enter my bedroom.

I don't flick the light on, nor do I look at my belongings. There is no need to look at the dresser that is pushed against one wall, my bookcase, or the cut outs I had pinned on my memory board. I know it's filled with pictures and other small trinkets I left behind. Instead, I sit on the bed and take another swig of tequila, remembering all the times Ethan climbed through my bedroom window.

CALLIE ANDERSON

Chapter Three

PAST

When I woke up the next morning, he was gone. I had awoken in a panic, worried that my mother would barge into my room and see a boy sleeping on my rug. But as I sprang from the mattress, I realized he was no longer there. I ran to the window and lifted it open. There was no sign of Ethan. At first, I thought I imagined the entire thing. That it was lack of sleep mixed with a wild dream.

I spent the day convinced that it was all a dream, until that night a soft rock tapped against my bedroom window. I was sitting on my bed, re-reading the same paragraph in the most recent Harry Potter book over and over. I couldn't focus. My eyes kept looking at the glass waiting for something to change. When the rock hit the glass, I nearly screamed. I hopped off the bed and opened the window, only to be greeted by his infectious smile. My heart did something it had never done before. I felt dizzy and my hands began to sweat.

"Hey," he whispered, and my stomach twisted at the sound of his voice.

I could see the family room light was still on from the way it lit up my back yard, which meant my father was still watching TV. "Shh." I motioned for him to come up.

Like he had done the night before, he ran, jumped on the railing of the deck, and pulled himself up on the extended room over the den.

Running to my bedroom door, I closed it and pulled my chair against it. It wasn't locked but it would warn us if my mother decided to come in.

"Hey," Ethan whispered. His hand brushed his soft brown hair away from his eyes. With the bedroom light on I could finally see his face. He was older than me, maybe by a year or so. I was turning ten at the end of August. His eyes were a mix of green and hazel swirled together in perfect harmony. He was the most beautiful boy I had ever seen.

"Leslie?" Ethan said, his eyes still glued on mine. "Are you going to scream?"

The nausea in my stomach and the rapid heartbeat in my chest made it impossible to breathe. Slowly I shook my head. "No, Ethan." I ignored the way his name slipped from my mouth in the most perfect tone. "I thought I made you up." I confessed.

"Are you known for making up imaginary boys who crawl in through your window?" He smiled at me, and in that moment I promised myself that I would always be funny around him so I could stare at his smile.

I scoffed and nervously began to twirl my hair. What were these thoughts that were consuming my ability to think normally? "It's not that. When I woke up this morning, you were gone and I wasn't sure if I dreamed up the whole thing."

Ethan chuckled and walked around my room like he had the previous night. This time, though, the lights were on and he could actually see the things that were scattered around. He took his time looking at the pictures I had on top of my dresser, and the ballet magazines. "You like to dance?" he asked as he lifted a picture of me from my first dance recital. I was three years old. My mother said she knew I was talented and I had a bright future ahead of me from a tender age.

Marching over to him, I yanked the photo away. "I don't like it. I live it. It's who I am." I said just like my mother had taught me.

"You're a ballerina? Is that even a real thing?"

"Yes and yes." I crossed my arms over my chest, feeling defensive.

"I'm only teasing you." Ethan ran his hand over my white furniture. "I actually came here to thank you."

"Oh." I sat on my bed. He continued to pace my room, his eyes roaming over the stack of CDs and books sitting on my bookcase.

"No one has ever done something like that for me before." He pulled his gaze away from the stacks of CDs and looked over at me. His eyes were hooded, and though I had seen a teasing glint before, this time I saw pain.

Nervously, I brushed my hair behind my ears and looked down at the carpet. "It was nothing, really." I didn't want to show him pity. He didn't deserve that. "You know . . ." I paused until I found the courage to look up at him. "My window will always be open for you. If you ever need to get away, or if it gets too bad in there, you can always come here."

"Thanks," he whispered. "No one has ever been this nice to me before."

"I'm sorry." I didn't know what else to say. "Can you get some help? Maybe you and your mother can go to the cops?"

Ethan chuckled and sat next to me on my bed. My cheeks warmed from his proximity. "My name is Ethan Prescott. Like the town we live in. My father owns everything and everyone. He's a horrible man who runs this city. No one would ever believe us."

"What about running away?" The second the words were out of my mouth I regretted them. If he ran away, I would never see him again.

"I've thought about it, but I can't leave my mom and my brother with that monster. He would make them pay for my actions."

"Does he hit you?" My voice was barely a whisper.

"Sometimes, but I know what ticks him off so I stay away. He doesn't touch my little brother anymore, either." Ethan answered. "Charlie's different from most kids. He's special and requires more attention. I could never run away and leave him all alone."

"I'm sorry."

"It's okay. We've been through worse, and besides, now I have you." He looked into my eyes. "No one has ever shown me any kindness before." He reached across and cupped my hand in his. My heartbeat intensified and the only logical explanation was that I was having a heart attack. "I owe you big." A smile grew on his face, and I couldn't stop my cheeks from burning. His hand felt perfect against my skin. It was warm and soft and I knew if laced his fingers with mine it'd be a perfect match.

We sat like that for a few minutes. My neighbor. My first friend. I was deep in thought when my mother tapped against my bedroom door.

"Leslie?" she said and pushed against the door, but my chair temporarily blocked her from swinging it open. "Why is your door blocked?" Ethan and I sprang to our feet.

"Oh!" My heart rate sped up and I thought I'd be sick. "One second!" I called out frantically. Turning to Ethan, I mouthed the word. "Hide."

I cleared my throat and walked over to the door. I pushed my chair aside and pulled open the door. Darlene stood on the other side, a warm mug of tea in her hand.

"Yes?" I said.

"Why was your chair blocking the door?" Her gaze scanned the room. "Why do you look flushed? Are you not feeling well?" She reached out and rested her palm on my forehead. "You know you can't get sick. That will ruin the schedule for this month."

"I'm fine, Mom." I moved to the side and she dropped her hand. "I was . . . um, I was doing a few core exercises and needed the space."

A wide grin grew on my mother's face. "That's my girl, always so focused on the task at hand."

I nodded, afraid if I opened my mouth I would confess that somewhere in my room was a boy I desperately wanted to kiss.

"Don't stay up too late, sweetie. Tomorrow we have an early start," she added before she turned and headed down the hallway to her bedroom.

Closing the door behind me, I pressed my body flush against it. My breathing was irregular and a bead of sweat dripped down my back. "Ethan?" I said, my voice so low I doubted he could hear me. After replacing the chair in front of the door, I stepped further into the room.

His head popped in from the window and his beautiful smile greeted me. "Coast is clear?"

I nodded. "She's off to bed."

"What's the task?" he asked.

"What do you mean?"

"You told your mom that you were working out, and she said you were focused on the task at hand."

My nervous hand reached for my hair as I tried to calm my breathing. My heart pumped the adrenaline and lust through my blood. "I dance ballet. It's my life." Ethan's eyebrows furrowed and I realized I needed to explain. "My mother was a performer. She worked at the Lincoln Center in New York City in her early twenties. She met my father when he was in the city on a business trip. After a year of dating, my father asked my mother to marry him, and soon after that my mother found out she was expecting. A child meant she couldn't perform for a year or two, so she quit before they let her go. After I was born, she devoted her life to making me the best dancer. She opened her own studio and I dance there six days a week."

"Wow." Ethan stretched his hands overhead. "Do you even like it?"

"Yes," I defended my passion, but his question puzzled me. No one ever asked if I liked it. It was simply what I did. "I was made to be great." I walked over to the dresser and took the photograph of my mother and me at my first competition. "See?" I said and handed him the photo. "At the age of four I was a better dancer than most of the teenagers."

"That's your mom?" He asked admiring the picture.

"Yes, I look more like my dad. He has the darker hair and what not."

He chuckled. "Okay, Freckles." I squinted at him. "What? You do have freckles." His fingertip ran down my nose. "They're really cute."

My heart did a somersault in my chest. Turning toward my pillows, I began to strip my bed so Ethan couldn't see the warmth that ran across my face. "Are you staying or do you need to go home?" I asked, afraid to look over at him.

"I'm staying." His voice ran through my body like an electric current.

Unable to speak, I turned my light off and tossed his pillow on the ground. I slid under the covers and I watched as Ethan make a bed on the rug next to me.

"Goodnight, Freckles."

"Goodnight, Ethan."

I lay there for a few minutes, unable to speak. Unable to move. All I could hear was the rhythmic sound of our breathing.

"Leslie?" Ethan said after a few minutes had passed.

"Yeah?"

"Will you dance for me?"

"Maybe one day," I whispered and closed my eyes. One day I would do anything he asked.

Chapter Four

PRESENT

The sound of a door slamming wakes me from my deep slumber. My mouth is parched and my head is pounding. I'm still drunk, *or severely hungover*. Heels click against the wood floors, and my hands brush the sleep off my face, gathering my thoughts.

Where am I?

My vision is blurry and I realize I slept with my contacts in again. *Fuck.*

"Passed out hugging a bottle, Leslie? How ladylike of you." My mother's voice shoots through my ears and I wince. *I'm in my childhood bedroom.* The previous forty-eight hours flood through my mind, and I gasp, sitting up on the bed. With both hands, I try to hold my pounding head.

"How's Dad?"

My mother looks at me in a disapproving manner. Her hands cross at her chest and she purses her lips at me. "I called you," she says. "I called you seventeen times. I haven't seen you in almost eight years. Do you know how that feels? You left me, Leslie, after everything I did for you. You up and left me, and when I called you, you didn't answer."

"It took you eight years to call, Mom," I say with a hoarse voice and my eyes closed. "And I didn't leave you. I disappointed you by breaking my ankle and tossing all your hard work down the drain."

"That's beside the point. I called and you didn't answer. Not only is your father in the hospital but I was worried sick something happened to you, too." Her eyes cut through me.

"Is Dad okay?"

"They took him to surgery this morning. I took a cab here to get you." She flicks the light in my bedroom on. "Go shower; you reek. We need to get back to the hospital right away."

I groan from the bright florescent light as I stand and make my way out of my bedroom.

My mother is a creature of habit. Once she finds something that is up to her standards, she never looks for an alternative. The shower curtain is the same one she purchased ten years prior from Bed, Bath and Beyond. Her Chanel No 5 religiously sits in the same spot on her side of the vanity, and she's used the same shampoo for as long as I can remember. I'm nothing like my mother. I change the curtains in my bathroom every season. During the holidays it looks as if Santa lives in my bathroom. I use different shampoos all the time, and I most definitely don't wear fancy perfume.

Sighing at the differences between my mother and me, I undress and climb into the shower. The warm water slides down my body and washes away the grime and exhaustion from the previous day's travel and hospital visit. Not to mention it helps with the headache that was beginning to form due to lack of food and the consumption of alcohol.

Once I'm finished, dressed and proper, I walk down the stairs. My mother has also showered, and she holds a warm cup of coffee.

"I made a pot," she offers.

"Thank you," I answer.

When I pass her, I stop and look over my shoulder. "Merry Christmas, Mom."

"You too, Leslie. Go and get your coffee. We need to get back immediately."

The sun is still hidden beyond the horizon. As we're pulling out of the driveway, I hold my breath and focus my gaze anywhere but on Ethan's home. My mother notices my hesitation and clears her throat. She doesn't say anything until we're on the freeway.

"Have you spoken to him?" She doesn't move an inch.

"No," I reply.

"Since?"

Inhaling slowly, I try to steady my crazed heart rate. "Since I left for Los Angeles."

"Really?" Her voice increases an octave and I glance over at her.

"Yes, really." I let a few seconds pass before I ask, "Why?"

"Oh, it's nothing." She shakes her head. "He disappeared after you left. I figured he went after you. That's all."

He's gone. A wave of relief washes over me, I want to ask her where he went and where he is now, but I stop myself. The chance of seeing him again has vanished. The sobering realization brings sadness to my heart and a cold shiver up my body. He's moved on with his life, and what we once shared disappeared right along with him. The secrets we held, the love we shared, have all dissipated.

I moved on, damn it. The best I could at least. I forced myself to forget about him the second I got to Los Angeles. I enrolled in every class available to me and dove head first into a major that seemed as if it would make me forget the life I once lived and the future I was supposed to have. I did a semester abroad in Brazil where I met my best friend, Emilia. I fell in "love" with a boy named Harry who, for a short time, made me forget Ethan. He was as damaged as I was and I clung to him. I tried to fix him and failed miserably. He overdosed on drugs, and I blamed myself for his shortcomings. Now I realize I loved

Harry but I was never *in love* with him. He was my Band-Aid. Focusing on him kept me from facing my issues.

My mother's words were an affirmation that, once again, I had lost someone I loved more than anything. I had lost my very first friend. He was gone, and the chances of seeing him again were slim. The secrets we shared and swore to never tell a soul would stay hidden, never to be spoken again. I had let Ethan go, but I wasn't ready for him to let me go.

It was selfish to assume he wouldn't.

Chapter Five

PAST

The school year was about to start, and Ethan informed me that we were in the same grade. The fact that I remained cool when he informed me of this glorious news had me skipping around my room the second he left. He told me that due to his brother's disability, he felt more comfortable being placed in the same grade as Charlie. He said that's what his mother made him tell anyone that asked. The truth was he had gotten in a few fights in and out of school that made him miss too many days. Therefore, the school board had no other option then to keep him back a year. When he noticed that I winced about him fighting he said it was his way of watching out for his younger brother. No one messed with Charlie because they knew Ethan was a loose cannon.

It was the first time in forever that I had a friend to go to school with and a boy that spends night after night in my room. Instead of being dropped off at school, I begged my mother to let me ride the bus. I might have also notified her that our new neighbors had a son who was also in my class and we could ride the bus together. My mother was hesitant. The bus stop was a few blocks away, and she didn't want me to walk out of fear I might fall and hurt myself. Ballerinas needed to be perfect. But my father heard my pleading and assured her I would be fine. He said having friends my own age was important and he offered to talk to our neighbors about a drop off and pick up bus schedule. Though unconvinced, my mother allowed it. And I, a ten year old, love-struck pre-teen, was thrilled.

It was the second week of school, and Ethan and I were inseparable. He quickly memorized my schedule and walked me to almost every class. At lunchtime we sat together, talking about everything and anything while eating. I was mesmerized by his charm. The way he smiled, and the way his eyes lit up when he was talking about something he was passionate about. He made friends with everyone so easily. Most of the girls I knew from dance, the ones who never cared to be my friend, quickly decided I was worth something now that Ethan was my friend. I couldn't fault them. He was gorgeous and his personality shone. So, for the first time in my life, I was somewhat popular—*thanks to Ethan*.

One afternoon after we got off the bus, Ethan decided he wanted to race home. Running wasn't my forte. I could hold a plank for five minutes but I couldn't jog five steps to save my life.

"Hey, wait up!" I shouted to Ethan who was a few feet ahead. My tennis shoes pushed on the cement as I chased behind him.

"Come on, slow poke." Ethan ran backwards with ease. His mother trailed behind us with Charlie as we walked home from the bus stop.

Ethan ran up the pathway that led into his father's garage. Joyce, Ethan's mother, didn't protest so I followed behind him, my book bag slamming on my lower back with each step I took. My heart felt as if it would explode from the strain of running, and the bright sun made it nearly impossible to see in the garage.

"Eth—"

"Shh." I heard his voice. "Come here."

I noticed him squatting behind his father's Harley. "What are you doing?" I whispered and crouched down beside him.

"Nothing, but we can't leave now. My father just walked in." He shifted and I noticed his father among a sea of men. Six in total if you counted his father. Unable to swallow over my fear, I clenched my arm around Ethan. There was something terrifying about his father's demeanor. His shoulders were broad, and his face permanently held a scowl. But my fear wasn't due to his looks. No, it was because I knew the kind of man he truly was. He was an abuser.

"Where's my money, Joey?" Jerry, Ethan's father asked. His voice caused goosebumps to rise all over my body.

"I'll get it to you, Jaws," Joey responded in a low shaky voice.

The hair on the back of my neck rose with fear. What kind of man was given the nickname Jaws?

"*You'll get it?* When? And where? Do you have a hundred grand laying around?" Jerry took a step closer to Joey, his finger pointed in his face. "You're a fucking liar. Maybe I should pay that little wife of yours a visit. I'd say her pussy's worth a couple of bucks." I cringed the at the harsh words and instantly felt embarrassed.

Joey took a step forward. What Jerry said clearly struck a nerve. Two of the men reached out and grabbed Joey's arms. "I'll get it to you, I swear. Just stay away from my family."

"Getting it to me is not the same as having it." Jerry said through gritted teeth.

My eyes had adjusted to the dim garage, and I could finally make out the features on his face. He looked a lot like Ethan. The same dark hair and defined jaw, but he was missing the warmth Ethan portrayed.

"And you don't tell me what to do," Jerry stated. The garage was so quiet, the first blow to Joey's face echoed in the silent space. My eyes closed shut of their own accord and I swear I heard the crushing of Joey's bones. I pried my eyes open, trying desperately to find a way out of there with no luck. Jerry continued to release his rage on Joey. His fists pounded into his face as blood splattered to the ground. My eyes refused to believe what I was seeing.

Joey's bloody face wasn't enough for Jerry. He moved to his tool box and pulled out a crowbar. "I've given you six months to pay me back. You know what happens when you don't pay your bookie? You rot in the fucking desert!" he bellowed and swung the crowbar at Joey's leg.

Anger ricocheted from Jerry's voice, and I gasped when Joey screamed out in pain. Ethan gripped my body and covered my mouth. "Shh," he whispered in my ear, and my body began to shake. What kind of monster was his father?

One of Jerry's goons shoved a dirty rag in Joey's mouth as Jerry continued his assault. Blood dripped down Joey's face and his legs were badly broken, but Jerry didn't let up until Joey's head hung low and he didn't move.

"Get rid of him." His voice was authoritative even when he was out of breath.

My body was frozen in place and a chill ran up my spine. *Get rid of him? As in kill him?*

"Okay, Boss," the man holding Joey's limp body responded.

A tap on the door startled us all. It came from the door that connected the garage with Ethan's home. Tears threatened to pour from my eyes. The guys rushed to cover Joey's body and stood behind Jerry, who was wiping his bloody hands.

Joyce appeared in the open doorway, her gaze focused on the ground. "What?" Jerry barked.

"Have you seen Ethan and his little friend from next door?"

I began to tremble. *What would he do if he found us?*

Jerry lifted his arms. "They're not here. Ethan knows not to come into my office." He marched over to her and pressed his pointer finger to her forehead. There was still blood on it. "Why can't you ever do one fucking thing right? All I ask for is food on the table, my boys taken care of, and my dick sucked. Get the fuck out of my face."

The guys behind him chuckled.

"I'm . . . I'm sorry," Joyce stuttered, turning away and closing the door behind her.

"What the fuck are you assholes laughing at? Get him out of here!"

To keep from passing out, I counted the seconds it took for them to leave. One hundred and sixty-seven to be exact.

When the garage door closed behind them, I gasped for air. Pulling away from Ethan, I ran out the back door with everything I had left in me. *Why had he gone inside his dad's garage? Why did I follow him?* The second the warm air hit my skin, the contents of my stomach erupted onto the grass. Ethan was behind me but I refused to look at him. I wiped my mouth with the back of my hand and ran up the deck and inside my house. The air-conditioning tingled my skin as I pressed my body against the cool glass. My legs were shaking.

My mother appeared from the kitchen. Her mouth moved but I couldn't make out what she was saying. My heart racing in my chest made it impossible to hear a sound "Leslie!" I blinked away tears. "My goodness, what's the matter?"

My knees buckled and I dropped to the floor. My breathing was erratic and my mother rushed to my side. "Leslie, talk to me!" Darlene pleaded as she brushed my hair to the side. She took me into her arms and I sobbed.

"It's okay, sweetie. It's okay." Her voice soothed me. When the sobbing stopped, she pulled me away from her chest. "Tell me what's going on?"

I swallowed back the golf ball lodged in my throat. I should have told my mother everything, but I knew she would take Ethan away from me. She would make me stop being his friend, and a world where Ethan wasn't my friend was a world I didn't want to live in.

"I . . . I . . ." I paused while I tried to come up with an excuse. "I got sick on the way home from school and I don't think I'll be able make it to dance tonight," I finally said.

"It's okay. You will be okay." She gave me a reassuring smile. "Why don't you take a nice warm shower and I'll call you when dinner is ready."

"I'm not really hungry."

"Okay." She brushed my hair with her fingers. "Take a shower and go lie down. I'll leave your food in the fridge. If you get hungry, you can warm it up."

In the shower, I let the warm water cascade down my body

as the images of Jerry's brutality flooded my mind. He was a cruel monster, and I couldn't stop wondering what happened to Joey. *Was he dead when they took him out of there? Did they kill him?*

I pushed the visions out of my head and dressed before crawling into bed. I had been in my room for an hour, the comforter curled around me, unable to move from my spot. My only solace was the brilliant red and orange hues of the sunset I could see through my window. Though it was a warm afternoon, I felt an Artic chill through my bones.

Ethan tapped on my window, but I didn't move to open it for him. I couldn't move. Joey and his fate consumed my mind. Ethan waited a few seconds before he pushed the glass pane open and climbed inside.

"Hey," he whispered. Tears filled my eyes and I lowered my chin. "Please, Freckles." He rushed to my side and draped his arms over my shoulders. Pulling me into his chest, he whispered. "Please don't cry."

"I'm sorry," I muttered as I let him hold me. "I didn't know your father was such a cruel man."

"*I'm* sorry," Ethan apologized. "I should've never gone in there. I wanted to show you his Harley. I didn't know he was home. He's never there during the day."

"Don't apologize for him. We need to tell someone, Ethan." I pushed away from his chest. My body craved his touch but anger began to fill me.

"You can't say anything." Ethan's eyes were wide.

"But—"

"You can't, Les!" he pleaded. His hands rested on my shoulders and I saw the pain in his eyes.

"He hurt him." I shook my head. "He told them to get rid of him."

"Leslie, if you tell a soul, he will kill me." His words were like the stab of a knife, deep in my heart. "And then he will kill my mother. And Charlie."

"But we can't let him get away with it." I didn't want Jerry to hurt Ethan or his family, but he needed to pay for what he did.

"What choice do we have?" Ethan released my shoulders and ran his hands through his hair.

"We can go to the cops," I suggested.

He rested his elbows on his knees. His eyes were glued to the sun like mine had been earlier. He too felt defeated. Shaking his head, he looked over at me. "We can't. My father owns them."

"So we don't say anything?" I asked, my eyebrows furrowed with confusion.

Ethan sighed in defeat. "No, not ever."

"Ethan, I don't know—"

"You can't say anything, Les. Please!" His eyes looked deep into mine, pleading with me. I didn't want to ruin the friendship I had made with Ethan. And the last thing I wanted was for Jerry to hurt him.

"Okay." I nodded.

He reached across the bed and grabbed my hand. "Promise?"

"I promise."

It was a simple sentence that forever bound us.

CALLIE ANDERSON

Chapter Six

PRESENT

My mother and I take turns pacing the small waiting room. The doctors said it will be an eight-hour procedure, but when six hours pass and no one appears with an update, we begin to worry. The effects of the tequila vanished a long time ago and I find myself craving more. I need something to help me escape my current reality.

"Did you have big plans for today?" my mother asks when it's her turn to walk around.

I sigh and twirl my hair around my finger, it's a nervous tick I've never been able to get rid of. My father's in surgery, I'm in a town I swore I'd never come back to, and I'm forced to have a conversation with a woman who is utterly disappointed in me. "No, I usually don't do much," I say in a low voice. "I'm normally busy with work so there's not much time for anything else. I was in Los Angeles visiting a friend for Christmas when you called."

"What do you do?" She doesn't look at me when she asks. My own mother has no idea what I do for a living. I doubt she even knows where I live.

"I'm a national account manager for a company based in Chicago."

My mother stops and looks over at me. "Chicago?"

I clear my throat. "Yes, I moved there about three years ago."

She huffs in disappointment. "It's like you're a complete stranger to me."

I shrug, not knowing what else to do. The disappointment is thick in the small room. Never did she imagine I would work a nine-to-five job.

"Does your father know?"

"Yes." I nod. "I'm surprised he never told you. I guess you never cared to ask."

"Don't." She raises her hand. "Don't turn this around on me. You're the one who left and never came back."

"Yes, you're right." Tears begin to form in my eyes. "I never looked back because eight years ago, when I was the one in *this* hospital and needed you to comfort me, *you* abandoned *me*. When they told me I would no longer dance, you walked out of my room and never stepped foot back in. You left me crying and alone when all my dreams were broken."

"You shattered your own dreams, Leslie. You were a love struck puppy following that boy around. It was his fault. I devoted my life to making you great."

"Yes, Mom," I say with a sob, and then I stand to face her. "You were the best coach I could have asked for. I trained hard to please you. I ate less to please you. I worked harder to please you. In that hospital room, though, I needed my mother, not my coach."

"Excuse me." A voice cuts through our argument. We both turn to face the doctor standing in the doorway. "I'm sorry to interrupt, but I'm here to give you an update." His eyes are kind and I know he is doing everything he can to maintain a stoic expression.

My mother holds her hand over her heart and we both wait

for any news on my father.

"There was a complication during surgery." I gasp and wrap my arm around my mother. "Lawrence went into cardiac arrest. We were able to resuscitate him but his heart didn't beat for a while which means his brain wasn't getting the adequate oxygen it needed. Unfortunately, we won't be able to tell if there is any neurological damage until we're finished with surgery and he regains consciousness."

The doctor continues to speak but my hearing stops working. My father could have brain damage. Everything moves in slow motion, and I do everything in my power to hold my mother up. Darlene has many flaws, but she is a dedicated wife to my father. If anything happens to him, I don't know how she will recover.

"When can I see him?" my mother asks. Maybe she is stronger than I give her credit for.

"He's still in surgery but as soon as he's in the recovery room I'll notify you."

The doctor walks out of the room, and my mother turns toward me. My hands rest on her shoulders and I realize we are supporting each other, both physically and emotionally. Tears drip down her cheeks, and for the first time in many years, we hug and cry in each other's arms.

The week passes in a blur and I find myself going through the motions and functioning on autopilot. After my father awoke from surgery, it was evident that he did, in fact, suffer brain damage. His speech is impaired and he has lost most of his mobility. He'll be transferred to a rehabilitation wing of the hospital, but the doctors have to ensure his heart is strong enough before they release him.

The stress weighs heavy on my shoulders. My week of vacation is almost up, and I'm not ready to leave their side, not when they need me the most. My mother spends countless hours at the hospital. We take shifts sitting with Dad and keeping him company but it's heartbreaking watching him try to communicate to no avail. Most nights when I come home, I find my mother curled up on the couch crying.

Yes, Darlene is complicated in her own way, but she's still my mother and needs me here. It's not easy being the caretaker to my parents, especially when not so long ago, I felt as if I didn't belong with them. It isn't that I don't love them; it's the constant feeling that I let them down—all because I fell in love.

Ethan.

My love for him has turned to hate over the years. He broke a piece of me. A piece that has never mended.

The pure dread of reliving or seeing anyone from my past is the reason I never turn on a single light in the house while my mother is at the hospital. The sooner my father gets better, the sooner I can go home. Away from this town and all the memories it holds.

I'm cleaning the kitchen counter when the house phone rings. At first, I debate whether I should answer it, but I see the telephone screen and realize it's my father's health insurance company.

"Hello?" I say holding the phone between my shoulder and ear.

"Hi, may I speak to Mrs. Sutton?"

"Mr. Sutton isn't here. Can I help you with anything?" I wipe the dishcloth along the countertop.

"My name is Ana with Gate United Health. I'm calling from the claims department. Is this a bad time?"

"No, not at all."

"I'm calling regarding the recent claim submitted to us by Freeman Hospital. It states that Mr. Sutton will be transferred to a rehab facility within the next few days. Unfortunately, we can't approve this claim at the moment."

"Why not?" I rest my lower back against the counter.

"I'm afraid your insurance is scheduled to be terminated at midnight tonight."

"I'm sorry, what? How? Why?" I can't mask the confusion in my voice.

"We were notified that Mr. Sutton's employment was recently terminated. In order for the coverage to continue under a portable plan, the application needs to be submitted by the end of the day today. The package was sent out last week and I'm calling to make sure we get everything squared away."

My father lost his job? Does my mother even know? I move from the kitchen and sit at the table. "So, his coverage will continue as long as the forms are submitted today?"

"Yes, along with the premium."

My hand massages my scalp. "Can I do this over the phone or online?"

"I can email you a link if you'd like."

I sigh with relief. "That would be perfect." I provide Ana with my email address. The second I hang up the phone, I rush to my father's home office, log on to his computer, and fill out the forms. Luckily, his personal information is at my disposal in the stacks of papers on his desk.

Once I'm finished, I sit back on the leather chair and glance at the papers on his desk. My father isn't an irresponsible man. He spent hours teaching me the value of a good job when I was younger. My shoulders sink as the stress keeps piling on them. How will he find a job with his condition? My mother hasn't worked in years. After I left, she closed down her studio. That studio was her happy place.

I glance at the time and realize my mother is probably ready to come home for the night. Jogging to the kitchen, I grab the keys and head over to the hospital to tag her out. My mind replays the conversation I had with Ana, followed by panic. *What will my parents do to survive?*

The hospital is busy when I arrive. Ambulances light up the sky and I can tell it'll be a busy New Year's Eve. Waving at the security guard at the main entrance, I make my way to the elevator.

My mother is sitting on the recliner when I enter the room. Her hair is pulled back like always and she looks so peaceful. The frown lines that have taken a new space on her forehead have disappeared. I feel an ache in my chest as I walk over to her. My hand rests on her shoulder and she looks up at me.

"You're back already?" she whispers.

I nod. "How is he?"

Her muscles tighten under my skin. "Better, I guess. He's recovering but still not well enough to transfer to rehab for another week."

I bite my lip and release a breath I didn't know I was holding. "Mom, do you think I can talk to you?"

"Is everything all right?" She turns to face me, her eyebrows furrowing as she waits for me to answer.

"Yeah. Um . . ." I pause, not knowing how to explain it all to her. I pull a chair toward her and take a seat. "When I was at the house, the insurance company called." I take her hands in mine. "They notified me that Dad is no longer employed and his health insurance was about to lapse."

My mother sighs. "Oh, my God. I can't believe I forgot to send that in."

"So, you knew about him losing his job?"

"Yes, of course." She swallows and holds her head up. "This is all my fault." Her voice cracks.

"Mom."

"No, it is." She shakes her head. "I received the papers regarding our insurance termination, and when I confronted him about it we argued. During our argument he started to feel the pain in his arm. Your father was under a lot of stress."

"It's okay. It's not your fault, Mom." Tears pool in my eyes. "And he will be fine."

"I don't know what to do. Even with the insurance, his medical bills will cost us a fortune."

"I can help. I have some money in my savings. I can take a few weeks off from work to help. And Dad has always been really good with his money. I'm sure you guys can dip into your savings."

My mother's lower lip quivers and she lowers her head. "Leslie, we have nothing."

"What do you mean?"

"We put all our eggs in one basket. Calvin, your father's business partner, drained the company's assets. Your father took out another mortgage on our house and emptied our savings so he could continue to pay the employees. I have no idea what we'll do." My mother reaches in her purse and pulls out a tissue.

"What if your father isn't the same after rehab? What if he can't work anymore? We'll have to file for bankruptcy. We'll lose everything."

The weight of the world rests on my shoulders. "Don't say that." I shake my head. "What about . . . What about your dance studio?"

"I haven't been there since you left. We were renting it out for some time, but it's been vacant for a while now."

"You can open it back up. Teach again. You were great."

"What about your father? Who will be with him? I can't be both places at once, Leslie." My mother raises her voice, frustration pouring out with every breath.

I sit back, feeling defeated. A few minutes pass before I speak. "I can take a leave of absence. FMLA will give me six months. That should be plenty of time to figure things out. I can help you at the studio." My voice is so low that it's barely a whisper. As if on cue, my ankle begins to throb and I find myself stretching it.

"Are you still dancing?"

"I haven't since . . ." I shrug, not wanting to admit that I haven't slipped on my ballet flats since the accident. "But I can teach. Those who can't do teach, right?"

My mother nods and the conversation between us dies. Realization sets in. I'll be re-opening her dance studio. A studio she bought for me. A studio where I spent countless hours dancing, rehearsing, and where the wood floor is embossed with my sweat, blood and tears.

I abandoned it, and now I am finally coming back.

"I have to make a quick call," I notify my mother and then walk around the corner to dial Chloe's number.

"Happy New Year!" Chloe sings into the phone.

"Hey, Chloe." I say barely above a whisper.

"Everything okay? How's your dad?"

I sigh and pinch the bridge of my nose. "I'm going to have to stay here a little bit longer. Things are much worse than we thought."

"Oh, no, Leslie. Is there anything I can do?"

"No." I press my back against the cool cement wall. "I'm

going to call Sherry in HR tomorrow and file for FMLA. Can you please just make sure Drew doesn't screw up any of my accounts."

"Babe, your father is in the hospital. Don't you dare worry about any of your accounts. I got you covered."

Slowly I massage my scalp. "Thanks, Chloe." I hang up and slide my phone into my purse.

I'm staying in the one place I swore I'd never return to.

Chapter Seven

PAST

Two Years Later

The tapping on my bedroom window woke me from a deep sleep. This was the fourth time this week that Ethan was seeking escape from his father and my heart was breaking for him. It had been a two years since the first time he climbed into my room.

My fingers held the white wood frame and slid it up the track. "You okay?" I mumbled when he was inside. Things had gotten worse since I witnessed the whole garage incident, and my heart constantly raced, wondering if he was alright.

"Yeah." He spoke softly, and I knew from the sadness in his eyes that he was lying. But at least he was safe.

Tossing him my extra pillow and the quilt that rested at the bottom of my bed, I crawled back under the blankets. "Do you think it will ever stop?" I asked, looking up at the glowing stars my dad and I had stuck to my ceiling on my eighth birthday.

"Probably not." He exhaled, briefly I closed my eyes praying that I could take away his pain. The pain I assumed was rooted deep in his chest.

"Why don't you call the cops?"

"We've been over this, Les. What are they gonna do?" I heard him shuffling on the floor.

Rolling toward him, I tucked my hands under my cheek. "You can tell them the truth. We can tell them what we saw; we can make them look for Joey."

"My dad is a bad man, Leslie. Even if they did believe us, he would buy his way out of trouble and then me, my mom, and my brother would pay for betraying him." Ethan lifted his hands and tucked them under his head.

"I'm sorry, Ethan."

He didn't respond. The hatred he felt for Jerry didn't allow him to say it was okay anymore. We all knew it wasn't okay.

At an age when you need your old man to show you the ropes, his father opened Ethan's eyes to abuse. Each night Jerry laid a finger on Joyce was another nail slammed into Ethan's coffin.

"It will be okay," I still whispered in the darkness of the room.

"Yeah." He paused. "When I get the hell out of this town."

Ethan and I had the same discussion for two consecutive years.

The banging on my bedroom door startled me. I sprang from bed with my fist clenched to my chest. The sun was bright in my room. I was late.

"Leslie?" My mother rattled the bedroom doorknob. "Why is your door locked?"

I glanced around my bedroom and took in my surroundings. Ethan was on the floor fast asleep.

"I'm sorry, Mom. I'll be right there," I said and tossed my pillow on Ethan.

"What's going on? Are you okay? Why is there a lock on your door?"

"Mom, I'm fine! Give me a minute." Ethan jumped up from the floor. His eyes were as confused as mine. I yanked the quilt off the floor and tossed it on my bed. "Hide in the closet," I mouthed to him. His long legs sprinted across the room and he ducked inside the closet. I brushed my hair back and gently opened the door.

"What are you doing?" My mother pushed open the door, her arms crossed at her chest.

"I was sleeping." It was the truth.

"Why was your door locked?" She didn't wait for me to respond. "When did you buy a lock for your bedroom?"

"It's always had a lock." I lied hoping she never noticed that I had Ethan install a new one and walked over to grab my tights and leotard.

"I don't want you locking this door. Do you understand me?"

"Mom, that's not fair. This is my room. Sometimes I need privacy."

My mother's stare cut through me. In any other circumstance I wouldn't fight her, but if I didn't lock my door, I would never sleep when Ethan was in my room. The fear of her barging through my door would keep me awake all night.

He needed me.

And I needed him.

"Don't you sass me, young lady! Your father will hear about this. Get dressed. I'll be downstairs."

I nodded and rushed to the bathroom once she began to walk down the stairs. I wasted no time as I brushed my teeth, changed, and pulled my hair up into a bun. I ran back to my room as fast as I could. I needed to tell Ethan not to leave until the coast was clear, but when I swung the closet door open it was empty. He had left without saying goodbye.

The horn honked in the garage and I knew my mother's patience was wilting. Grabbing my flats from the closet, I ran down the stairs, through the house and into the garage.

"Sorry," I muttered when I closed the car door.

"This is unacceptable, Leslie," she said as she pulled the car out of the garage. "How do you plan on getting into Juilliard if you can't even wake up on time?"

"I'm sorry, I didn't hear my alarm. It won't happen again." I bowed my head. I knew there wasn't a thing I could say that would justify not being on time. Her lecture lasted the entire ride from our house to the studio. She never mentioned anything about Ethan climbing out of my room, so I figured we were in the clear.

Once at the studio, my mother turned the lights on and I dropped my bag on the chair. The sleek wood floors ran across the studio and a floor to ceiling mirror lined the wall. The studio wouldn't open for another hour, but this was my time to warm up and rehearse. After fifteen minutes of stretching, I was ready for my routine. My mother turned the music on and scrutinized me from her chair. It was a seven-minute performance that she made me repeat over and over.

"Again," she demanded.

"Point your toes," she ordered.

"Tight arms," she barked.

"From the top!" she yelled.

I wasn't allowed to complain. Or grunt. If she said I needed to point my toes, I made sure my toes were as stretched as humanly possible. At the top of the hour she turned the stereo down. My muscles ached but with a good pain. They were warm and ready to push through the classes.

Cracking my neck, I walked over to my duffle bag and pulled out my water bottle, my towel, and a protein bar. My stomach was growling with hunger.

"Don't you dare eat that," my mother barked from the other side of the room.

"But I'm hungry."

"You are a dancer," she reminded me. "That's three hundred and fifty calories of junk that will go straight to your hips. You're not allowed to gain a single ounce."

"Mom," I couldn't help but whine. "I didn't get to eat breakfast."

"Go in my office. There's a banana on my desk, and some

almonds in a bag."

I tossed the chocolaty bar in my bag and walked over to her office. "Oh, and Leslie?" I looked back at her. "Make sure you only eat twenty almonds."

I sighed. "Yes, Mother."

By one in the afternoon all of the classes were finished and I'd danced with all of them. For the beginners, I was an instructor. I spent the entire hour demonstrating proper form. My mother insisted I hone my craft, even if I spent the hour practicing a *plie* with a bunch of five-year-olds.

My mother was busy in her office catching up on paperwork while she ate her salad. The front door jingled when it opened. "We're closed," I called out before I turned to face the front entry. To my surprise Ethan stood at the door. My eyes widened and I ran to him. "What are you doing here?" I asked in a low voice.

"I wanted to see where you run off to every night and weekend." He looked around the room. My eyes locked with his in the mirror and I watched as he glanced down my body. Though it was a subtle glance it didn't go unnoticed. "This is a nice place. I've never seen you like this." His gaze pulled away from my legs and met my eyes once again.

A shiver ran up my spine and I felt my face grow warm. "It's no big deal."

"Will you show me your routine?" I looked away from the mirror to face him and was met with his sad eyes. Slowly, I watched his mouth curl up in a perfect smile.

"It's not perfect yet." I tried to hide my insecurities.

"I won't know the difference." Ethan shifted on the balls of his feet. "Please?" How could I say no when he begged.

Without a word I walked over to the stereo and skipped over the tracks till I found my song. My legs felt like Jell-O as I took the center of the dance floor. Ethan's eyes were on me and I needed it to be perfect. I inhaled and exhaled slowly before the music began. My eyes closed and I let the movements pour out of my body. Each step was delicate. Every movement crisp and defined. I used the entire dance floor. My heart raced in my chest because I knew Ethan was watching me dance for the first time. With one last pirouette, I crumbled to the ground on the final note as the song ended.

Ethan clapped. "That was amazing!"

I glanced up at him and laughed. I opened my mouth to speak, but my mother stopped me.

"That was your best performance today." Her voice bellowed through the quiet room.

"Mom." I rushed to my feet.

"It's still not perfect but definitely better than this morning." She walked over to Ethan. "I don't think we've properly met. Darlene Sutton." She extended her hand to him.

"Ethan Prescott." He placed his hand in hers and bowed.

"You're the boy Leslie walks home with, right?"

"Yes, ma'am."

"And what can I do for you?" Her lips pursed as she eyed him. "I don't suppose you're interested in ballet classes for yourself?"

"Oh, no, ma'am." He scratched the back of his head. "Um, Leslie and I have a project due for science. I went by the house to see when she wanted to go to the library and start the research, but since she wasn't there I figured I would try here." I furrowed my eyebrows.

"Science project?" She looked away from Ethan and over to me. "Why is it not on the calendar at home?" I opened my mouth to explain but she lifted her hand and stopped me. "Juilliard needs you to have good grades too, Leslie. Go to the library and get it done quickly. I expect you home by six."

I nodded, then walked over to my bag and yanked out an oversized shirt to put on.

Ethan wore a wide grin. "It was a pleasure meeting you in person, Mrs. Sutton."

"Good-bye." My mother waved him away, her face puckered in distaste.

When we were outside and around the corner, I looked over at Ethan. "Can I ask you two things?"

Amusement was plastered on his face. "That was one already."

I shook my head, annoyed. "One, did you really bow when

you met my mother? And two, what science project? We're not even in the same class."

Ethan chuckled and raised his hands. "Yes, I bowed. Your mother is seriously intimidating. Worse than my father, and that's saying a lot because my father is a piece of shit." I nodded, agreeing with his last statement. "And as for the science project, I figured it was a long shot, but now we have the afternoon to ourselves. What do you want to do?"

I couldn't hide the smile on my face. I didn't remember a time when I was free to do whatever I wanted with a friend. The options were endless. We could go to the movies, to the mall, or simply walk around. But my stomach growled so loudly it made the decision pretty obvious.

"I guess we're going to grab something to eat first." Ethan laughed.

"Sorry, I woke up late." I glanced at the cement floor.

"Come on," Ethan grabbed me by my hand. "I know the perfect place." The butterflies in my stomach flapped their wings as I followed him to a pizzeria in the center of our town. It was a popular spot since it was hard to find great New York-style pizza so close to the Mexican border.

"For here or to go?" the host asked as we walked in. Frankie's was owned by Isabella and Marcus. They had lived on the east coast most of their lives, but after retiring to Arizona they realized what they missed the most from the Big Apple was pizza and decided to open up a pizzeria.

"For here," Ethan said, pulling me out of my trance. Glancing around the room, I noticed a few kids we went to school with hanging out together. Yet another thing I never got to experience, thanks to my mother.

Worried that someone would spot me and report back to my mother, I kept my head low as we followed the host to our booth. *That constant feeling that everyone was always watching my every move.*

"What can I get you kids?" an older lady asked.

"Two Cokes and a large pie," Ethan stated.

"Coming right up."

"Actually," I said in a low voice. "Can I please have a water with lemon? And do you have any salads?" I kept my eyes glued to Isabella, but I could feel Ethan's gaze burn into me.

"Um, we don't usually make salads, but let me see what we have in the back." She walked away from our table.

From across the table I could see that Ethan had his hands crossed at his chest. When I finally mustered the courage from deep inside, I glanced up.

"Why did you order a salad? Your stomach was growling a few minutes ago. I thought you would have loved a slice of greasy heaven."

"My mother doesn't want me to gain any weight, and pizza is very fattening. On average, one slice of regular pizza has about two hundred and eighty-five calories. Two slices of pizza are equivalent to swallowing three spoonful's of oil. Have you ever seen a fat ballerina?" I tried to defend my mother's need for me to be thin.

Ethan cracked his neck and looked over at me. Never had his stare been so prominent. His nostrils flared and for a split second he looked identical to his father, rage and all. "I'm going to say something you may not like, but I feel you need to hear it. Your mother is stupid. I can count your ribs, for crying out loud. And before you try to argue with me, I saw your body when you were dancing in that ballerina jumpsuit thing." My face warmed because of his words. "There isn't an ounce of fat on you. You *need* the fatty pizza." He threw his hands up in the air. "As a matter of fact, I think we need two pies," he said in a louder tone.

I laughed at his dramatics but then crouched down when I spotted a few other classmates looking our way. "Fine, we can order pizza, but only one."

"Deal." Ethan slapped the table in triumph.

"But no Coke." His excitement wavered a little but he didn't push me.

"Excuse me." He waved down our waitress. "I'm sorry, but due to her lack of sleep she's a bit off today. You see, she thought this place was known for their salads. She was mistaken. We'll have one pie, a Coke, and a water."

She looked over at me and I nodded enthusiastically. When

she was a few feet away, I looked over at Ethan. A wide smile covered his face. "You're in a happy mood. I don't think I've ever seen you so chipper."

"It's not every Saturday that I get to spend the afternoon with you."

I opened my mouth to speak, but the rapid beat of my heart made it impossible to breathe.

"Can I ask you for a favor?" Ethan said after a few minutes. "I know how determined you are to be great, but don't miss out on living your life because of it."

"Extraordinary," I muttered and Ethan gave me a puzzled look. "My mom doesn't want me to just be *great*. She wants me to be *extraordinary*."

"And you are, trust me when I say that. But you also shouldn't starve yourself. I think you might be the skinniest girl I've ever seen."

Unable to determine if his comment was an insult or a compliment, I sat quietly.

"Are you angry?" I shook my head. "Don't be mad. I think you're perfect." Ethan stopped himself from continuing, scratching the back of his head. I found he did this when he was nervous. I wasn't mad. Not when he said I was perfect.

The waitress placed the pizza between us, and the awkwardness that threatened to ruin our afternoon subsided at the sight of the bubbling cheesy goodness. I took my time eating my slice. The cheese felt warm and velvety in my mouth, and the crust had a perfect crunch to it. I savored every bite. Ethan was on this third slice by the time I finished my first. Unlike I intended, I wound up eating two slices while Ethan polished off the rest.

I offered to split the bill with him but he took the check and paid it all. Once we were outside Frankie's, Ethan began to walk away from the center of town and toward the back streets where it was less crowded.

"It's nicer to walk through town, you know?" I said when we rounded a corner.

"I know." Ethan looked over at me. "But my father owns most of it and I don't want him to see us."

"What does your father do?" I asked. I had no idea what his dad did other than intimidate people. I was afraid of what Ethan's response would be.

"A little bit of everything. My great grandfather moved here when there wasn't much of anything. Over the years, he became involved in the community and built businesses. My family owns most of the storefronts in the square, and my dad personally runs a few businesses himself."

"Why do you say he owns the cops, too?"

"The sheriff in town is my uncle. Or a distant cousin that I call my uncle. He and my dad are childhood friends. When he first started off on the force he got into some really bad gambling trouble, which my father eagerly bailed him out of with the assumption that he would help my father out when required. Not to mention, my father donates a considerable amount of money to the police department when needed."

"Wow."

When another block passed and we were closer to the downtown square, Ethan glanced over at me. "You look beautiful . . . when you dance," he stated.

My feet felt like they were glued to the ground. I tucked my hair behind my ears and tried not to read into his comment. "Thanks." My voice was shaky with nerves. Being around him made me giddy. "It's not perfect yet, but I still have some time."

"What more can you do to it? It looked perfect to me. I knew you danced, and ballet was what you lived and breathed, but when I *saw* you dance . . . I never expected it to be like that." Happiness pinched at my heart. For once in a very long time someone other than my father thought I was great.

"I wanted a partner for my audition to Juilliard," I said, referring back to his question. "It's not for a few years, but it's hard to find someone around here who is willing to take the trip with me to New York for the audition and actually knows a thing or two about ballet."

"What does your partner have to do?" We approached the downtown square and sat on a bench to watch a few toddlers running around as their mother's chatted.

"Throw me around and whatnot," I responded.

"I can be your partner," Ethan said matter-of-factly.

I turned to face him. "Have you ever danced before?"

"No." He shrugged. "But if it's a few years away, I can start practicing now."

"Really?"

"Of course." A wide smile grew on his face and my stomach flipped with excitement. "I'd do anything for you, Les."

I leaned in and bumped my shoulder to his. It was an odd movement, but I figured it was better than hugging him in front of all these people.

"Plus, how hard can it be? You weigh less than a feather." He threw his arms around my shoulder and brought me closer to him.

My stomach turned and the butterflies were flapping their wings in my belly. Ethan had his arms on me. An inferno coursed through my body. Slowly, I pulled away from him at the fear of breaking out in complete hyperventilation. I was dizzy. Being around Ethan made it impossible to consume all the oxygen my body needed.

"It's not so easy." My voice was unsteady. I stood and turned to face him. "Every move has to be calculated, finessed with attitude and balance." I threw my hands in the air demonstrating *port de bras* and lifted onto my toes in *relevé*. "We would have to dance in perfect harmony where the audience simply sees a performance and the judges see the technique."

Ethan stood. He threw his hands in the air and I laughed. His posture was wrong, and his arms were forced over his head. "I can't stand on my toes." He chuckled when he tried and fell back on the balls of his feet.

Shaking my head at his attempt, I leaned forward, bending at the waist. I pushed my leg straight in the air.

"Wow." Ethan said. I inhaled to hold the position longer when Ethan laced his hands around my waist and lifted me off the ground. My posture faltered and I laughed with both fear and excitement due to his unexpected lift. But when I was almost six feet in the air, I realized that Ethan was stronger than I thought. He grunted. "Am I doing it right?"

"You can put me down." When both of my feet were safely on the ground, I slapped him on the shoulder.

"What was that for?" he complained.

"For starters, you could have hurt yourself." I tried to keep a straight face. "Also, you can't just lift me without telling me."

"Sorry." I knew from the sneer on his face he wasn't sorry. "I was online looking at a few ballet dances and I saw how the men just lift the girls up."

"You looked up ballet?"

"Yeah." He shifted his weight to the back of his feet. "I wanted to learn more about you."

"Thanks," I said, my glance locked on the ground.

"You're pretty interesting, Leslie." He threw his arm over my shoulders. "Come on, let's get going. I don't want your mother to be upset with you."

Chapter Eight

PAST

One Year Later

Ethan and I grew closer with each passing day. We found any excuse to spend more time together. We both volunteered at school for extra credit and to be part of the food drive during the holidays. It kept us out of the house and with each other. Though he still climbed into my bedroom at least three times a week, the complaints about his father had stopped. I think it had to do with the fact I knew what kind of man Jerry was and there was no need to say anything else.

School was easier because of Ethan, too. I had always been an honors student but now I also had friends. Well, I had Ethan's friends. I no longer sat in the cafeteria alone. Kids didn't talk to me simply because they needed something from me. When head cheerleader, slash, the most popular girl in school, Erica Adams asked to hang out after school, I felt as if my eyes would bug out of my head. I didn't want to be the popular girl, but high school was approaching fast and I didn't want to be the loser with no friends.

After my math class one afternoon, I was surprised to find that Ethan wasn't waiting near my locker. Wondering if he had gotten in trouble again with Mr. Collins in biology, I grabbed my books for my next class and closed my locker door.

It was then I saw him.

With her.

Erica.

An indescribable emotion washed over me.

Anger.

Sadness.

I felt it in the pit of my stomach.

Erica threw her beautiful blonde hair back and laughed at something he said. I stood there paralyzed at the scene before me. She didn't want to be my friend. She wanted to be his girlfriend. I hugged my books to my chest and walked past them. I kept my head low and willed my feet to move quickly so I wasn't seen.

"Les, wait up," Ethan called out behind me, but I didn't stop. I hurried down the hallway and straight into a bathroom. The scent of antibacterial soap wafted through the small three-stall restroom. The first bell rang, warning students there were three minutes to get to class. Having no desire to leave, I dropped my books on the counter and looked at myself in the mirror. Tears welled in my eyes and I couldn't explain the feelings that coursed through me.

Erica and Ethan. My mind replayed it over and over like a broken record. E & E. I could already imagine her doodling all over her composition notebook like a love struck fool. E2. Erica loves Ethan. Erica and Ethan Prescott. I would lose my best friend.

I was hurt. No.

I was angry. No.

I was jealous.

Erica was pretty, and popular. Her hair was shiny and flawless. And her breasts had begun to develop at a rapid speed. I on the other hand had wild untamable hair and my body was lanky. She had everything I didn't. Her mother wasn't a crazy strict dance coach who didn't let her do anything but dance and school work. The bell for class sounded. I was officially late. It would be my first tardy ever, but like most girls, I'd blame my period. Not that I knew anything about that, but I had seen a few girls show up late to class and blame it on cramps. I gave myself one last look in the mirror, grabbed my books and walked out of the bathroom.

The second I swung the door back, I was greeted by Ethan. I sucked in a quick breath. He stood across the hallway, one leg propped up on the wall. His books were in one arm and his eyebrows furrowed when he saw me.

"Are you okay?" he asked, kicking off the wall.

"You're late to class," I barked and walked past him down the hallway.

"I don't care. You ran off; I thought you were sick." He trailed behind me.

"I'm fine, Ethan."

He stopped. "Geez."

I should have felt guilty for treating him like that. He didn't deserve my sass, but I couldn't control the jealousy thing. This was all new to me.

"Why don't you go see if Erica is all right?" I said, looking over my shoulder at him. I spun my head forward and headed for the stairwell, I wanted to skip class and sit in the nurse's office until it all seemed right in the world. Ethan's footfalls approached and I tried to walk down the stairs faster but he beat me to the first landing and jumped in front of me.

"What's that supposed to mean?"

The words spewed out of me. "I'm fine! I don't need you waiting around for me."

"Fine?" He cocked his head to the side and a sly grin grew on his face. "You ran into the girl's bathroom to hide from me. I wouldn't call that fine."

"I had cramps," I said louder than I intended. "I'm not hiding from you. So if you don't mind, I have to go to the nurse now."

"Whatever." Ethan stepped to the side. "Hopefully the nurse

has something to cure your jealousy, too."

I was halfway down the second flight of stairs when his comment registered in my head. "Jealousy?" I looked up at him. "Me, jealous of you and Erica?" I chuckled and prayed to every God out there that I could lie thought my teeth. "Ethan, you're my friend so I'm going to tell you how it is. Don't flatter yourself. If Erica wants you, she can have you. Feel free to crawl into her window at night." I turned back down the stairs.

We didn't speak for the rest of the day. He wasn't on the bus home, and after school I begged my mother to stay at the studio for a few more hours. She seemed happy with my dedication and didn't have an inkling that my need to stay longer was to avoid seeing Ethan outside our house.

That night, I tossed and turned in bed. I was mad at Ethan, but my anger was pushed aside when the hours passed and he never showed. I grew worried. When I went to bed, I locked my bedroom window, but I spent most of the night staring at it, waiting for him to show up. By two in the morning, I crawled out of bed and opened it. I was afraid I'd taken away his safe place and that was worse than him dating Erica. Peering my head out the window, all seemed calm at the Prescott's home.

The following morning I was late to the bus stop and Ethan was already sitting with some kid named Michael he had become friendly with. He didn't even glance my way when I passed him. Instead, he pulled a baseball cap out of his bag and placed it over his head.

I wanted to cry.

I wanted to yell.

It was our first argument.

The school day wasn't any better. My classes dragged, and to make matters worse, Ethan completely ignored me. He didn't wait after any of my classes, he ditched gym, and when I did see him in the hallway he was always with Erica. What hurt the most was that he sat with her at lunch, leaving me all alone.

Trying to stop myself from crying, I pulled out the book we were reading in English class and worked on the assignment. "Hey, is this seat taken?" I glanced up and noticed Michael standing in front of me. I glanced around my empty table.

Everyone who usually sat with me at lunch had gravitated toward Erica's table.

"They're all empty," I said and looked back at my book.

"I know, but usually you sit next to Ethan, so I wasn't sure if he was coming back." Michael sat beside me. "Is that Mrs. Evan's homework you're doing?"

I closed the book. Ethan was sitting a few tables behind us. Our eyes met. Though Erica continued to speak, his eyes remained focused on me.

"Yes." I pulled my attention away from Ethan and looked at Michael. "I figured I'd get a jump start on it since I'll be busy later."

"With dance, right?"

"Ye—"

"Can I sit with you, Les?" Charlie interrupted me. He was Ethan's younger brother. We'd sat together at lunch since the first day he started here. Ethan never spoke of his disabilities so I had no clue what they were, but lunch was the only time we saw him during the day. He rode a different bus, and his classes were longer and on the opposite side of the building.

I smiled up at him. "Of course." This time, I didn't need to look at Ethan to feel his gaze on me.

"Thanks. We sit at this table. Not there. Only this table," Charlie said and placed his tray in front of him.

"We can always sit here, Charlie." I noticed him glancing at my tray. "You can have my cookie if you want."

Charlie clapped his hands and took it from my tray. "You're the best, Les."

"Anytime, Charlie," I said with a smile on my face. At least I still had Charlie.

Glancing back at Michael, I smiled. "Sorry, what were you saying?"

"Nothing." He shook his head and glanced over at Ethan. I didn't like their exchange. There was something in Ethan's eyes that haunted me.

"Everything okay, Michael?" I asked when Ethan looked over at Erica and smiled.

"Yeah, everything is fine." He slouched down and picked at

his lunch.

By Friday, Ethan and I still had not spoken. My window had been open all week but he never crawled through it. There was a rumor floating around school that he had been in a fight. I didn't believe it, but when I spotted a cut on his eyebrow, my stomach dropped. Ethan was loved by the entire school, he was friends with everyone, and getting into a fight was something I could never see him doing anymore. I had an inkling that it was his father's backlash, and the guilt weighed heavy on my heart. Because I was jealous of him and Erica, he had nowhere to run.

At lunch, I walked into the cafeteria with Charlie. As we made our way through the crowded lunchroom, my eyes met Ethan's and he scowled. He was sitting with Erica and her friends again. I looked away and headed toward our usual spot. Michael was waiting for us.

"Hey." I placed my tray next to his. "I hate this school sometimes."

"I got you an apple." Michael held up the Granny Smith for me.

"Thanks." I took it and placed it on my tray. Michael was still smiling at me. I shifted on my seat. "Do you want my juice?" I offered wondering if he was expecting an exchange.

"Actually, I was wondering." Michael cleared his throat. "Tonight, a bunch of us are going to the movies." He paused and took a sip of his water. "I was thinking, if you're not busy, maybe you want to come with me?"

Charlie snorted. "You're asking her on a date. Date. Date. Date."

I looked over at Charlie and laughed awkwardly. "Um . . ." I'd never been on a date before. "I have dance practice until seven. I can ask my Mom to drop me off?"

Michael's eyes beamed with excitement. "Okay. The movie starts at 7:30, and my mom is doing the pick up so she can totally drive you home."

"Great," I said nervously.

"It's a date, then."

I smiled and looked over at Charlie for some sort of help. I was going on my first date. With Michael. He was a nice guy, and I saw him as a friend, but he wasn't the person I'd imagined my first date would be with.

After much pleading with my mom, my father and I finally convinced her to let me go. Once I was finished with dance, I quick-changed out of my tights and into jeans before my mother drove me to the theater.

"I'll pick you up here after the movie." She handed me a twenty-dollar bill. "I don't care if Mrs. Tulip is taking everyone else home. I'll be here to pick you up. Do you understand?"

I sighed and jumped out of the car. "Yes, Mom." I closed the car door.

Walking inside the theater, I waited by the kiosk for Michael. It was the meeting point he'd suggested. Though the theater was crowded with the Friday night crowd, I didn't see a single person I knew. There was no sight of anyone from my school.

I waited.

And waited.

And waited.

When seven thirty came along, I realized Michael wasn't planning to show up. I'd been asked on my very first date only to be stood up.

Unwanted tears swelled in my eyes. Hurt and disappointed, I walked out of the theater. I couldn't go home. My mother would never let me out again. Walking a few feet away from the entrance, I sat on the curb and lowered my head to my knees. The tears flowed from my eyes and onto the asphalt. I was mad at the world, at Michael, and most of all, I was mad at myself.

I sat and wallowed for a few minutes, and didn't lift my head until someone sat beside me. I half-hoped it was Michael, but I was greeted with Ethan instead.

I rubbed the tears away from my eyes. "What are you doing here?" I cleared my throat and looked out into the parking lot.

"I came to get you since Michael didn't show."

"Where's Erica?"

"Come on, Freckles. I don't want to fight anymore." His

voice was low and it tugged at my heart. Glancing over at him, I noticed the cut on his eyebrow.

"When did it happen?" I gently rubbed the scab with my thumb.

"The day we fought. He yelled at Charlie and called him stupid, so I got in his face. It's not as bad as it looks."

"I'm sorry." My lips quivered and my emotions were all over the place. "My window was open all week," I admitted.

"I know." He took my hand in his. "I wasn't sure whether you did it out of obligation or if you really meant it."

We stared at each other for a few seconds. "You're always welcome to stay in my room regardless if we are fighting. Even if we never speak again and I hate you, I will never turn you away. I don't want him hitting you."

"Thanks."

"Wait." I pulled my hand away. "How did you know I was here?"

"I told Michael to call it off. And when I saw you weren't home—"

"You what?" I stood and took a step back.

"I don't want you going out with him." Ethan stood and crossed his arms over his chest.

"So you told him not to come?"

"No, I told him to call you and tell you not to come."

"Who are you to tell him anything? He asked me to the movies. What's the big deal?"

"He's my friend and I don't want him dating you," Ethan stated matter-of-factly.

"I got stood up because of you?" I threw my hands in the air and groaned. "You don't have that right." I turned and walked away from him.

"Leslie!" he yelled behind me, but I continued to walk away.

"Screw you!" I yelled, refusing to look back at him.

"Les." Ethan grabbed my hand.

I spun to face him. "Don't." I tugged my hand away. "Do you know how humiliated I was back there? How stupid I felt waiting around for him to show?"

"I'm sorry." His voice lowered an octave and his eyelids were hooded.

"Why?" I refused to let his sad eyes change the way I felt.

"Why, what?"

"Why did you tell him not to come?" My arms crossed at my chest. I needed a valid reason why my best friend would be so mean to me. When a few seconds passed and Ethan didn't speak, I turned away. "Whatever." I mumbled under my breath.

I took two steps before Ethan grabbed my hand and pulled me into his arms. I didn't have a chance to protest before his lips were on mine. His hands cupped my face and mercifully all my anger toward him disappeared into the thin, warm air.

It was my first kiss.

The first time I heard my heart thunder in my ears.

It happened so quickly, his lips on mine, his scent overpowering all of me. Before I knew it, it was over and his green eyes were staring down at me.

Slowly, Ethan brushed my hair away from my face and a grin grew across his lips. "I didn't want him to be your first kiss," he whispered, and I could smell my strawberry lip balm on his breath. "I don't want you kissing anyone but me."

"What about Erica?" I said breathlessly.

He pressed his forehead against mine. "She's not you," he said looking deep into my eyes. "She will never be you."

"Okay," I muttered and I felt my cheeks curl up into a grin.

Ethan smiled at me, our noses flushed. "Everyone seems to know that you're my girl but you. Be mine, Freckles," he whispered and placed his arms around my lower back.

I bit my lower lip and nodded, afraid that anything I said would ruin this moment. Ethan kissed me once more and I closed my eyes, forever etching this day in my memory.

And just like that Ethan and I were a couple.

CALLIE ANDERSON

Chapter Nine

PRESENT

The keys dangle from my hand as I open the studio door. Stale air greets me when I step into the studio that was once my home away from home. Locating the switch, I turn on the lights and gasp at what I see.

Time seems to stand still.

There is no shine to the wood floors laid parallel to the mirrors, and the dust that covers every surface is like the cloak that covers my dreams. The music that once vibrated through these walls has long ceased, and the irony is not lost on me: when I walked away from this dream everything else died. My mother shut the studio down when I left, and it looks as if she hasn't been here since. Though she said she rented it out, I know that by the amount of dust that it was a lie. It saddens me to see something she worked so hard for tossed away so easily.

I take a few seconds walking around, the familiarity of each step reminding me of the years I spent here. I let the emotions crash over me as I drag my fingers along the ballet barre installed in the back of the room. The throbbing in my ankle brings fresh tears to my eyes, and I look at myself in the mirror. For a split second I see a younger version of myself in a leotard and I'm reminded of how everything has changed.

"Enough with the pity party, Les. It's time to get to work." I brush back the tears that threaten to fall. I'm here to save my parents, not dwell on the past.

My mother casually mentioned that the studio needed a clean up before we could open the doors again, but by the looks of it, I'll be here for the remainder of the week. I toss my hair into a messy bun and get to work.

With a full day behind me, the floors are vacuumed and waxed. The mirrors are clean and streak free, and I can see the potential the studio still has. It looks like it once did, beautiful and filled with endless opportunities. I feel anxious, and hopeful for a successful grand re-opening, but I doubt I'll ever be the dance instructor my mom is—*or was*.

Walking over to the sound system in the far right corner of the room, I plug my phone in and slide my feet out of my tennis shoes. There is only one way to find out if I still have it in me. Whether I can teach or if I'll be a complete failure. I wait for the song to load, crank up the volume, and hit the play button. Naturally, my feet and arms take first position, and then I press up on my toes and wait for the song to start. Closing my eyes, I allow the melody to take over my soul. It's a routine my mother and I choreographed.

It's my audition for Juilliard.

It's what got me my dream before it was taken away from me.

My toes extend and my arms move effortlessly through the air. I push through the pain and each position is delicate as it leads me into the next. The rhythm takes over and I leap across the floor. Extending my toe, I fan out my leg and fall to the floor dramatically before getting back up. The tempo of the song changes and I push myself, arching my back into an arabesque. It's near the end, so I lift up as I set up for the fouette spin. I'm rusty and my ankle wobbles as I try to balance myself. But I fight through the pain and let the rhythm of the music guide me across the floor. With one final spin, I imagine myself being lifted into the air. I hold my breath and let my body float off the ground effortlessly, even if only in my mind.

It was how Ethan and I practiced it that entire summer. We had spent countless afternoons under the massive tree in my back yard doing the routine until it was perfect. It was how I envisioned the piece. Ballet was my life and when I was down, he was there to lift me up. He was my foundation. The one who built me up when my mother tried to tear me down. It was only right that the routine end with a lift. It was how I imagined it. Through every hour of torturous practice, the blood, sweat, and tears, I would rise up like the lotus flower.

I gasp and open my eyes when I feel myself being lifted from the ground. His hands are at my waist, extending me over his head. I lose my balance and screech with fear. Slowly, Ethan lowers me back to the floor. My body brushes against his and I take a few steps back.

Stunned.

Breathless.

Consumed by his presence.

He's here. Standing before me as if nothing ever happened. As if eight years never passed. As though the last time I spoke to him, I wasn't begging him to come to me.

We don't say anything to each other as the song comes to an end and the studio is silent. My heart races in my chest and I can't seem to catch my breath. His presence is unbearable, and for a moment I think I'm imagining it.

It's a mirage. He's not really here. It's the fumes from the wax.

"Hey, Freckles." His voice is more masculine than I remember. The way my nickname slips off his tongue causes me to bite back a sob. The man before me looks nothing like the boy I left behind.

"Ethan," I manage even though every fiber in my body is telling me to run away.

His gaze scans my body and I take a moment to do the same. He is older, more handsome, stronger, and the scruff growing on his cheeks makes him look delectable. Every single emotion crashes through me.

Hatred.

Love.

Pain.

Longing.

Repulsion.

Desperation.

I want to run into his arms. I want him to kiss away the pain like he always did. But I stop myself. The pain radiating up my leg keeps me grounded to the floor.

"I heard about your dad. How is he?" He tucks his hands into the pockets of his jeans and shifts his weight from one leg to the other. My eyes are fixated on his arms when I catch a glimpse of a tattoo peeking out from under his sleeve, but I can't see what it is.

"He's fine." I clear my throat and hope my voice sounds less shaken than I feel. "How's yours?" I cock an eyebrow at him.

"Still breathing."

I huff. "How unfortunate."

"You're still dancing?" A small grin curls up on his face and for a split second he again looks like that boy who made me fall madly in love with him.

"No." I shake my head. "Not since . . ." My words fail me and I lift my ankle to crack it. I inhale and push the thoughts out of my mind. "How did you know I was here?"

"It's a small town, Leslie. People talk. And when they see you, they tell me."

"My mother said you left."

"I keep to myself. I moved across town and I don't go to that house anymore. Not to mention your mother rarely leaves the house anymore."

My eyes trail down his body and I notice his shirt. It's from a business his father once owned. The anger rises, heating my blood.

He'd become his father's son.

BROKEN DREAMS

"You're picking up your daddy's slack, I see." I shake my head in disgust. Anger erupts through my body and I can't hold back anymore. "You're working in his shady business! What the hell happened to you?" I grind my teeth and try to keep my voice calm but fail. "You hated everything he stood for. You hated how he ran this town. You wanted to leave this god awful place, and yet here you are as his *fucking* replica?"

"Leslie—" He takes a step forward and I step back.

"Don't touch me!" I can't stop the tears that pool in my eyes. "You're just like him, aren't you? Did you earn your spot by killing an innocent person? Sorry I missed your initiation." I begin to tremble so I walk to where my phone is plugged into the sound system.

"I'm nothing like him," he claims.

My feet fail me. I'm paralyzed. Rooted to the spot. "Oh yeah?" I don't look back at him. "Tell me you don't own this town." I wait a few seconds before looking back at him.

"It's not what you think." His eyes are hooded.

"Really?" I cross my arms over my chest. "You know what I think? I think you're a coward. Growing up, all you wanted was to leave this fucking horrible town. And yet here you are running shit like your father once did."

"I didn't have a choice." His voice rises. "After that night in the garage-"

"Get out!" I scream. The pain in my ankle is unbearable. "Get. Out. Now."

"Let me explain."

"Explain? You want to fucking explain? Too little, too late, buddy. I don't want to see you. I don't want to be anywhere near you."

"I'm sorry . . . for everything." he says softly before turning around and walking out the door. I wait until I hear the revving of his car before I break down and cry.

I arrive home from the studio drained. My muscles ache with a familiar pain they haven't felt in years. I find my mother in the living room sitting in my father's recliner.

"Hi," I say, surprised to see her. "You're home already? I thought I was going to pick you up after his dinner? How was he today?" My father was transferred to the rehab center on the other side of the hospital a few days ago once the new insurance kicked in. My mother usually spends her entire day with him.

She looks over at me and I realize she has been crying. Her eyes are puffy and the tip of her nose is red. "Mom, what is it?" I crouch down and grab her hand.

"It's just painful to watch, Leslie." She sniffles back. "Your father isn't the man he once was. And I know he's on the road to recovery, but to see him like this . . . It breaks my heart. I couldn't wait for you to come and get me. I needed to leave."

I rub my hands over hers to soothe away her pain. "He's going to get better, Mom. The doctors are very hopeful that he can make a full recovery."

"I hope you're right." She slides a tissue under her eyes and wipes away the tears.

I give her a small smile. My eyes scan her face. I can see that her cheeks are sunken in and I can't remember the last time I saw her eat. "I'm gonna make us some dinner." I stand and let go of her hand. "If we're going to help Dad, we need to be healthy ourselves, and that means we need to eat."

"I'm not hungry," she mutters.

"Mom, we need to nourish our bodies. You can't live off coffee." I walk out of the living room and toward the kitchen.

"You seem to be living off tequila just fine."

I look back at her and can't help but laugh. She's right, I have consumed copious amounts of it since I arrived. "Fine, no more coffee for you, and no more tequila for me." She nods her head in agreement.

In the kitchen, I cut up vegetables and defrost some chicken. Tossing it into a pot, I add some chicken stock, and just like that we have chicken soup.

My mother is sitting at the kitchen table when I bring her a bowl. Without saying a word we consume our dinner. It's the first time in what feels like a lifetime that my mother and I have shared a meal. It seems odd yet comforting.

"That was delicious." My mother wipes the corner of her mouth with her napkin. "I don't remember teaching you to cook."

I feel the corners of my mouth curl up in a grin. "I worked for a catering company through my last year of college. I can make phenomenal whipped cream, but I don't think you'd approve of the fat and calories."

She laughs. "No, you're right. I would not approve, but the soup was splendid." The puffiness around her eyes has vanished and some color has returned to her cheeks. "I'm going to head up." She stands, taking her empty bowl with her. As she passes me, her hand lands on my shoulder and she grips it firmly. It's only for a split second but I know it means so much more. It's an olive branch to a potential relationship between us.

Chapter Ten

PRESENT

My mother approved the changes I made, and the dance studio is ready for re-opening. She has been so preoccupied waiting on my father hand and foot that she didn't even question what genre of dance I would be teaching. Prior to my accident our dance studio primarily taught ballet, but it has been closed for years and there have been many changes in professional dancing. I want to bring that change and revamp the studio. I want to make it my own.

We're in the car on our way to the hospital, when my mother spots the flyers in the back seat of the car. "What are those?" she asks.

"I want to hang up a few flyers around town." I shrug. "I figured parents would see the ads I have running in the local paper, but if the little girls see it, they might ask their moms to sign them up for dance."

"I guess that fancy education your father paid for is paying off after all."

"Can't you just say 'I'm proud of you' or 'Smart thinking'?" I grip the steering wheel firmly as I stop at a red light. "Do you always have to make a backhanded comment?" I glance over at her.

Her lips purse together and she pulls her gaze away from mine and focuses out the window. A few miles pass before she opens her mouth to speak again. "You haven't stopped by to see your father."

"I haven't had time, Mother," I lie. I want to stay far away from that place, and she should know why better than anyone.

"He's going to know that you haven't been visiting him."

"I've been busy with the studio. Once that is up and running again, I will go visit him. I think Dad understands that." I have my own reasons for not wanting to go into that place that holds painful memories. I lived there for an entire summer as doctors told me I would never dance again, as my mother was too unstable to have me home, as Ethan never came to visit.

After dropping my mother off, I make my way back to the center of town. I'm on a mission to get these flyers hung up. I stop by the school and greet some of the teachers who are still there from when I was in school and I ask if I could hang a flyer in their classroom. Everyone seems happy to help.

By late afternoon I've made my way through the entire town. With no flyers left, I decide to stop for lunch. There's so much variety, but I finally settle for a pub. An ice-cold beer will definitely help with the exhaustion. The pub is dark, and the smell of stale peanuts and old cigarettes linger in the air. There are big wooden booths that line each side of the bar and a few high top tables scattered around. An oval bar is the center of the room.

"Can I help you?" the bartender asks.

Hesitantly, I step further inside and my eyes squint due to the darkness. It's empty, so I assume the lunch rush has died down.

"Um, I'd like to order some lunch."
"Do you want a table or are you taking it to go?"
"I can eat at the bar." I walk up to pull a stool back.
She places a menu in front of me and walks over to grab me a glass of water. Her hair is platinum blonde and her dark eye shadow makes it impossible to recognize her. But as soon as she slouches to one side, I know exactly who she is.
"You're Erica, right?" I say with a hint of excitement in my voice. "We were in school together." She stops and looks at me like I have two heads. "I'm Leslie. Leslie Sutton."
Erica sighs and cocks her head to the side. "I know exactly who you are. Now what do you want to eat?"
Ouch. I don't remember her being that much of a bitch. I curse myself mentally for not befriending more people and being so caught up with Ethan's ass. "Can I just have a cheeseburger and a Stella, please?" I close my menu and do my best to ignore her as she walks around the bar mumbling under her breath. I pull out my cell phone and check my messages. I smile at the new picture of my niece Lyra that her dad sent me. She's not my blood relative, but I *am* her TiTi. After I reply, I check my mailbox. I have two new emails regarding potential new students for the studio.

Dear Leslie,

I'm inquiring about the ad I saw in the Tribune News this morning. I have three girls who don't really care much for physical activity but they love to dance. I would love to come by the studio and chat more. Please email me back with your availability so we can set something up. Thank you in advance,
Margie

Dear Leslie,

I caught a glimpse of your flyer outside of Al's Bakeshop and I was wondering what kind of dance programs you offer. We're new to town and my daughter loved taking hip-hop/jazz at our previous community center. Let me know when I can swing by the studio so we can talk some more.
Best regards,
Jackie.

I can't help the excitement I'm feeling. Not only did someone see the ads in the paper but the flyers I posted are working, too. My fingers click on the third email but I don't read it. My attention is pulled away due to a banging on the bar top. My head pops up immediately and on the other side of the bar, Erica stands with her back facing me. Two men surround her, and a sinking feeling takes over when one of them looks directly at me, and a sly grin grows on his face.

Michael.

I try to smile but I can't, there is a look in his eyes that terrifies me. It's like he's almost pissed to see me here.

Erica hands him my beer and he walks it over to me. "Well, well, well, look what the cat dragged in." The stench of old cigarettes and liquor permeates from his pores.

"Hi, Michael." I reach for my beer. It's been years since I've seen him, but he still looks like the same boy who asked me on my first date so many years ago.

"I'm surprised you even remember my name." He steps closer, invading my personal space. His voice is low and terrifying when he speaks again. "I'm surprised you know anybody, really, since when you did live in this town, you only focused on one thing. One person, really. Ethan."

I lean back and hop off the stool. There's something about the way he is looking at me that makes a chill run up my spine. "It's good to see you too, Michael. Now if you'll excuse me. . . ." My gaze pulls away from his as I notice the other guy heading toward us. It all brings back memories I've spent years pushing away. Never will I ever let a man invade my space again. Everything in me tells me to get the hell out of here.

Erica appears on the other side of the bar, holding a white plate with my food. My hunger has long vanished as my heart is racing and I want to run.

"For someone who won't be here long, it looks like you've been very busy." Erica pulls a flyer from her back pocket and tosses it at me. "Will you make me chase you out of here like last time, *Les*?"

"Last time?" I can't help but look at her as if she's an idiot. I refuse to let them know the affect they are having on me. "I don't know what delusional world you live in, but I left for school. Unlike you, I didn't stay in this minuscule town and become a nobody. I got a degree, I got a job, I moved on with my life. No one chased me away."

The other guy chuckles and it seems to fuel her rage. Crossing her arms over her chest, she squints at me. "Sure you did. I suppose you're also over Ethan, which is why, out of all the restaurants in town, you came to his place."

I close my eyes for a brief moment. "Fuck," I mutter under my breath. Reaching inside my purse, I pull out a twenty and toss it on the bar before I throw my purse over my shoulder. "It won't happen again," I say, hoping my voice sounds as condescending as I mean it to be.

When I turn to leave, Michael and his friend block my path. "You're not welcome here," Michael hisses in my direction.

"Excuse me?" My shoulders tighten and he takes a step forward.

"The only person you cared about was Ethan, the only friend you had was Ethan. You've caused him enough damage that we don't need you around him anymore." He grabs my forearm. "Do I make myself clear?"

"Don't touch me!" I snap.

Erica giggles. I glare at her. "Me and Ethan are together now. I keep him happy, if you know what I mean. Stay away from him. Go back to where you came from. No one wants you here."

My fists clench at my sides. There's a bottle of mace inside my purse but I know I won't be quick enough to grab it. It's of no use to me. Bile rises in my throat. "Oh, it looks like we've made the dance queen mad." Erica laughs.

"Back the fuck off," Ethan's voice bellows through the quiet pub. My knees wobble and I glance in his direction. He is in dark jeans with a black T-shirt and his strides are powerful and calculated. His gaze never meets mine.

Michael and his friend take a step back, and I find myself finally able to breathe again. "Come on, E, we were just having a little fun; some friendly hazing. You know we were just messing with her," Michael says with a squeaky voice. I can see the fear in his eyes.

Like Jerry, Ethan strikes fear when he enters a room.

Ethan walks right between Michael and me. His shoulders are broad, shielding me from harm's way. As always, he is my protector. "What the fuck do you think you're doing? I don't pay you to sit around here and fucking bullshit the day away with Erica. Your job is under the hood of the cars." Ethan's voice is threatening and authoritative. "Get to fucking work." Michael and the other guy rush out of the pub. Ethan glances over at Erica. His jaw twitches. "What are you looking at? Don't you got shit to do? The new shipment of liquor came in. Go restock the back room."

Erica mumbles something and storms out of the bar.

When we no longer hear her heels clicking on the wood floor, Ethan turns to face me. His features soften when our eyes meet. "I'm sorry about that," he mutters. I stand there speechless for a few seconds staring at the man in front of me. He is everything I love laced with everything I despise.

Jerry.

He is identical to his father, and the resemblance makes me sick.

"I have to go." I hold firmly to the strap of my purse and jog out of the pub. The warm air hits my skin and I feel like I'm going to pass out. I walk up Main Street completely dazed and confused. After walking for five minutes, I realize my rental car is parked in the opposite direction. Frantic, I turn and am greeted with the kindest smile I've ever seen.

Charlie.

He was running after me. He stops dead in his tracks and opens his arms wide for me. "Leslie," he says, folding his arms around my back.

"Oh, Charlie! How are you, my friend?"

"So much better now that you're here." I pull away from his arms and glance up at him. He's a full foot and a half taller than I am. His shaggy brown hair is curled at the ends, and there are a few shaving nicks on his face. He looks so much like Ethan but still has a boyish touch.

"You look good, Charlie, so grown up." I can't hide the smile that grows on my lips. Out of everyone Jerry touched, Charlie was the only one who stayed pure.

"You're just being nice. I still look the same. A little taller, and I got hair in places I didn't know I could have." His eyes are wide.

I stumble back and laugh. Of course Charlie would be inappropriate at the most appropriate time. "Charlie . . ."

"I know. I know. I know. I can't talk like that in public. Ethan yells at me all the time."

My smile falters and I reach for his hand. "He yells at you?"

"No, not yells. Not like Dad. Never like Dad." I sigh with relief. "He just makes sure that I take my bath, I take my medicine, and I stay out of trouble."

I don't ask him anything else because a part of me doesn't want to know what Ethan does with his life now. *The less I know, the better.* "Well, it was really nice seeing you, Charlie." I lean forward and kiss his cheek. "I'm so happy I bumped into you."

"Me, too."

I take a few steps away from Charlie, but he calls back for me. I turn my head and he says, "Michael's a punk. Don't be scared of him. He wouldn't touch a fruit fly. But if he messes with you, let me know and I'll take care of it."

I simply nod and continue to walk down the street.

My foot lifts off the gas and presses gently on the brake as I turn onto my street. The houses all come into view before I gasp. Ethan rests against the hood of his car, his gaze focused on his old house. My heart races as I approach him.

He straightens when I pull my car into the driveway. I inhale some courage and step out of the car. We don't speak. His eyes scan my body before he holds up a white paper bag. "Hungry?"

"Why are you here?" I ask him.

"I figured since you left without touching your food you'd be starving."

"Your employees lack customer service," I snip, hating the

encounter with his *girlfriend*.

"Can we talk?" Ethan cocks his head toward the backyard and I nod. As much as I try to hate him, deep down inside I never learned how. He follows behind as I lead the way. I walk past the deck and toward the field of tall grass that leads to the beautiful mountains. It was where we sat when we were kids. We spent countless hours after school back here, doing homework or making out until our lips were bruised.

We find our way under our tree and sit. Refusing to look at him, I bring my knees to my chest. Ethan opens the bag and hands me a turkey club sandwich.

"You still like these?" he says, holding up a bag of salt and vinegar potato chips.

"Yeah." My voice is low. Being near him causes my brain to turn to mush.

"Is it weird being back?" he asks before taking a bite of his sandwich.

"You have no idea." I open the bag of chips and shove a few in my sandwich. "My mother is still the same. Crazy as always."

"How's Los Angeles?"

I look up at him. There is so much to say to one another, so much I want to ask, but too much time has passed and he isn't the same person he was before. "I moved to Chicago a few years ago," I say before taking a bite.

"Oh."

We are silent for a few seconds before I ask, "How's life here?"

"It's okay." He shrugs and I lift my eyebrow. "I'm not like him, Freckles," he adds like he knows exactly what I'm thinking.

"That's not what it looks like." I chew my bite slowly before swallowing. I'm remembering the powerfully scary man who walked into the pub earlier today.

"I would never." He shakes his head in defense. "You know how much I hate him."

"So, Michael and Erica?" I can't help but want to know more about them.

"They work for me. After Jerry . . . After you left, I had to pick up the slack." His words hurt me. "Everyone counted on me once my mother was taken away by the state and Charlie had no one to look out for him, so I dove head first into the business."

I give him a concerned look. "What happened at the pub today isn't okay."

"Michael thinks because we're friends, he's the hot guy in town. He's harmless."

"Harmless? Invading my personal space isn't harmless. It's all too familiar. And Erica?" My voice grows with annoyance.

He sighs. "She doesn't care for you very much."

"What did I ever do to her?" I ask before taking another bite.

"You didn't do anything. It's more that I refuse to let you go."

Taken aback, I lick my lips repeating what he said. "You *did* let me go."

"Not really." He looks deep into my eyes. For a moment I'm lost in the green hue that holds specs of gold.

Shaking my head, I say, "From what I remember, I asked you to come. I begged you to come and you never showed."

"Les . . . It wasn't that simple."

Swallowing the golf ball lodged in my throat, I nod. "I see." A part of me wants to scream. I want to rehash the past and say the words I never had a chance to say.

"I don't do what Jerry did." He tries to change the subject.

"If you say so."

"Les."

"You don't owe me any explanations, Ethan." Having a normal conversation with him is impossible. The past is still the past and it's something I will never get over. I crumble up the wrapper and stand. "I have to go. Thank you for lunch, and thank you for saving me from your friends."

"What are you doing?" He rushes to his feet.

"I'm not going to sit here and pretend everything between us is fine. I'm tired of being the bigger person and swallowing back everything I feel. I needed you. I needed you to be there, and you weren't. I needed you to be my anchor, and you left me. What happened to Jerry was because of me and never did we talk about it. I was shoved in a hospital room and the last image

I have of you is you in that garage. You dove into the family business because everyone was looking at you. You were there for everyone *but me*."

"Les. I fucked up, but let me explain. " He reaches out to grab my hand but I take a step back.

"No. Don't chase after me now. I don't need your explanations eight years later. I learned to build myself back up, no thanks to you. I'm here to work and help my parents. When everything is back to normal, I'm out of here."

And with that, I turn and make my way toward the house. I don't glance back. I refuse to let him see me falter.

Not anymore.

Chapter Eleven

PRESENT

That tequila bottle is half empty but I pour myself another shot. I know I made a deal with my mother to give up tequila but that was before Ethan appeared. I'm attempting to drown out Ethan from my head but failing miserably. After I rushed off from our picnic, I stopped at the liquor store before picking up my mother. I decided on the drive from there to the hospital that it would be a night for forgetting. Even if it meant I drank the entire bottle.

I hated being around Ethan.

I hated that I still loved him as though a day had never passed.

But most of all I hated every single feeling I still had for him deep inside of me.

After dinner, my mother excused herself to her room, and I made my way to the tequila bottle I had stashed inside my purse. Sitting in the living room, I stare at the blank screen on the television, a shot glass in one hand and the bottle in the other as

I contemplate my life. I'm tired of running. But it's what I do best.

My mind spins. One moment I'm considering how much I love Ethan, and the next I'm imagining him and Erica. My blood boils with anger. I feel like that Katy Perry song. *I'm hot and I'm cold* . . .

I'm a freaking mess, that's one thing I know for sure.

I should get some rest since tomorrow will be packed with meetings with potential new clients for the grand re-opening. But instead of going to bed, I pull out my phone and open Facebook. I'm not usually on social media. I actually find it repulsive.

That's a lie.

I avoid it so I don't become a stage five clinger and stalk people. When I first moved to Los Angeles, I spent hours on Facebook waiting to see if Ethan popped up. The app became so addictive I blocked everyone from Prescott and changed my contact name so no one would find me. After a few years, I stalked Harry, my ex-boyfriend, until I drove myself mad. It's toxic, yet I refuse to deactivate my account.

Unable to control myself, I unblock all the friends from Prescott, and enter Ethan's name in the search bar. His profile appears, and like countless times before, nothing has changed. An old picture and no updates on his life or places he has checked into. Feeling like a daredevil, I take a swig straight from the bottle and click through the pictures he's been tagged in. My stomach turns.

It's pictures of him after I left. His life when I was gone. He looks serious in some, standing behind the bar as some guy takes a picture. In a crowd as someone takes a group shot. There are also plenty of him with Erica. She must love tagging her boyfriend all over social media.

I grind my teeth and click on the next photo. I can't help but scrutinize the last picture longer than most. It was taken two years after I left, and thanks to Facebook I even know the date and time it was uploaded. It's a picture of Ethan and Stephanie.

Stephanie was my friend who transferred to our school the summer of my junior year. She was in my dance class at school, and was also a regular victim of my mother in the studio. Aside from Ethan, she was the only person I considered a friend.

My drunken eyes study the picture. "Stephanie and Ethan," I slur to the computer screen. They're sitting rather close to each other. She's leaning into him and her silky blonde hair rests on his shoulder. They are both smiling into the camera and a part of me feels jealous.

Was she my replacement once I was gone?

Like me, she had planned on a dancing career for herself. She was supposed to go to Miami after high school, not stay here and take pictures with my boyfriend. Ex-boyfriend, I remind myself.

"Grr," I growl at the computer screen like a dog. This is why I hate social media. A simple picture has made the green-eyed monster that lives inside me rear its ugly head.

My fingers race over the keyboard on my computer and I can't stop them. So I give in to the jealousy and send Stephanie a Facebook message.

Me: Hey stranger, how's life?

The second I hit the send button, I don't blink waiting for her to respond. It's a disease, really; I'm wasting precious time over a picture that is six years old.

Three little dots appear immediately and I can only assume she has a notification setting on her cell phone.

Stephanie: OMG!!!!! Leslie! How are you?

Me: I'm good. Back in town. Temporarily, of course. My dad had a heart attack so I'm helping out my mom.

Stephanie: Oh no! I heard about your dad, I'm sorry. How does it feel to be back?

Me: You heard about my dad?

Stephanie: Yeah, you know how this town is. It lives for gossip.

Me: I didn't know you were in town. What happened to Miami?

Stephanie: It's a long story. Maybe we can meet and catch up?

I blame the alcohol for my need to know everything. I blame the jealousy that courses through my veins like blood.

Me: I'm free tonight if you want to grab some coffee.
Stephanie: Sure, that works. Do you want to meet at Beans in thirty?
Me: Perfect, I'll see you then.

We exchange numbers before saying good-bye. I run into the bathroom to shower off some of the drunkenness. Ten minutes later I'm dressed and out the door. I take the keys off the hook near the door, but walk past the car. Due to the amount of alcohol I've consumed, it's best to walk into town rather than drive.

The mile and a half hike sobers me a bit more, and when I see Stephanie all chipper and beautiful I pray that my pores aren't oozing with tequila. She's sitting at one of the tables outside of Beans. Her hands are laced around a large paper cup and when our eyes meet a genuine smile grows on her flawless face.

"Hi!" She stands and rushes over to me. Her tiny hands embrace me, and I'm greeted with her lavender scented lotion. "Oh, my God, look at you!" She says when she lets go. "You're still smoking hot!"

I shake my head and laugh. "Shut up! You know I can never compete with that gorgeous hair of yours."

"Please. Blonde is boring and flat. Your untamable long, black hair is sexy. I seriously can't believe you're back in town." She hugs me once again. "I'm so happy to see you. Come on, we need to catch up."

After I order the largest Americano on the menu, I sit outside with Stephanie.

"So." Her eyes are wide and she is swaying from side to side. "How's life? You live in LA now, right?"

"Life is good, I guess." I blow on my hot coffee. "I moved out of LA a few years ago. I had a job opportunity in Chicago, so I took it." I take a sip of my coffee and realize my life is pretty boring. I'm at the stage where my friends are getting engaged, getting married, having kids, travelling the world. I go to work. I hang out with my coworkers, and on occasion I let said coworkers set me up on blind dates because they feel I'm wasting my beauty.

"How are you?" I ask, quickly changing the subject. "I'm surprised to see you here. We had plans to get out of this town."

"I know." Stephanie sighs. "Miami didn't happen." She pouts.

"Why not?" I try to tone down the eagerness in my voice.

"I realized that summer it wasn't for me. I was getting ready to ship everything to Florida and it hit me. I loved to dance, but I didn't want to do it professionally, not like you." She shakes her head. "Yeah, I was a good dancer and it was fun, and I loved to compete, but it wasn't my passion." She lifts her hands. "I hate the humidity. I'm petrified of hurricanes. And I just didn't feel right. So instead, I went to Arizona State."

"Oh, wow," I say but in the back of my mind all I want to do is ask her about the picture with Ethan.

"Yeah, I was close to my parents and it was such an easy drive to come home when ever I wanted. And after the whole thing with Jerry, the town got so much better." She crinkles her nose at the mention of Jerry. I pull my gaze away from hers and glance down at my coffee cup. "I'm sorry. I didn't mean to bring him up. I should've known better."

I shake my head. "It's okay, really. It was such a long time ago it doesn't bother me anymore," I lie.

"So, were there any hot guys in Los Angeles?" She winks at me, and we both know she is desperately trying to change the subject.

"There was one, but it didn't work out. I was too focused on my career."

"Or maybe you were still holding on to what you left here."

"I didn't leave him here. He never came after me." Stephanie's lips purse and I want to ask her what it means, but her phone vibrates and she glances down at the screen.

"Crap, hold on," she says, bringing the phone to her ear. "Hi, honey." She smiles at me and I can hear a man's voice on the other end of the line. "I'm having coffee with Leslie . . . She was my first friend here and then she went to school in Los Angeles. This is the first time she's back. How's Seattle? . . . Oh, no! . . . Okay, well, can I call you when I get home? . . . All right. I love you! Bye, honey." She places the phone on the table and smiles up at me. "Sorry; the hubby." She raises both eyebrows with excitement.

"You're married!" I can't hide the excitement in my voice.

"Yeah, we eloped last year in Hawaii. His name is Bruce, and we met my last year at Arizona State. I had an internship with his firm. He travels a lot for business, which was why I chose to move back home so at least I can be close to my family. It's hard when he's gone for long periods of time, but I don't work anymore so when I miss him, I just get on a plane and go see him." Her eyes sparkle as she talks about him.

"I'm really happy for you," I say with every ounce of genuine enthusiasm I have inside of me.

"Thanks." She takes the tip of her coffee. "I'm sorry we lost touch."

"I think that was more my fault than yours. I was locked away in that hospital for so long, and the second I had a chance to escape, I ran and chose to never look back. I didn't want any reminders of the life I had." I chuckle. "Hell, I never spoke to my mother."

"Well, she didn't take it very well. I don't think anyone did; definitely not Ethan."

"I didn't know you guys were close?" I ask because it's festering inside me and the ugly green monster has won.

Stephanie glances at me before looking down at her coffee. "We weren't at first. But when you left, we became friends." I can't help but furrow my eyebrows at her. "It's not what you think." She raises her hands to reassure me. "He needed a friend. I think for a long time he was just trying to replace you. He was looking for the next best thing. And I think at one point, he thought it was me. He even tried to kiss me once. He was drunk, of course, and I slapped him upside the head. He missed you a lot and constantly talked about you. Still does, you know."

"I saw him today. I accidentally walked into his pub and was greeted by Erica and Michael."

"Ugh." Stephanie rolls her eyes dramatically. "I still hate that girl." Stephanie crosses her arms. "She's like a damn gnat that won't die!"

"Apparently, Ethan doesn't."

"I think he takes pity on her. Her dad reminds him of Jerry."

"And she keeps his bed warm," I add, letting her know that I know about them.

"I think she only does when he's desperate and drunk." She tries to ease the blow.

"What he does with his life is not my concern," I say, trying to convince myself. "He doesn't owe me anything."

"So you ran into him . . ."

"Yeah," I continue. "Michael and Erica were giving me a hard time. Michael was making these threats about me not being welcomed, and Ethan broke it up. I ran out, and when I got home he was there waiting for me with food." Stephanie sighs and I see the puppy eyes growing on her face. "We had lunch, and then I just lost it."

"Why?"

"It's been a long time, and I have so much anger and pain built up because of him. And when he's around he makes me feel things again, and I've worked very hard to forget these feelings."

"Maybe you should stop trying to fight everything. Maybe your feelings are meant to be. The history between you two goes back almost twenty years."

"Whatever; enough about me and Ethan. Let's talk about anything else."

"How's your mother?" Stephanie asks with a smile.

"I drink almost a bottle of tequila a day because of her. I'm probably becoming an alcoholic, but whatever." I laugh.

Stephanie giggles. "Girl, if I'd known you were that much of a lush, I would've invited you out for a cocktail, not coffee."

"I'm always down for drinking when I'm around my mother."

"Well, let's get going then. I know just the place."

"As long as it's not a place Ethan owns."

"No, not at all."

I chug the rest of my coffee and follow Stephanie to her car. We head down Main Street toward the end of town to a tiny little complex that I didn't even know existed. It faces out into the mountains with condos above the storefronts. Stephanie parks the car in front of Rosa's Wine Bar.

"This is new," I say, closing the car door behind me.

"When Bruce and I got married, my parents wanted me to have a traditional wedding. Since we chose to elope, my father bought us a piece of land as our wedding present. I didn't want to build a giant house since I knew it would be empty a lot, so we invested and built condos. We rent out the storefronts, and my sister-in-law runs Rosa's Wine Bar."

I nod, studying the sleek architecture. The building isn't massive, only a few floors up and the length of a city block. Inside, wine bottles are scattered throughout the room, and three rustic light fixtures hang from old beams in the ceiling. The atmosphere is laid-back with a few couples spread around the lounge area.

Stephanie waves to a female standing behind the bar and then points to an empty table across the room. "This must be heaven," I joke when we sit down.

"I like to say it's my little piece of heaven." A waiter walks over and greets us with a menu, but Stephanie declines. "Can you tell Rosa that we want the wine sampling for two." She looks away from the waiter and then over at me. "Trust me, it's the best thing here."

"Sure, that works," I agree.

Our waiter brings us two trays each carrying four different wineglasses. Each glass is filled with a little more then your regular sip. "This is the Merlot sampling," he says, placing the trays in front of us. Another waiter behind him places a wooden block filled with assorted cheeses and various nuts. He explains which cheese is paired with each wine before heading to the back.

When Stephanie said a sampling, I simply envisioned four glasses. I didn't realize we would be sampling the best of every variety of wine Rosa carried. I reach for my first glass and take a small sip. The wine is filled with a variety of aromas and I taste the wild black fruit in its undertone. "I think I found my new go-to location," I say as I reach for the dried apricots that are hidden behind the Manchego.

"I'm here almost every weekend." Stephanie raises her glass and we cheer to our little piece of heaven.

We start with the Shiraz, followed by the Cabernet, and Pinot Noir. Jason then returns with the rose wines. They're sweeter, and I have to admit that at this point they're all starting to taste the same. By the time we move on to the white wine, my buzz is in full effect. My cheeks are warm to the touch, and I have to hold back the urge to giggle.

When Jason places the dessert wine in front of us, I push my tray forward. "I'm tapping out. I'm officially way too drunk," I say and I know my words are slurring. "I need to get home. I have to be up tomorrow for the grand re-opening." I press my palms to my eyes.

"Oh no!" Stephanie protests. "Tomorrow is Saturday and it's only ten-thirty. You can hang a little longer, can't you? Please?" I glance up at her and shake my head. "My condo is right upstairs. You can spend the night in the guest room. It'll be like old times and we'll have slumber party where all we do is talk about boys. Well, I'll talk about Bruce and you can talk about Ethan," Stephanie rambles.

"If Darlene wakes up and I'm not home, she'll hang my head over the mantel. You know how she is." I take a sip of water that Jason has kindly put in front of me. "I should call a cab."

"Don't be silly!" Stephanie shakes her head and digs in her purse. "I invited you out, I will call you an Uber."

I thank Stephanie and excuse myself to use the restroom. Keeping one eye closed, I try to walk with grace toward the door with a big W on it. Inside, I splash my face with cold water but it does nothing to help. The reflection in the mirror frightens me, and I run my fingers under my eyes, wiping away the mascara.

"I'm really freaking drunk," I mutter.

I don't remember how I find my way back to Stephanie, but when I do she forces me to drink two glasses of water before leading me outside. "Come on, babe, your chariot awaits." The fresh air cools my skin and I inhale it, hoping it helps. Stephanie holds the back door open for me and I climb into the back seat. I fall on the cool leather and I pray I do not pass out.

"You take care of my girl," I hear her say to the driver.

He chuckles and I feel my body warm. That chuckle sounds so familiar. I attempt to pry an eye open to see who he is, but I'm only greeted with the black leather from the seat in front of me.

I moan, unable to lift myself up. "I'm going to feel like hell tomorrow," I say and close my eyes.

Sleep.

It's the only thing my body craves.

I push off the seat and wipe the drool from the corner of my mouth. I blink a few times and wait for my vision to become clear. Confused, I stare outside and see that we are parked in my driveway. Glancing back at the driver, I suck in a quick gasp of air.

"Goddamn it! Stephanie called *you* to take me home?" I wince when my head begins to pound.

Ethan flicks the car light on and looks back at me. "Did you have a nice nap, Freckles?" The boyish grin causes my head to spin but I choose to blame the alcohol. "I forgot how cute it is when you snore."

"One, I don't snore," I say and cover my eyes. "Two, why are your lights out?" Surprisingly, I'm shocked that I'm no longer as intoxicated as I was at the bar.

"I didn't want to wake anyone. Besides, I figured I'd let you sleep it off for a bit so you wouldn't wake your mother."

"How long have we been sitting here?" My throat is parched.

"An hour or so."

I glance at the clock in his car, which reads two in the morning. I try to remember what time I left Rosa's and realize it's a lot longer than an hour. Inhaling, I dig through my purse for my keys. "Thanks, Ethan. Stephanie tricked me into drinking."

"Anything for you." He kicks his car door open and reaches back for mine. "Come, I'll walk you to your door." He sticks out a hand for me.

"Who said chivalry is dead?" I give him my hand.

In one sweeping motion, Ethan has me out of the car and into his arms. The scent of him is intoxicating and I stumble to the side. "You're going to wake your mother if you can't walk straight." He brings me closer and his low voice causes a shiver to run down my spine.

"The doctor prescribed her Ambien," I whisper, avoiding his gaze. "She won't wake up." I realize the proximity of his face. Testing my heart, I look up at him. Our eyes lock for only a few seconds, but a lifetime of love flows through us. I desperately want to rub my fingertips along the scruff coating his cheeks, but I force myself to take a step toward the house.

Ethan and I stand at my front door, and with his help I'm able to stick my key into the lock and turn it. "Thank you for saving me tonight," I say over my shoulder.

"I'd do anything for you. You know that."

"Back at ya." Without any hesitation, I lean in and kiss his lips. It's a quick kiss, one I have offered millions of times before. And though my body feels as if it's about to explode, I choose to ignore it and push the door open.

"Good night, Les," Ethan says and turns to walk toward his car.

I thought tequila was the liquor that made you do insane things, but clearly it is wine.

"Hey, Ethan?" I call back to him. He stops and looks over at me. "I miss you climbing through my window."

He chuckles and I walk inside.

Tossing my belongings on the console table, I kick my shoes off and make my way up the stairs. My pants are tossed to the side by the time I reach my room and I'm swearing to never drink again.

I'm digging through my suitcase when I hear a tap on my window. I jump and look over at Ethan. His body is illuminated by the full moon, and I'm transferred back to ten years ago when I would wait patiently for these moments.

I push the window open and allow him in. "I thought you were heading home," I whisper. His eyes are locked on my legs. "Crap." I slap his shoulder. "Stop being such a dog. I didn't know you were coming up, and I was changing into my pajamas."

"Hey, that's not my fault." He slides his jacket off his

shoulders. "As long as it's visible, I'm going to stare at it without any shame." My face warms and I back away from him.

"I thought you were going home?" I ask again.

"No, I only wanted to park my car around the corner. I don't want the neighbors talking to your mom." Ethan's voice is low and raspy. "Mrs. Greeley is still nosy."

I slide my pajama pants on and turn away from him. Discarding my shirt, I slip my bra off and pull a T-shirt over my head. The entire time, his gaze heats my skin. My heart is racing a mile a minute, and I don't know what to think. I don't want him to leave, but I also don't want to have any false hopes about something that ended so tragically.

When I'm ready for bed, I look back at him. It's my turn to gawk since he in standing shirtless with only his boxers on. The ache between my legs makes it impossible to speak. Instead, I walk over to my bed and draw the comforter back.

"I must be very, very drunk since I'm letting you stay the night." I say as I climb into bed.

"You'll be fine. You're the only girl I know who can drink her heart out and never puke." He slips in next to me.

I slap his bare chest and my hands land on his tattoo. The heat from his body radiates off his skin and I curl closer to him. "When did you get it?" I ask. I want to turn the light on and inspect every millimeter of his body; every muscle that has tripled in size from the last time I saw it.

Ethan huffs and stretches his arms out so I can lay on his chest. I don't argue. Even if it's just for one night, I want to hit pause on everything that ever happened between us.

"A year after you left. When did you get yours?"

"What are you talking about?"

"I know every freckle you have, every beauty mark. I spent many nights in this room studying your body. The room is dark, Leslie, but I'm not blind. And for whatever reason, you still have that nightlight plugged into the wall. I saw the shadow of it when you took off your bra."

My heart is thumping in my chest. "A year after I left," I say.

Ethan shifts on the bed and brings me closer to him. My forehead rests against his cheek, and my hands traces the ink on his chest. "What did you get?" I ask, trying to envision what it is.

"The same as yours." He kisses the tip of my nose and a grin grows on my face.

"You don't know what I have." My lips press on his.

"Of course I do."

He kisses me back and I moan into his mouth. It's familiar and painful at the same time. I spent many years forgetting what his lips felt like. I ran from the pain he caused.

It's too much to bear.

Pulling away, I look into his eyes. "I've spent eight years trying to forget you," I remind him. "I taught myself to hate you." I lie.

He ignores me for another second and kisses me once more. This time our tongues meet and he presses his firm body against mine. I melt into him and he pulls away. "You want to hate me because you love me." He pulls me closer to him. "Let's pretend that, just for tonight, we're still teenagers." He kisses the top of my head and I sigh into the nook in his neck.

"Tomorrow I go back to not speaking to you."

"You're not a good liar, Leslie." His voice is soothing.

"Shut up, Ethan."

"I love you, too."

We both know we have permanently inked ourselves with a Lotus flower.

CALLIE ANDERSON

Chapter Twelve

PAST

Three Years Later.

Ethan.
Ethan.
Ethan.

I was consumed by all things Ethan. My world revolved around him. When I was in school, I was with him. When I was at dance, I was thinking of him. When I was home, I rushed to my room and waited for him. He was my world, and we spent every possible second together. We spent hours making out hidden in the tall grass behind my house. We spent nights sitting out on the extended roof outside my bedroom window looking up at the stars. He was my everything and there wasn't a thing I'd change about our love. It was infectious and beautiful.

I was a sophomore in high school, finishing up my year before the summer started. I was worried about the summer. My mother had insisted I spend three weeks at a dance clinic, and I didn't know how much time I would get to see Ethan. We both knew this summer would put a strain on our relationship. It was the last summer before our senior year and his father wanted him to get his hands dirty with the family business. While most juniors going into their senior year were applying to colleges Ethan wasn't allowed. He was to stay home and take over the kingdom his father had built. Jerry wanted Ethan to be like his old man. And that made me tremble with fear.

Over the years, we'd learned that Jerry ran a few drug trades outside of town, but no one within a ten-mile radius caused any trouble in this town without dealing with Jerry. Ethan also learned that Jerry owned many things in town including a mechanic shop, a local bar, and even a few apartment buildings in the center of town. Though most of the businesses ran legitimate books, Jerry was known for laundering money. He also had the Police Department on his payroll, which meant they looked the other way as Jerry buried the bodies in the desert.

On Ethan's first day of work, I stayed busy the only way I knew how. I danced.

I danced until my feet bled.

With fear and anger coursing through me, I figured I'd transform the energy into something productive like videotaping my audition for Juilliard. With the videotape recording, I left everything on the dance floor—the fear of losing Ethan to his father; the rage I felt toward my mother for continuously making me redo everything even though it was perfect; the dream of getting out of this town as soon as I was old enough. I challenged myself; I pushed harder. Tears dripped from my eyes and I knew this would be the tape I submitted to Juilliard. There was no other way I'd be able to capture this emotion again.

When the song finished, I dropped to the floor as I gasped for air and warm tears dripped down my cheeks.

"That's how you'll get into Juilliard." My mother's voice startled me.

I didn't respond. Her compliment did nothing to alleviate the pain in my chest. I knew I was getting into Juilliard. There wasn't a doubt in my heart. But I wasn't sure if Ethan would still be by my side.

Later that night, I waited in my bed for Ethan to appear. My sore legs shook with anxiety as I waited for him to come in through my window. I pushed every thought out of my mind and focused on the glass. I needed to see him. I needed for him to be okay.

When he appeared in the window frame, I jumped off my bed and ran toward him. My arms laced around his body. "I was so scared." My voice came out in a frantic whisper. Unable to control my tears, I let go and cried into his chest.

Ethan draped his arms over me and enveloped my small body into his masculine frame. "It's okay." He kissed the top of my head. "I'm okay."

I rose on my tippy toes and kissed him on the lips. The sadness I saw in his eyes caused fear to permanently wrap around my bones. "Talk to me." I sniffled back.

He shook his head as though he was trying to shake away the memories. "No one is safe in this town as long as my father is here. We should get out of here." His voice was cool and calm. It was terrifying to see him like that. His large hands framed my face and his eyes scanned mine with fear. "We should leave and never come back."

My jaw quivered and my hands dug around his frame. Closing my eyes, I pressed my head to his chest. "Where do you want to go?" I would follow him to the moon and back if he wanted me to. He was what mattered most. He was more important than anything else in my life.

"Let's go to New York." His voice held a steady tone.

"What?" I pulled away from him and was greeted with his green eyes. There wasn't an ounce of doubt in them.

"You want to go to school there, and I can find a job. I'll go to school at night, and we can still be together," Ethan said as though he had planned it all along.

"Yeah?" I asked, my vision temporarily blurred with fresh tears.

"I'm serious, Leslie. Let's get the hell out of this town and far away from my father."

There was a pinch in my chest. It wasn't painful. It was tight like a hug right on my sternum yet made it difficult to breathe. It was the kind of pain that even rubbing your chest did nothing to alleviate. It was then I realized it wasn't a pain at all.

It was love.

I was in love.

Over the years, I'd somehow fallen in love with Ethan. It wasn't that fleeting kind of high school love. It was an eternal love. So powerful, so all-consuming that it physically hurt. I curled my lips into a grin and looked at him. He was the only person I ever wanted to love. Ethan kissed the top of my head and then the tip of my nose before staring at me with his tantalizing eyes.

"I love you," I confessed. The words slipped out in perfect harmony. It was the first time in my life I had ever uttered those words to a boy, and I meant them with every fiber of my being. His hands cupped my face; his thumb grazed my soft cheek. Gently, he rubbed it against my lips.

"I love you, too," he said before he leaned in and captured my lips with his.

His words made my insides tingle. I wanted to be with Ethan. I wanted to spend the rest of my life feeling for Ethan the way I did in that moment.

Slowly, I led us to the bed and straddled him. My hands ran through his hair as my lips kissed his. Gentle at first, slowly, memorizing every centimeter of his lips. Ethan's hands slid up my back, and when he grunted inside my mouth I nearly lost it. I opened my mouth wider for him and pushed my body down on him. My tongue swirled around his until we were both panting for air.

I could feel him under me. His fingertips dug into my skin as he deepened our kiss. We had never gone this far before. He had moved from sleeping on the floor to sleeping next to me where he would hug me all night long, but never had we crossed the line. Some people at school talked about it. Some were doing it all over town, but Ethan never pressured me.

I wanted him to.

I wanted him more than anything in the world.

I wanted him more than I wanted to dance.

I tugged at the hem of his shirt, lifting it over his chest. His hands met mine and he stopped me. "Les . . ." He said my name against my lips.

I didn't respond. Instead, I pulled my shirt off. Ethan's eyes scanned my body and I felt my skin warm beneath his gaze. His hand slowly moved down my back and around my body. He sucked in a gasp of air and our eyes locked. He had never seen me like this before. Ethan had been climbing through my window every day for the past six years, but I was becoming a woman. His fingertips ran up my stomach, and I trembled at his touch. Everything seemed to be more intensified than before.

"Not like this, Les," he whispered as his hand cupped my breast. "Not in your room in the middle of the night." The trail of his fingers felt like an inferno. "I want our first time to be perfect."

I shook my head. "You're a boy. Why do you care about it being perfect?" I couldn't mask the annoyance in my voice. I took my shirt off the bed and slipped it back on.

"It's for you. I love you, Leslie, and I don't deserve someone as good as you. I'm the devil's spawn and you're this beautiful person. You were there for me when I needed you the most. You're my best friend, and never once did you judge me because of my father. Instead, you love me more for it. I don't want your first time to be something that you look back on and regret." He lifted me up and laid me on the bed. His body towered over mine, and his lips trailed up my neck.

"I want your first time to be something you never forget. So when I say not now, it's not because I don't want to." His lips captured my earlobe. "I'm fighting everything inside of me not to take full advantage."

"I'm sorry." I laced my arms around his neck. "I guess I got a little excited."

Ethan chuckled and lay his head on my stomach. "One day

we'll get out of here. We'll leave behind the darkness we came from. We'll make it on our own."

"Like a lotus flower," I said as I ran my fingers through his hair.

Ethan moved to look up at me. His eyebrows were furrowed together. "A lotus flower?"

I smiled. "Yes, it's a flower that grows beneath muddy water and then rises to the surface. It's beautiful, purifying. At night it goes back down into the water, and when it rises again the next day it's clean, soil free." I sighed at the realization. "That's us. The soil and murkiness is my mom, your father, and this town we live in. We will rise from it all and shine bright."

"Shine bright," Ethan whispered.

Chapter Thirteen

PRESENT

His side of the bed is cold, and without opening my eyes I know he is gone. The scent of his cologne lingers in my room. Ethan was here. We spent the night in each other's arms.

I roll to my back and stare at the glow-in-the-dark stars that are still stuck on my ceiling. Though it is against everything I force myself to believe, Ethan has come to my rescue. It's impossible to stay mad at him. Not when he is my protector, my knight in shining armor. The one I can always count on to bail me out of trouble.

My mind wanders for a few minutes as I remember his chiseled chest and the tattoo that ran across his heart and up to his shoulder. I want to see his body in broad daylight. I want to be in his arms again. I can't stop the crashing waves of emotion that threaten to drown me. I love him, there is no denying it. I have loved him every single day since I met him. It's a constant battle between my heart and my brain, and at this very moment my heart is winning the war.

Frustrated, I take a pillow from under my head, hold it over my face and scream. "Goddamn, mother of pearl, what the fuck is wrong with me?" Inhaling the pillow, a stronger scent of Ethan travels up my nose and all the tension in my body fades.

I'm fucked.

That's the only way I can describe it. Everything inside me is warning me I still need to hate him. I need to blame him for all of it. But my heart tells me a different story. It reminds me of the love I have for Ethan. The love we shared. He was the first man who ever held me in his arms and made love to me. He was my first love, the one who is impossible to forget.

The alarm on my cell phone buzzes and I grunt with pain as I get out of bed. I need to push away all the confusion and focus on the grand re-opening. Surprisingly, when I stand I realize I only have a minor headache that will be cured once I chug a bottle of water and down a few aspirin.

When I make my way downstairs, my mother's in the kitchen, ready for her day. Unlike her regular routine of spending her day with my father, today she's coming with me to meet with the clients. I'm a temporary fix, so she will need to know all of the details once the studio is up and running.

"Are you feeling okay?" she asks when I groan at the sunlight.

Blocking the bright stream with my hands, I head straight for the coffee pot. "Never better," I lie.

"I'm ready when you are," she says in her Darlene tone. I don't need to look over my shoulder to know she is eyeing me.

"What is it, Mom?" I pour myself a large cup of coffee.

"You're wearing jeans."

I sigh and open the medicine cabinet. "I am."

"How can you wear jeans to a ballet studio?"

Annoyed, I turn around too quickly and my head throbs. "Mom, it's a grand re-opening. People will be walking around, meeting with us and looking at the classes we offer. I don't need to be in tights and a tutu."

"Maybe not, but you should look professional." Her lips are pursed.

"Well." I fold my hands, silently pleading for this argument to go away. "I didn't pack for this. The clothes I have here are limited, so this is the nicest thing in my suitcase."

Annoyance appears on my mothers face. Her eyebrows pinch together and she shakes her head. "Fine. Let's go."

When her back is turned, I glance up at the ceiling and pray to the heaven above. *Please let this day go smoothly.*

Thirty minutes later we pull in to the studio, and by the audible gasp from my mother I know she approves of what I have done. The banner I hung is bright and colorful with the words Grand Re-Opening written in bold gold letters, and there is an arch of balloons that leads you to the main door.

My mother steps out of the car and I can see that her eyes have filled with tears. "You like?" I ask and walk around to her.

"I haven't been here in so long, Leslie." She glances over at me with a smile on her face. "It all looks beautiful."

"Come on." I loop my arm with hers. "I want you to see the inside before anyone gets here."

The studio is as different as night and day. The floors sparkle, the mirrors are streak free and the air is fresh. My mother meanders around, letting her hand graze the surfaces as she takes it all in.

"I didn't change anything inside. It simply needed some TLC. The layout you had is the best one for the space."

"Your father would be proud," she says. It's the best compliment she could have given me. Darlene would never admit she's proud, but I know that's what she meant.

"Thanks." I unlock the front door. "We are officially open for business."

We meet with twenty new clients who are interested in the programs we offer, from ballet to jazz. Some people drop by simply to wish us good luck. When Stephanie strolls in wearing a pair of oversized sunglasses covering her face, I know she's still hurting from the previous night.

"Everything looks beautiful." She leans in for a hug. "How

are you, Mrs. Sutton?" Stephanie smiles kindly at my mother.

"Oh, Stephanie, what a wonderful surprise!" My mother's voice is filled with joy. *She was always my mother's favorite.*

"Delivery for Leslie Sutton," a man announces as he walks in with a large bouquet of pink and white lotus flowers hidden in a sea of white lilies. I glance at Stephanie, and though she is focused on the conversation she is having with my mother, I notice the way her lips curl up into a grin.

"That's me," I say.

The delivery man hands me the vase, and the scent that permeates from the flowers is intoxicating. Long lotus stems flow from the glass vase, and neatly tucked inside is a card. Centering the arrangement on a table, I read the card.

Have dinner with me tonight?

I can't help but grin. There is no name on the card, but I know exactly whom they are from. I slide the card into my back pocket and return to the conversation with my mother and Stephanie. When another potential client appears, my mother chooses to give them a tour of the studio, and Stephanie glances over at me.

"From the smile on your face, I'll assume the wine didn't do much damage to you last night." Stephanie bumps her shoulder to mine.

"Remind me to never drink with you again." I shake my head and laugh.

"You're fine. I'm the one who had to down a cheeseburger in order to get out of bed."

"But you do it with such grace," I tease, and stand in position one.

Stephanie sticks her tongue out at me. "What did the note say?"

"He asked me to dinner."

"Are you going?" Stephanie lifts on her feet. "Of course you're going. It's dinner with Ethan. What am I talking about?"

"I don't know." I can't hide the hesitation in my voice.

"You owe him." Stephanie jumps to his defense. "He drove you home last night."

"*You* called him to pick me up." My hands rest at my hips in defense.

"Whatever." She shrugs. "You still owe him."

"But—"

"No buts." Stephanie raises her hand to stop me. "I don't understand why you two can't figure it all out."

"You really have to ask?" I hike up my jeans and show her the scar that runs up my leg.

"That's not his fault, and you need to stop blaming him for it. That was all Jerry." She purses her lips and I know she's right.

I sigh and swallow away the thoughts of it all. "He knew I was leaving. We had a plan and he didn't come after me."

Stephanie takes a second and cracks her knuckles. Her eyes scan the room looking for my mother before glancing back at me. "This isn't my story to tell, but you have a few missing pieces to that story," Stephanie says in a low tone.

"What do you mean?" My eyebrows furrow and I lean further into her.

"You need to ask Ethan what happened after you left."

"I know what happened. He took over for his father."

Stephanie shook her head. "Ask him what *really* happened."

I open my mouth to ask her what she means, but my mother appears. "This is my daughter," she says, introducing me to the potential clients. "She used to train here seven days a week when she was younger. She was offered a prestigious position to dance for Julliard."

"I'll see you later," Stephanie mouths to me, and she is out the door before I have a chance to stop her.

"Pleasure to meet you," I say to the woman and her husband. Their two young daughters are hiding behind them, and I peek around to greet them. "Hi," I say in a soft voice before crouching down. "I love your dress." The one girl smiles at me, and I look up at their parents. "I can keep them company if you need to discuss anything further with my mom." I look back at the girls. "Do you want to see the all the colorful tutus I have in the back room?" Both of theirs eyes widen.

"Thank you," my mother says, leading the parents into the office.

"Come, girls." I stand and lead them to the back room. They

both gasp when I flick the light on and notice the number of costumes that line the rack. "These are all from when I was younger."

"Do you still dance?" the older one asks.

"Only when I want to be really silly," I joke. "Go on. You can try the tutus on if you like."

They both run to the shiny, beaded clothing. I watch as they take turns pulling different costumes from the hangers. A feeling of nostalgia washes over me and I lean into the doorway. That was me once, the excited little girl who couldn't wait to try on the new dance costumes.

My phone buzzes in my back pocket and pulls me from my thoughts. A new text message appears with a number I have never seen before.

Unknown: Hi.
Unknown: How did you sleep?
Unknown: I'm waiting on a response.

I smile and hit the reply button.

Me: I slept like a baby :) I didn't know how to get in touch with you since I didn't have your number.
Ethan: Stephanie sucks as a wingman.
Me: I'm assuming that's how you got my cell phone number?
Ethan: Actually, I guessed it.
Ethan: How's the grand re-opening?
Me: Perfect. Thank you for the flowers.
Ethan: Does that mean yes?
Me: Maybe.
Ethan: That smile is telling me a different story.

I spin around, looking for him. The room is empty, and my mother is still chatting away in the office.

Me: Are you here?
Ethan: I can see you from my office. I'm directly across the street.

Hitting the call button, I dial his number and look up at the building across the street.

"Hi." His voice is low, and it immediately causes my body to shiver.

"You can't see me smiling from your office," I protest and walk closer to the glass window.

"No, but I can now."

I look up and find him standing by the window.

"Have dinner with me, Les?"

"Okay," I whisper. "I should get back. My mom left me in charge of two little ones."

"Okay. But, Les?"

"Yes?"

"I behaved last night because you had a few drinks in you. But I want you to know that I plan on kissing you like I used to."

I swallow back and bite on my lower lip to stop the massive smile from growing on my face. "I'll see you later, Ethan."

"I'll pick you up at eight."

I turn away from the window and press my phone to my chest. Stephanie said I need to ask Ethan the real reason he never came after me all those years ago, and this is my chance.

Him offering to kiss me is simply an added bonus.

CALLIE ANDERSON

Chapter Fourteen

PAST

One Year Later.

A mild storm had hit Texas and we were getting the aftermath. The air was muggy, the weather abnormally hotter than usual as I walked into my house with a film of sweat on my skin. My mother had spent the last few hours punishing me with drills. She didn't care that sweat was dripping from my body. In her mind it was weakness leaving my body. The harder I practiced, the better I'd be.

The cool conditioned air alleviated the stickiness I felt. My father sat on a barstool near the island. The smile on his face was one I could never forget. There was something in his eyes that told me he was proud.

"Hey, kiddo," he greeted me. "How was dance?"

"Hot," I complained and tossed my duffle bag on the counter.

"Something came in the mail for you today," my father said in a tone that sounded excited and hopeful all in one. I stopped dead in my tracks and looked back at him. He used two fingers to push a large envelope a little closer. By this time, my mother was at his side, her hands resting on his shoulders. Her eyes were kind, and it seemed as if the weight of the world had been lifted from her shoulders.

"Open it," he said, and there was a faint smile in his eyes. My gaze moved from my father to the envelope to my mother. There was a look in her eyes, one I had never seen before. A look of joy, excitement and honor all wrapped and tied with a bow. I stepped closer to the envelope. My legs were wobbly, and I knew it wasn't because of my recent dance practice. My eyes landed on the word Juilliard. The envelope was bigger than I imagined it, eight and a half by eleven inches.

"Go on," my mother prompted.

I swallowed back all the fear that consumed me in that moment, and slipped my finger under the paper and tore through the flap. My hands were shaking by the time I pulled out the sheets of paper.

Dear Leslie,

Congratulations! It gives me tremendous pleasure to inform you . . .

Unable to read the next line, I jumped up and down. "I got in! I got in! I got in!"

My mother rushed to my side. Her arms clung to my small frame in a vice grip. "I'm so proud of you," she whispered into my hair, and I felt her body shake as though she was crying along with me. This was as much an honor for her as it was for me. She had been by my side through it all. She was my coach, my leader, my best friend, and my worst enemy. I wouldn't be the dancer I was if it weren't for her.

Slowly I pulled out of her grasp and looked up at her. "Thank you, Mom." She cupped my cheeks and kissed my forehead.

My dad was still sitting nearby, a wide smile plastered on his face. "You did it, kiddo."

I rushed into his arms. I had done it. I had spent my entire life preparing for this moment. I was going to New York. Ethan and I were going to New York. I needed to tell him.

"Come on." My mother tapped my shoulder. "Go get in the

shower and I'll make us some dinner. We need to celebrate."

I nodded and rushed out of the kitchen and up the stairs. Taking them two at a time, I darted into my room and opened the window. My gaze landed on his house. The lights were on but I couldn't see him. Leaving the window open, I ran to the guest room. It was the only room in the house that gave me a direct view to Ethan's bedroom. I had asked my mother to switch my room to that one but she forbade it. She knew as well as I did that it was in direct sight of his room, and that would only cause trouble. My parents were aware Ethan and I were friends, but none of our parents knew we were dating. I was afraid my mother would say he was a distraction and keep him away from me. And Ethan never wanted his father to know he was dating me. He constantly said it was the only way to keep me out of harm's way.

The light in his room was off, but I left the guest room window open as well. It was our own version of the bat signal; an SOS of sorts.

Once I showered and changed, I made my way back downstairs. Walking past the living room, my father called me over to him. "Come here," he said in a hushed tone.

I strolled into the living room. On the coffee table there were three other envelopes similar to the one from Juilliard. "I know Juilliard was your first option, but I wanted you to see these as well."

In the beginning of my senior year, my dad and I decided that besides Juilliard, I should also apply to a few other schools. Juilliard was my first choice, but I needed a backup plan. There were thousands of applicants who applied yearly, and only twenty-four applicants were accepted.

Twenty-four.

Twelve men.

Twelve women.

I knew it was the reason my mother had instructed such an intense regimen my whole life. She knew what it took to get in to Juilliard. She had once been one of those twenty-four.

There was always the chance I wouldn't get in, and for that I needed a backup plan. Behind my mother's back my father and I applied to some other schools. I sent applications filled with an essay and recommendation letters to Michigan State, UCLA, and Northwestern University. Aside from dancing, I figured a degree in business would be my fallback. If I couldn't be like my mother I sure as shit wanted to be like my father.

Glancing down at the coffee table, I saw all three envelopes: UCLA, Northwestern, and Michigan State. The envelopes were identical to the one that came in from Juilliard. "Go ahead, Les, open them," my father said with such pride in his voice.

Each of the letters read like the other.

Congratulations . . .

The smile grew on my face. I had accomplished so much. Juilliard was where I was going. I had been training for that school since I was three years old, though I couldn't help but feel a sense of accomplishment when I saw that the other schools wanted me, too. Dance notwithstanding, I was qualified to go anywhere I wanted.

"I'm really proud of you, kid," my dad said when I laid the last letter down.

Once dinner was over and the kitchen cleaned, I sprinted up the stairs and headed straight for my room. I expected Ethan to be there, waiting for me by my bed like he normally was, but when I pressed the door open, the window was still open and there was no sight of him.

My heart pounded in my chest. I could hear it in my ears, and when I finally caught my breath, I heard the scream next-door. I ran to the window and couldn't find Ethan in my backyard. Jerry's voice bellowed again, and chills ran up my spine. He was pissed.

I darted out of my room and ran to the guest room. I kept the lights off so no one could see me. Inching ever so slowly toward the window, I spotted Jerry. He was angry as he paced around Ethan's bedroom. My heart sank to the floor when I spotted Ethan sitting on the edge of his bed. His head was crouched over as his father continued with the verbal abuse.

My hand rushed to my mouth to muffle my screaming. My mind ran a mile a minute wondering what the hell was going on. Jerry's words were muffled since Ethan's window was closed, and Ethan never replied. He never made eye contact with his father. He simply sat there, his head lowered and his arms resting on his knees. Unable to help him, I stood behind the curtain. Tears streamed down my face.

Ethan looked so helpless. So vulnerable.

I lost track of how long I stood there, but when Jerry walked out of the room and a few minutes later got in his car and drove away, I did the one thing Ethan made me swear to never do. I ran back into my room, slipped my feet into sneakers and climbed out my bedroom window.

I needed to be by his side.

I needed to comfort him and tell him no matter how terrible his father was it would all be okay.

I slid down the extended roof that covered the living room the way I had seen Ethan do, then walked over to the corner and climbed down the gutter. Barring a few scrapes on my legs, I safely hopped off and landed on the deck. My parents were in the living room and luckily hadn't spotted me. Not that they would have been able to stop me, anyway.

With shaky legs, I ran across our yards, and climbed into his house the same way he climbed into mine each night. I jumped on top of the garbage cans, anchored my foot on a loose brick and pulled myself up to his window. I tapped gently until he looked back at me.

The lights in his room were still on and I gasped when I saw the swelling around his right eye. Briefly, I closed my eyes to stop the pain in my chest. Fuck you, Jerry.

Ethan ran to his window and lifted it open. "What are doing here?" he asked as he pulled me into his room. His voice was filled with fear, something I had never heard from him before.

"Your eye," I whispered as I tried to catch my breath. I was hyperventilating. I reached out to touch it and Ethan grabbed my hand.

"It's fine, Leslie." He brushed my touch away.

"Don't do that." I couldn't stop the tears that filled my eyes.

"Don't do what?" He moved over to the wall and flicked off the light.

"Don't push me away." I ran my fingers under my eyes. "I saw your father in here. I saw him yelling at you, and I saw him leave." I walked over to him and grabbed his hands. "Don't push me away because I'm not going anywhere, Ethan." He lowered his head. Slowly I lifted my hand to his unharmed cheek.

"Tell me what happened?"

He shook his head and pulled me closer to him. Our bodies collided in a tight embrace, and he kissed the top of my head. "Talk to me," I pleaded.

"I got accepted into NYU." His voice was low and hoarse. I blinked away the tears that wouldn't stop and let him continue. "I didn't want to go to New York with you and weigh you down. I wanted to be someone you were proud of. We could go to school together and live there. You'd have your goals and I'd have mine. But my father arrived home before me. He grabbed the mail and all hell broke loose when he saw the acceptance letter." His voice cracked and I hugged him tighter. "No son of mine is going off to some fucking college, he said. And when I tried to say I didn't need his help, that I had managed to get a few grants and I was planning to apply for student loans, the blows came crashing down."

"Oh, Ethan," I cried into his chest. "Where was your mom?"

"With Charlie at therapy." Ethan kissed the top of my head once more. "I'm sorry, Leslie. I just wanted to make you proud."

"Hey." I pulled away from him and looked into his eyes. "We will get through this, I promise. And I'm so proud of you. You can be anything you want to be, and if your heart is set on NYU, that's where you'll go. Your father can go screw himself." Ethan chuckled and I kissed his lips. "No matter what, you and I are getting out of this town."

"Promise me I'll never lose you, Freckles."

"I promise," I whispered and met his lips again. This time I kissed him with wanton, desperate hunger. I wanted to show him he would never lose me. That he was the only person I ever needed in my life. He growled when I bit down on his lower lip. I pushed our bodies together and lifted the hem of his shirt.

"Make love to me, Ethan," I whispered against his lips.

He pulled away slowly, his eyes staring deep into mine. "Leslie . . ." It almost seemed painful for him to say my name.

"I want this. I want you forever. Make love to me." I pulled his shirt over his head.

"Not here." He shook his head.

I knew he wanted to make our first time beautiful, but as long as I was with him anywhere would be beautiful. Grasping his hand, I placed it over my heart. "You are the only thing I love in this world. It doesn't need to be hearts and flowers, all I need is you. It's all I've ever needed."

Ethan sighed and pressed his hand to my heart before he wrapped both arms around me. His hands slid down my back until they found the hem of my T-shirt. Slowly, he pulled it off, and then his hands trailed down my body. Goosebumps rose on my skin.

"Are you sure about this?" he asked.

"More sure than I am about anything else." The words came out like a beautiful melody.

Ethan lowered himself and wrapped his hands around my thighs. In one quick motion, he lifted me off the ground and carried me to his bed. Ever so slowly he laid me down. His body towered over mine and his lips met mine with so much love. He took his time kissing me. His lips trailed every inch of my body, and when he moved down to my stomach, he gently tugged on my tights and lowered them.

I wasn't embarrassed. I wasn't nervous. I had waited for this for as long as I could remember. There wasn't an ounce of hesitation in my mind. Ethan lowered his pants and walked over to the nightstand.

"Are you sure about this?" he asked me again.

There was no way I was backing out now. Not ever. It was me and him always. "I'm sure."

Ethan removed his boxers and took the condom from the nightstand. He walked over to the bed, laced his fingers around my panties and gently pulled them off. His eyes were glued to mine as he climbed on top of me. We didn't speak. He simply gazed into my eyes and I opened my legs for him.

I whimpered from the pain and Ethan kissed my forehead. My fingernails dug into his back as he pushed inside of me.

"Do you want to stop?" he asked. I knew he hated that he was hurting me.

"No." I shook my head and found his lips. "Kiss me," I said. "It doesn't hurt when you kiss me."

And he did.

"I love you, Leslie."

"I love you, too."

I cried from the pain. For his pain. For the love we shared. Inch by inch, as slow as humanly possible, Ethan made love to me.

It was painful.

It was beautiful.

It was us.

It was everything I had ever dreamed of.

I cried.

I laughed.

I fell even more in love with Ethan.

Once we were done, he held me in his arms. His hands traced my bare back. "Why didn't you tell me you applied to NYU?"

"I wasn't sure I'd get in."

"Why not? You're smart, you get good grades. Of course they would want you."

"I guess it was the fear of getting your hopes up and then letting you down."

"You can't possibly let me down." I glanced up at him and his lips kissed mine.

"I'm going to call them and let them know I'm going." For the first time since I crawled into his room there was confidence in his voice.

"Yeah?"

"Yes. I'm eighteen and my father can go fuck himself. I'm

not staying in this town."

"Nine more months and we'll be on a plane to New York," I whispered in bliss.

Ethan brought me closer to him and kissed the tip of my nose. "Nine months and we'll be out of here."

It was a promise. It was a definite plan.

At least that's what we thought . . .

Chapter Fifteen

PRESENT

Every article of clothing I came with is scattered on my bed. I quickly realize that nothing I packed is appropriate for a date with my first boyfriend, slash the love of my life, slash the guy who broke my heart.

Jeans and T-shirts and one casual dress are all I brought. Nothing screamed, *"I need to have you now!"* or, *"My God, I lost her once and I won't lose her again! Not when her legs are so fucking hot!"*

After trying on everything I had, plus everything my mother owns, I resort to Plan B. Pulling my phone off the charger, I send Stephanie a message.

Me: SOS! I need a little black dress to wear tonight.

She replies within seconds.

Stephanie: I'm on my way.

Twenty minutes later Stephanie knocks on the door with a suitcase at her side.

"Are you moving in?" I ask her.

"No." She shakes her head and tugs on the handle. "But I brought you every dress I own. You'll find something here for sure."

"You're my fairy godmother." I hold the door wide and she wheels the oversized suitcase in through the foyer.

"Where's your mom?" Stephanie asks as we both take hold of the suitcase and clumsily walk it up the stairs.

"She popped an Ambien after dinner." I sigh and pull the suitcase up another step. "Sometimes I feel I need to be more concerned about her pill popping now that my father's in rehab."

"That bad, huh?"

"I think she's really depressed. My mother used to look at my father like he walked on water. Him being so fragile and helpless has really taken a toll on her." I exhale as we make it to the top step.

"Do you think he'll get better?"

I sigh and let my shoulders slump. "The doctors are hopeful, but we really won't know for a few more months."

Stephanie gives me a kind smile. "If you ever need anything, Les, you know I'm always here for you."

I nod and force a smile. "Thanks. I hope once he's out of rehab things will go back to normal and I can get back to my life." I lead us to my room.

"You're not gonna stay?" Stephanie asks when we enter my room.

"My life is in Chicago."

"Yes, but your parents need you here. And Ethan is here."

"I won't leave until my parents are okay. I have a job that I need to get back to, though. I have responsibilities." I shove all my clothes in the hamper. "And Ethan and I don't exist anymore. We're having dinner as old friends."

"Dinner as old friends?" Stephanie crosses her arms over her chest. "Ha!" She throws her head back dramatically before she eyes the only decent bra and panties I had packed and lifts them. They're nothing fancy; a lace black bra with a matching lace thong. "This definitely screams dinner as old friends." Her lips purse together in amusement.

"Shut it!" I snatch it from her hands. "It's not even that cute, and it's the only thong I have," I lie.

"Fine, so the bra and panties are old, but why did you text me with an SOS telling me to bring you hot dresses?" Stephanie shifts her weight from one foot to the other. "If it's just dinner with an old friend, why aren't you wearing jeans and a T-shirt? It's what you wore when we had drinks."

"You know, I really hate you sometimes." I stick my tongue out at her. Stephanie is no help as I drag the suitcase onto the bed. "And this is Ethan we're talking about. I've been with him before and it didn't end well," I add in a strained voice.

Stephanie laughs even harder this time. "You don't hate me. You just hate that I know you better than you think." She winks and pulls out a dress. "And you were with childhood Ethan, the eighteen-year-old boy who lost his virginity to you. Not the twenty-seven-year-old man he is now." She lays another dress out on the bed. "Call it what you want, but you're looking to get some. Who knows, maybe in Chicago old friends means fuck buddy."

"We're not having sex!" I take a dress and hold it up to my body. Stephanie scrunches her nose before shaking her head. "We're only having dinner, and I want to look nice. Is it so bad that I want to get out of this house and out of the crappy clothes that I packed and look decent for one night?"

"Oh, honey, of course not. If that's the story you want to stick to, then sure," Stephanie says in her sweet innocent voice with a devilish grin on her face. "Just make sure everything has been shaved and waxed off because you know sometimes dinner with old friends leads to breakfast with old friends."

"Crap!" I grunt and toss the dress at her, but she's right. *Who am I kidding?* It has been months since I've had sex. And if last night is any indication, when I'm around Ethan there is no denying him. "I'm gonna take another shower, I'll be ten minutes," I say as I tug the towel off behind the door.

Stephanie's laughter bellows from my room.

By eight o'clock that night, I have on the shortest black dress Stephanie owns. My dark hair is blown out, and Stephanie has spent a good twenty minutes focusing on my eye shadow alone. I don't even recognize myself in the mirror when she's done. My clammy hands tug on the hem of my dress, bringing it down an extra centimeter.

"Stop doing that!" Stephanie yells at me before swatting my hand away.

"Maybe I should go with the other one. It was a little longer." I can't hide the anxiety in my voice.

"You are wearing this one. It makes your legs look like they're a mile long. Plus, it's not that short. Just don't bend over so you don't have any Britney Spears incidents."

"I can't believe you convinced me to do this."

"I didn't do any convincing." Stephanie shakes her head before pointing to my crotch. "That is all your Regina." *Her word for vagina.* I crumble up a T-shirt on my bed and toss it at her. "All right, I better get going before Ethan arrives." She walks around my bed and kisses me on the cheek before eyeing the dress one last time. "That poor boy doesn't know what's coming for him." She winks, and wraps her hands about the handle of the suitcase.

"Thanks for everything, Stephanie."

"Not a problem, babe. Oh, and you can keep the dress. I don't want it back after he's had his stuff all over it." She makes an awkward motion with her hand and I can't help but laugh.

The second Stephanie is out of the house, panic sets in. I'm actually doing this. I'm putting fear aside and I'm going out with Ethan. "Fuck," I curse out a sigh. I pace around the living room until his car approaches, then take a few calming breaths and walk over to the door.

As I pull it ajar, he is stepping out of his car and heading toward my house. Ethan stops dead in his tracks, his gaze landing directly on my legs.

"Thank you, Stephanie," I whisper and a grin grows on my face. *This is the perfect dress after all.* His eyes tell me everything I need to know. Closing the door behind me, I walk toward him. The strappy sandals click against the cemented sidewalk as I sashay his way.

"You're trying to kill me, aren't you?" he says as I approach. I bite my lip to hide my smile and place a soft kiss on his cheek. His hands rest on my hips and I feel my core ache with need. Stephanie was absolutely right. I'm only thinking with Regina now.

I take a step back and try to sound modest. "You like?" I pout and lean into him. His cologne is intoxicating but I refuse to let it weaken me. "It's not too much for dinner, is it?" I run my hand across his chest before making my way to the passenger side door, but before I reach the car, Ethan is right next to me, his hand lacing around the handle. He opens the door for me, and we exchange a quick glance. There's a hidden communication between us. We both know what we're doing. We both know that this night consists of us rehashing all the pent up desire between us.

"You look gorgeous," he says as I climb into the car.

"You don't look so bad yourself," I say before he shuts me in. I take the opportunity to gawk over him as he walks around the car. His dark blue jeans hug his hips, giving me a perfect view of his sculpted ass. The red button-down shirt hugs his chest and arms, and my mind wanders to what it must feel like to lick his taut chest. And then there is his perfect face. Ethan was always handsome. His face is perfection with a strong jawline, high cheekbones and piercing green eyes. But tonight the icing on the cake is his hair. It's the longest it has ever been. Ruffled and carefree.

He reminds me of my old Ethan.

My heart pinches with pain, and I ignore the ache of my ankle. Tonight I am pushing all doubt aside.

"You ready?" he asks and turns on the car.

The engine purrs and my body vibrates. I glance over at him and there is no denying that dinner with friends will become breakfast with friends. "Oh, yeah," I say and cock an eyebrow at him.

Ethan drives us into town, his hand laced with mine as the stereo plays in the back. I'm glad for the lack of conversation since the only thing on my mind is his body on top of mine.

Ethan pulls his car into an empty driveway near the studio. There are a few apartment buildings over the storefronts and I glance over at Ethan. "This is your office, no?" He nods. "Why are we here? Did you forget something?"

"I decided to cook you dinner." He shifts his car into park and smiles over at me.

"Bu . . . I got dressed up to go to your house?" I can't mask the disappointment in my voice.

Ethan shifts in his seat to face me. "No, you got dressed up so I can stare at your legs." He leans over and kisses my lips, then pulls away. "If you want, we can go somewhere to eat, anywhere you want, but I doubt anyone would give us any privacy," he whispers, and I can feel his breath on my skin.

My body temperature rises and I shiver. Our lips are only a few inches from each other. "Cook me dinner." I bite my lower lip as I imagine what dessert will be.

Ethan ushers me out of his car and I follow behind. He leads me up a flight of stairs and down a long hallway. "This is Charlie's apartment." He points to a door. "And this one is mine." He slides the key into the door across from his brothers.

"Charlie has his own place?" I ask and cock my head to the side.

"Yeah." Ethan glances back at me. "He has his own room in my house, but sometimes when he has his episodes he needs a place of his own."

The pinching in my heart is a reminder of how Ethan had always taken care of his brother. Even when we were kids, Charlie was always one of us. No one ever picked on Charlie because Ethan wouldn't accept it. "He knows you're coming over tonight, so he's in there. He won't bother us."

"Your brother is never a bother, you know that."

Ethan grins and nods before opening the door. "This is it."

I take a step forward and gasp when the light turns on. The interior of his apartment is nothing like the exterior. Where the building outside looks outdated with red brick and a green awning, the inside is sleek and modern. I'm greeted with dark-stained wood floors, cream-colored walls and dark brown furniture. There is a large leather sectional seated right in front of an entertainment system with a wet bar a few feet away. It's a bachelor pad, sleek yet tasteful.

I turn back around to look at Ethan. "This place is beautiful." I run my hands along the leather sectional. "A place like this doesn't belong in our town. It's too modern and sleek. I bet half of the things in here are custom made."

"I'm glad you like." He closes the door behind him. Immediately, I feel the walls closing in. My heart accelerates in my chest. We are alone, completely alone.

Just us.

I'm nervous and excited.

"Would you like a tour?" He extends a hand for me. I know from the grin on his face he can feel that I'm anxious.

"Sure." I smile and brush my hair behind my ears before placing my hand in his.

"There's no need to be nervous, Freckles. It's only dinner." Ethan winks and I shake my head before I slap him in the arm.

"You're such an ass." I laugh, but am thankful that he's broken the awkward tension between us.

"Living room, dining room, kitchen, self-explanatory," he says as he brings me closer to him. "This one is the bathroom." He opens the door to a half-bath between the dining room and the kitchen before heading down a hallway with three doors. "This is Charlie's room." He points to the door. "He doesn't like anybody in there, so I won't show you inside." I nod, understanding Charlie's issues with his own personal space.

"This is my office." He opens the door. There are television monitors mounted on the wall. Four to be exact. As I step closer, I realize they are security cameras. "That's how I knew you were at the pub. Charlie's job is to watch the cameras."

"Oh," is the only word I can form.

He's not like his father.

He's not like his father.

Aside from the TV's on the wall, there's a bookcase, and a large desk in the center. I walk over to the bookcase to examine his collection. It's not like Ethan to read memoirs or autobiographies. A small item catches my eye, and I stop dead in my tracks as every emotion washes over me.

Happiness.
Anger.
Disbelief.
My eyes are glued to the Swarovski crystal ballerina. It is *my* ballerina.

My father gave it to me for my eighth birthday. The small trinket fit in the palm of my hand. She's all crystal in arabesque position, standing on her toes with her leg extended back. It is also the first item Ethan picked up from my dresser the very first night he crawled into my room.

"When did you get this?" I can't turn around and face him. Too much has happened between us, and I don't know if I can hold back my tears.

"After you left, I went into your room one last time." His voice is as pained as mine. "I wanted a part of you to keep with me always."

He went back for this. After I moved to LA. I replace it reverently on his shelf, my vision blurred with unshed tears. I wish he knew he didn't need a crystal ballerina to keep a part of me. I would always belong to him. When God created souls, he created mine just for Ethan. He was my soul mate.

"Would you like a glass of wine?" he asks as I slide my fingers under my eyes and flick away the tears.

"Desperately." I laugh, and find the courage to cast him a glance.

He extends his hand and we lace our fingers together. Ethan pulls me closer to him and wraps his arms around my shoulders, kissing the top of my head. I let him lead me back into the kitchen and sit on the bar stool that is tucked underneath the island. He pulls out two glasses of wine and a bottle.

"Your house is gorgeous," I finally say after I have a grasp on my emotions.

"You missed the best part." The grin on his face is devilish. "You didn't get to see my bedroom."

I wait until he's poured me a glass before I say, "I'm pretty sure many girls have seen that bedroom. I doubt it's anything spectacular."

"Low blow, Les," he says with a deep chuckle.

And just like that we're back to normal.

Ethan opens the oven, and I get a glimpse of the roast. "It smells delicious," I say. "Do you need any help?"

"No, I'm okay. You still eat meat, right?"

"Yeah, why?"

"Well, you've lived in California for so long. People out there are usually vegetarians or vegans or whatever."

I shake my head at his ridiculous statement. "I'm a carnivore. I spent six months in Brazil eating picanha every day."

"Brazil?" Ethan shuts the cabinet and looks back at me.

We know so much about each other's lives, and yet times like this it's as if we're complete strangers. I know the look on his face when he's happy. I know how he looks when he's mad. I know that his eyebrows crinkle together when he's deep in thought. But there are eight years from our lives where he knows nothing about me or I about him. "I studied for a semester in Brazil. "

"I guess college did you well. You always wanted to see the world." Ethan turns toward the refrigerator and pulls out a few items. I take his compliment as a dig.

We wanted to travel.

We made plans to see the world.

"It's like the second we forget what happened between us and can move forward, something from the past fucks it up," I blurt out before taking a big sip of wine. "I wanted to trave*l with you*. But I went to Brazil to forget you."

Ethan sighs and takes my hand. The kitchen island is between us but it feels more like a mountain. His eyes are soft as he runs his tongue along his lower lip. "I didn't mean to upset you."

I wait a few seconds, my eyes locked on his. There is so much I want to say. So much I want to know. And then a thought pops in my head. "Stephanie said I should ask you what happened after I left, aside from you taking over your dad's business."

"Do you really want to know?" His eyes grow hesitant and I can feel the floor about to be pulled out from under me. Whatever he is about to say, I know it will hurt, but I need to know.

"Yes."

Ethan lifts the bottle of wine and refills our glasses. He takes a long gulp before he pinches the bridge of his nose. When he looks up at me, I swallow back the fear. "I went after you," he admits, and my chest tightens.

I shake my head, not understanding him. "You . . . What? When?"

"I guess I should start from the beginning." He sighs as if he is finding the courage himself. "It was three months after you left, the week before Thanksgiving. Jerry had been moved to his permanent residence, and the psychiatrists had my mother on every type of medication. But she was calm, and I was looking for an institution to put Charlie in." I see his Adams apple bob as he swallows.

"My mother was in no shape to take care of him. With Jerry completely disabled, the SSI from the state combined with the rent from the stores was enough to pay the bills. There was no need for me to be here anymore, so I packed a bag and went after you."

I close my eyes, remembering how sad I was my entire first semester. How every night I went to bed crying because I missed him.

"We hadn't spoken since you were about to board the plane. I figured you didn't want to see me, so I took my chances and decided to surprise you."

I lower my chin, my mind replaying that dreadful conversation we had.

"I didn't know exactly where you were and you had changed your number. Your parents were no help so I had no choice but to go in blind. I walked the campus for two days looking for you. Did you know there's more than one campus at UCLA? I found you on the third day. It was a hot Thursday. You were in the courtyard sitting on a blanket."

I shake my head and the tears are warm on my cheeks. But I don't stop him.

"You were reading some textbook. As I walked toward you, your friends joined you."

Shocked, I look up at him. The brain is a powerful muscle because within seconds I can remember that day. They weren't my friends but my lab partners.

"You were laughing. You were happy." Ethan's voice grows hoarse and I know it's killing him to go on. "From afar, I watched you join in their conversations as if you didn't have a care in the world." He inhales deeply and sighs. "And then I realized I had nothing to offer you. I didn't have a job. I didn't have a place to stay. I didn't have anything. You were at a school you didn't want to be at because of me."

"That's not true," I whisper but I'm not sure he hears me.

"I needed to make something of myself first before I could find you again."

"You came after me," I state in a shaky voice.

"Twice," he admits, and I snap my head up at him. The pain in his face is prominent and I know mine matches his. "Three years later I came back. I didn't have your phone number. Your father again shut the door in my face, and your mother wouldn't even look at me when I approached her in the supermarket. It was my luck that you rented an apartment under your name."

I stand and my legs are unsteady.

"I had made a name for myself. I had taken over my father's business, made it legitimate and became the man I wanted to be. So when I was ready, I came after you."

I shake my head again, hoping he stops.

"I drove non-stop for ten hours and arrived early on a Sunday morning. I pulled in to your apartment complex just as you and some guy were walking out of your apartment. You were wearing your pajamas and you stopped at your door. Then you threw your arms around his neck and he kissed you good-bye."

My hands grip the edge of the granite countertop as I steady my body.

"You were happy. You were in love. And I knew I was too late."

"Harry," I say in a painful whisper. I take a few minutes to absorb everything Ethan said, then stand tall. "His name was Harry," I manage. "It took three years before I could find someone who made me happy. The sad part is, I needed to stay busy and Harry needed someone to fix him. I liked him, but I loved fixing him more. I kept telling myself one day I would make him better than you. One day I would forget you ever existed." My voice breaks with each sentence. Ethan walks around the island and I hold my hand up to keep the distance between us. "I wish you would've walked over to me in the courtyard that day," I cry.

"Me, too." He nods. "But I don't think it would've done us any good. We had some growing up to do, me especially."

"Three years," I mutter. "It took you three years to come back. You could've called."

"I'm sorry."

I close my eyes, remembering everything that happened between us. "I went to Brazil to forget you. I met my best friend, Emilia. I was with Harry; she was with Weston. They were in a band. They moved to London to become famous. She and I drifted apart. Soon after that I moved to Chicago. For eight years all I've tried to do is forget the pain you caused. I tried to forget that god awful day I begged you to come with me to LA and you flat out said no and broke my heart. And it all could've all been fixed if you had only walked up to me in the courtyard."

"I'm sorry," Ethan says again.

"I don't want you to be sorry!" I throw up my hands and shout. "I want those eight years back! I could've been with you this entire time!"

"I thought you hated me for what happened to your leg."

"Fuck my leg! I hated you because you weren't there. But you were!"

"Fuck!" Ethan yells and runs his hands through his hair. "I'm here now, Les." He growls before he storms over to me. Grasping me in his arms, he yanks me closer. "I fucked up. Over and over I let you down when you needed me. I'm here now and I'm never letting you go again." His mouth crashes over mine and I cry from the pain and pleasure coiled within me.

Ethan grips my legs and lifts, sitting me on the island. My

black dress rises and bunches around my waist as my legs wrap around him and he claims my mouth again. I'm desperate for him. His hands are on my face, our lips crashing over each other as we drown in our kisses. His hands run up my thighs and I moan against his lips.

Every move is hungrier than the last.

Every kiss is desperate.

Every moan is exhilarating.

I yank his shirt over his head and he finds the zipper to my dress. I toss his shirt on the floor and then run my hands down his chiseled chest.

He is a man, no longer the boy I once knew.

"I need you now," I whisper in his mouth.

He yanks off my dress and tosses it behind him. His gaze is glued to my body and I can't wait another second. My breasts are heavy, only inches from his face, and I need his mouth on them. I reach behind me and unclasp my bra, my nipples hard from the cool air. Ethan growls under his breath, and cups one breast with his hand. I moan at his touch and throw my head back, waiting for him to have me. His warm tongue circles my nipples until I'm begging him for more.

"Please, Ethan, I need you," I bellow out in ecstasy.

He lifts me off the counter and carries me to the couch. I sit back as he tugs his pants off. My mouth waters, looking at his chiseled chest, defined abs, and the perfect V that peeks out from under his boxers. His hands trail my body, flicking my nipple as his right hand lifts my chin to meet his green eyes.

"I need you," he whispers.

My back is flush against the cool leather as he drops to his knees. I'm breathless, panting as his hands make their way to my thighs. My core aches to be touched. The way his fingers crawl up my body ignites an internal inferno. The way his eyes glare at me as if I'm beautiful tears down all the walls I've built around my heart.

His lips tease the skin of my upper thighs as he lowers my thong. The warmth of his tongue causes me to tremble. I feel his breath, feel his lips kissing my arousal. When he lowers himself to my core, I melt at his touch.

"Please," I beg. "I'm going to . . ."

Ethan's tongue twirls, circles, and licks every last drop of my orgasm. When the trembles subside, he positions himself at my entrance, pushing inside of me, fulfilling my hunger for him. A hunger only he can tame.

His pace is slow at first, allowing me to feel every single inch of him. Pulling out to the tip, he slowly pushes back in until I'm gasping for air. He grunts; I moan. We find our perfect tempo, and dance to it until we can't take it anymore. My back arches as another orgasm forms. I moan sweet renditions of his name, my skin igniting, goose bumps rising with each thrust. Ethan's eyes lock on mine as he drives deeper, savoring the seconds that have passed.

My hands run across my chest, cupping my breasts. I take my nipples between my fingers. My climax is near, and I'm relishing the moment until I can no longer. "I'm . . ."

"Me, too." He grunts, holding my thighs as he drives deep inside me one last time, releasing himself. Gasping for air, we come together, the world around us ceasing to exist as we travel to the abyss.

Chapter Sixteen

PRESENT

The memories invade my mind; it's the same nightmare that has haunted me for years. The pain is unbearable.. It shoots up my leg like battery acid being poured over my bones. I sit up on the bed and grab my ankle. Tears pour down my cheeks as I try to rub the anguish away. It's been months since I've had a spasm like this. My fingers dig along my shin, rubbing my muscles. It's my brain reminding me what happened.

I try to be quiet since Ethan is sleeping next to me, but I whimper through the pain. I don't want him to see me like this. Not when we have spent the last few hours making love to each other. From the couch, to the floor, to the kitchen counter, we took our time making up for lost years. Seeing me like this now will only bring up the past for him.

"Hey." He turns to face me. His voice is low and hoarse.

"Go back to sleep," I whisper, wiping away my tears. Slowly, I try to move away from him so he can't see what I'm doing.

Ignoring my request, he sits up on the bed and grabs my leg. "Where does it hurt?"

I don't want to admit to any pain, but swallow back my instinctive denial and lower my head. "Around my ankle and my shin."

His strong hands rub my ankle in a circular motion. We don't speak as the minutes pass and he works vigorously on my leg. His thumb kneads the muscles and the pain slowly drifts away. When he leans down and kisses the scar he has been tracing with his fingers, I cover my face and cry harder. That marred skin is a permanent reminder of all that has happened. All I have to do is look down and a wave of dreadful memories drown me.

"I'm so sorry, Les," he whispers, kissing my scar again.

I pull my foot away from his grasp. "I'm okay," I say in an attempt to convince us both. "I promise."

"Does this happen often?"

"It hasn't happened in a few months."

"Come here." He leans back on the bed and pats his chest for me to lay on. His oversized T-shirt hangs off my shoulder and I curl around him. Our faces are mere inches from each other. In his arms I feel safe. He brushes back my hair and kisses the tip of my nose.

"I'm so sorry for the pain I have caused you. You're the last person I ever wanted to hurt."

"I know," I whisper, and kiss his bare chest. His strong arms drape over my body and shield me from the pain.

A few minutes pass and my mind is racing. "Can I ask you a question?" I say and sink deeper into his arms.

"Anything." He kisses the top of my head. His fingertips rub gently along my skin.

"Whatever happened with the cops after the whole Jerry thing?" I wait silently for his response.

"Nothing."

"Nothing?" I look up at him and he shrugs. "Your uncle was the sheriff." I can't hide the shock in my voice.

"Yes, my uncle was the sheriff who was thrilled to not have to deal with Jerry's blackmails anymore." Ethan chuckled.

"They just looked the other way?" I can't hide my surprised

reaction.

"No. There were a few detectives on the case that Jerry took care of on the side. They wanted a full-blown investigation. I wouldn't say a word to anyone, and the only story they had was yours. My uncle closed the case and said it was self-defense. Since Jerry isn't able to say what happened, it was a done deal."

I nod and force everything out of my mind.

"What made you think of that?" He moves his hand from my back and uses it to brush at my hair.

"I guess the nightmare brought it all back." I sniffle back and exhale slowly. "My father kept me in the dark for so long I had no clue what happened. I grew depressed as the weeks passed, and when my father offered me a ticket to UCLA I never looked back. I guess I was curious to know if you ever got in any trouble."

"It's all over now. We are finally safe."

Closing my eyes, I hear his heart beating in his chest. The sound is soothing, but before I can protest and say that until Jerry's dead we will never be safe, I drift back to sleep without any more interruptions.

When I wake up, the sun is bright in his room and the bed is empty. The smells of bacon and fresh coffee waft through the room, and I extend my hands overhead, stretching before I crawl out of bed. A shirtless Ethan is in the kitchen standing over the stove. Not thinking twice, I walk right over to him and wrap my arms around his body. The scent of him is enticing; the muscles that wrap around his body are addicting. Gently, I bite his upper back.

"Good morning," he says. "Are you hungry?"

"Starving," I say and kiss his warm skin. At the moment I'm not sure if I'm hungry for breakfast or him.

Ethan turns the stove off and spins around. Instantly, his lips are on mine and his hands coil through my hair. "There's coffee, tea, and orange juice." He buries his face at the hollow of my neck and inhales. "I made bacon and eggs, but your scent seems more delectable.

We stay in each other's arms for a few more minutes before we move to the barstools. With our plates in front of us and our eyes locked on each other, we eat our breakfast. We don't speak but there's a sense of feeling between us. A sense of familiarity. A sense of home.

Ethan had always been my home. My entire life I felt a part of me was missing. I was always trying to be a better dancer for my mom, and the smartest kid in my classes to impress my dad. But never once did I feel I belonged. It wasn't until I befriended Ethan that I felt I was destined to be in someone's life. We were destined for great love. One that didn't require us to speak while eating.

Once I'm done with breakfast, I load my plate into the dishwasher. Ethan's lower back is resting against the edge of the counter, and when I turn toward him, he's watching my every move. "I should get going," I say nervously. Though I've felt at home this entire time, the nightmare from last night has caused my mood to change.

He doesn't speak. Instead, he reaches out for me. Unable to deny him, I place my hand in his and he pulls me into his arms. He cups my face and kisses my lips. "Can I see you again?" he asks between our flushed lips. He leans back and looks deeply into my eyes, making it impossible to deny him.

My teeth graze my lower lip as I look up into his tantalizing eyes. "I have to work later. And my mom stays late at the rehab center on Sunday."

"Monday night, then?"

I stand on my toes and kiss his lips. "We'll see." I wink and try to walk away. Before I'm about to turn, he drags me back into his arms. His mouth hovers over mine. Unlike before, his kisses are hungry and desperate. As much as I fight to pull away, I can't.

"Fine," I whisper between kisses. "Monday night."

I arrive home an hour later. Ethan drops me off and I rush inside, hoping my mother is still asleep. Tiptoeing in the house, I think I'm in the clear when I hear her audible sigh.

"Mom?" I step further into the house. "You're up early." I

BROKEN DREAMS

try to sound optimistic. I'm an adult, after all. There's no need to explain where I've been all night, but never having done the walk of shame before, I find it terrifying.

I locate her in my dad's recliner, her lips pursed with disgust when her gaze lands on me. "It didn't take long for *him* to find you, did it?" An icy chill runs up my spine. "Or should I say, it didn't take long before you were crawling into his bed."

I lean into the doorframe and cross my arms. "Good morning to you too, Mother."

"Don't you have any respect for yourself?" She stands and throws the newspapers on the coffee table. "Given everything that boy has done to you."

"He didn't do anything to me, Mother. His *father* did," I remind her.

"Funny." Darlene crosses her arms over her chest and matches my stance. "I remember you sitting in that hospital room and him never coming to see you."

I swallow back and try to stand tall, but she is throwing low blows. Low, hurtful blows.

"I remember you crying night after night and him not even calling you. That's what I remember."

I taste blood in my mouth as I bite the inside of my cheek. "Funny, I remember *you* walking away from me when I needed you the most." Tears pool in my eyes. "I needed my mother, and you were nowhere to be found." I match her blow for blow. "In that moment I didn't need him. I needed *you*, and you were gone." I take a step forward. "Where were you, Mom? Gone!"

"Because you threw it all away!" she yelled. "For years, Leslie, we worked on one thing together. Your goal was to get into Juilliard, and you did! Your bags were packed and you were leaving. I had done my job as a mother. I raised you to be responsible and to be respected. To be a beautiful and talented dancer. And then you threw it all away when you went to chase that boy."

"I didn't throw it away. We were leaving together!" I confess. "He was gonna stand by me as I followed my dreams. We were getting the hell out of this town and he was coming with me to New York. But you insisted on that stupid party."

"So, you're saying it's my fault."

"No! Its fucking Jerry's fault, and he never paid for what he did to me!" I cry. I raise my hands and take a step back. I can't rehash the past. Shaking my head, I turn on my heel and head up the stairs. There's nothing anyone can say to make me feel any less pain than I feel now.

Chapter Seventeen

PAST

One Year Later

Against my wishes, my parents decided to throw me a graduation party. Friends of my parents along with neighbors and colleagues all joined at our house for the festivities. My mother had spent the last three months planning this extravagant party, and every single client from the studio was invited. Look! Have your daughter train with me and I can get her into Juilliard as well! I assumed this was the invitations' underlying message.

Running my hands down my thighs for the third time, I tried to calm my nerves. I was in my room trying on the dress my mother laid out for me. It was peach-colored chiffon that tied around my neck. The A-line style wrapped around my chest and ribs before opening in a mesh skirt down to my knees. My mother had instructed me to wear my hair down and to pin a few strands back away from my face, and I was under strict instructions to make sure my makeup was light. There was a rule for everything, but I didn't argue.

Ethan had accepted his offer from NYU, and secretly we planned out the next chapter of our lives. In three weeks, he and I would be on a plane to New York, so for now I would wear whatever dress my mother wanted me to wear. I would smile and be courteous to their friends because I had twenty-one days left.

After I was dressed, I peeked out my bedroom window and noticed there was no sight of Ethan at the party. He had promised he would be there, and I didn't want to come down until I spotted him.

Light tapping on my door startled me, and to my surprise it was joyful Darlene. "Leslie, you don't want to keep your guests waiting." She walked over to me and moved a strand of hair behind my shoulder.

"Yes, Mother." I waited till she was out of the room before I pulled my hair back to the way I had it. "Three more weeks," I muttered under my breath and followed her down the stairs.

The house and backyard had been transformed. There were balloons, streamers, twinkling lights, and sparklers. Small round tables were scattered around the backyard for people to sit and mingle. Classical music played on the Bose surround sound my mother had installed for the occasion. My mother had hired the best caterer in Arizona, and we even had white gloved waiters who walked around serving hors d'oeuvres.

I smiled and greeted my guests, thanking them as they handed me envelopes. Though I carried on conversations with those my mother insisted I speak with, I kept my eyes out for Ethan. There was no sign of him anywhere inside the house. Scanning the room once more, I noticed Charlie near the chocolate fountain, his lips wrapped around a coated strawberry. He gave me a goofy grin and dipped another berry in the chocolate.

Joyce sat on the chair next to him. Her lips were pursed together and her fingers wrapped around a wine glass. From the way her eyes were half-mast, I knew she had popped one of her pills and chased it with some wine. I couldn't blame her for wanting to run away from her life, especially when I knew the man she was married to.

I walked through the kitchen and into the living room, and was greeted with a familiar face.

"Hello there, princess," Stephanie teased, then curtsied at me gracefully.

"Stop that, Steph. You know this was never my idea."

"Oh, I know." She looked around and spotted my mother. "But look at Darlene. I haven't seen her smile this much in my entire life. I actually believe she's been possessed by a ghost."

"Yeah, the Juilliard ghost." I couldn't hide the annoyance in my voice.

"Are you not having fun?" Stephanie pulled out a small flask from her clutch. "I can change that, you know."

"If my mother even smells a hint of alcohol on my breath, she will break every bone in my body. You know that." I shoved the flask back inside her purse.

"That is very true." Stephanie smiled. "But this is a beautiful party, babe. Loosen up a bit, okay?"

"Hey, have you seen Ethan?" I asked, ignoring her request. I couldn't hide the pinch in my chest.

"No." She shook her head and gave another quick scan of the room. "I figured he'd be with you. I have no idea where he is."

I sighed and forced a smile. "If you see him, tell him I'm looking for him."

"Will do, babe."

I continued to look for him, but he wasn't in the backyard or on the deck, nor was he anywhere in the house, and my heart began to ache with worry.

The clinking of champagne flutes startled me. "May I have your attention please?" my father said. The room got quiet and my gaze landed on him. Slowly, he walked toward me. Placing his hand on my shoulder, he raised his glass. "I'd like to thank you all for coming here tonight and celebrating my sweet little girl." He looked down at me with a loving smile.

"Leslie, I am so proud of the woman you have become. And I know you will continue to dance into the hearts of others as you have danced into ours. May you have all the success in the world as you embark on this next journey in your life. To Leslie." He raised his glass and the room filled with cheers.

"To Leslie," the crowd said in unison.

I smiled gracefully and thanked everyone for the well wishes before I stood up on my tippy toes and kissed my dad on the cheek. "Thanks, Daddy," I whispered. My mother placed her hands on my shoulders in a kind embrace. In that moment we looked like the perfect family.

When the people returned to their previous conversations, I slipped out the back door. By the looks of things, my mother was four champagne glasses in and would be oblivious. I ran across the grass that joined my yard with Ethan's, but all the lights were out inside. I sprinted around the front of the house and found that door also locked. Panic rose throughout my body.

Ignoring everything that warned me to run back to my house and ask Charlie, I tried the side garage door. The hair on the back of my neck rose as I held the door handle. I hadn't been in this garage in years. I could vividly recall the last time I was here—when Jerry beat Joey and told his boys to shove him inside his car. Desperate to find Ethan, I pushed through my fears and turned the knob.

The scent of oil and gasoline wafted through the air, punching me in the face. It was a smell I could never forget. It was a scent that was coiled around fear. Luckily, Jerry's car was nowhere in sight. I exhaled the breath that was lodged in my chest and jogged across the cement floor. I was halfway across the double car garage when his words stopped me dead in my tracks.

"He's not here." Jerry's voice was low, but it caused every fiber in my body to shake with fear.

Nervously, I brushed my hair behind my ears and looked him in the eyes. His expression darkened with an unreadable emotion. "Oh," I stammered. "Okay, then." I took slow steps backwards toward the side door, my eyes locked on his like the innocent prey waiting for the evil monster to strike.

"You don't have to rush out of here so soon," he said, and

began to walk toward me.

Instantly, my pulse beat erratically at the threat in his deep voice. I knew what this man was capable of. I knew what he did for a living. Unable to move, my feet felt as if they were stuck in quicksand. My fear had me paralyzed. My breathing grew irregular and my rapid heartbeat hummed in my ear.

"You have grown into a beautiful woman," Jerry said. His face was so close to mine I could smell the gin on his breath.

I swallowed back the contents of my stomach threatening to come up, and took a deep breath. "I should really get going." I managed to move a step back, but I couldn't get away fast enough.

His hands laced around my wrists. "You know, I never got a real good look at you." Panic rioted within me. "But I see now why Ethan wants to move all the way to New York. Is your pussy as pretty as your face?"

His inappropriate remark made my cheeks heat and tears formed in my eyes as panic set in. "Let me go. Please." I tried to tug my wrists away from him but it was no use. Jerry was much stronger than I was.

"Shh." He brought his face down to my neck. "The more you fight, the more it's going to hurt."

Bile rose in my throat and it felt like I couldn't breathe. "Help!" I screamed. Someone, please help me!"

"You hear that?" Jerry said in a calm, icy voice, which only intensified my fear. "Your mother hired a band, which means you can scream as much as you want. No one will hear you."

Tears swelled in my eyes. I shook my head and did the one thing I remembered from the self-defense course we took in high school. With everything I had in me I lifted my knee and aimed straight for his nuts. But Jerry was faster than I was. He dashed out of the way and grabbed me by my arms. Shoving me against the wall, I saw the devil in his eyes.

"You fucking bitch."

My head slammed against the concrete wall, and I whimpered from the sharp pain. His mouth pressed on mine. My nails scraped his skin repeatedly as I struggled to get away, but it did nothing to faze him. I was pinned between a horrific monster and a solid-stone wall.

I screamed, I begged, and my arms grew weaker with each passing second.

Jerry moved to unzip his pants and sheer black fright swept through me.

"Please don't," I cried. "Please don't do this to me!" His calloused hand slid up my thigh just as I bellowed out my last scream.

"You son of a bitch!" was all I heard before Jerry was yanked off my body.

I fell to my knees, scraping them on the concrete floor. As I blinked away the tears, I saw Ethan swinging at Jerry. His fist collided with his jaw, but Jerry threw a punch that tossed Ethan to the ground.

"Ethan!"

Jerry kicked him in the gut before he turned toward me. I watched as he wiped blood from the corner of his lip.

"Run!" Ethan shouted in agony. His hands were wrapped around his stomach. I scurried to my feet and dashed for the door, my legs shaking with each step I took.

"Oh, no you don't." Jerry's fingers coiled around my hair and tugged me back.

"Let her go!" Ethan shouted.

Jerry released my hair and I fell to the ground. Gasping for air, I looked back and watched Jerry wobble toward the massive tool shelf. Bright crimson blood dripped from the back of his head. My gaze moved from Jerry to Ethan, and fresh tears pooled in my eyes when I saw the damage his father had done to his face. One eye was shut and bruising. His lip was split in half. Then my gaze moved to the bloody crowbar Ethan held in his hand. The crowbar he used to hit Jerry's skull.

I opened my mouth to scream, but nothing came out. In that moment, the air in the garage vanished. Ethan tried to run for me; he tried to rescue me, but there was no point. There was no noise, only excruciating pain. It was then I glanced down at my leg and realized the source of the numbing pain. The tool shelf had fallen on me. Jerry had pulled it down and was lying trapped underneath it.

BROKEN DREAMS

Ethan dropped to his knees next to me. Without saying a word, we both knew this had broken us. I bit back a sob as the world around me fell dark.

Our dreams of escaping this town were dead.

Chapter Eighteen

PRESENT

Gasping for air, I wake up.

My hands rush to my chest and I try to calm my racing heart. "It's in the past . . . It's in the past," I reassure myself. The argument with my mother, along with the night I spent with Ethan must have triggered the memory I had buried so deep in my brain.

I roll off the bed and march down to the kitchen for a glass of water. *I spent most of the afternoon sleeping.* Locating my purse on the kitchen counter, I pull out my phone.

Ethan: Are you sure I can't persuade you to come over tonight?

My fingers hover over the keypad, but instead, I shake my head and lock the screen. I don't want to talk to him. Not when the wounds feel so fresh.

I walk over to the medicine cabinet and debate taking one of my mother's Ambien. I know they will help me sleep; drown out the voices and fears that linger deep inside. Holding the bottle, I weigh my options, and then place them back in the cabinet. I need to face my demons head on. I can't always turn to tequila when I'm down, and turning to sleep medication will just open a whole new can of worms.

My hands rest on the kitchen counter and I take a few calming breaths to help the anxiety attack that is forming deep in my chest. I know what I can do to fix this. Hating this part of me, the part that needs to run to feel safe, I shake the thoughts out of my mind and close the cabinet door shut before I run up the stairs. I crawl back into bed and stare at the stars that are glued to my ceiling. I can't be the same Leslie as always. I need to learn to grow. If being back here has taught me anything, it's that time does make us grow. I now, somewhat, have a normal relationship with my mother, Ethan and I are happy together. Wanting to run because of a bad nightmare is stepping backward, not forward. I toss on the bed and roll over until my eyes land on the window. I can't run away. It's time to plant my feet and face my demons.

I'm in the studio late Monday night with my beginner's ballet class. With their flats on and their hair pulled back in a bun, we practice plies and first position. My mind is everywhere but where it should be. Though I forced myself to stay and not run, my mind keeps imagining the possibility of leaving it all behind.

When I broke my ankle, Ethan was nowhere in sight and I couldn't take the pain of letting everyone down. So I ran. When Harry left for London, I couldn't take the burden of not being good enough again, so I ran to Chicago.

Running is what I do, and right now all I want to do is run away from this place again. Run away from Ethan. The simple memory of what happened between us makes me want to rip my skin off and run. It's a constant battle that, at times, I feel I'm losing.

I glance up at the clock and notice the class has run five

minutes over. "Okay, girls, that's it for tonight. Remember to practice your pliés at home."

I'm saying my good-byes to the parents when Ethan walks in through the studio door. Instantly, my heart flutters; we both know why he's here. I've been dodging his calls lately. Not because I don't want to see him, but because I know he can see right through me. He leans against the wall and waits until I'm finished. When the last parent and student are out the door, he walks toward me. His eyes are kind, and his hands are tucked away in his leather jacket.

"Hey," I say nervously. His eyes are compelling and magnetic.

He scoops me into his arms and kisses me tenderly. When he pulls away, I'm breathless. "What is it, Freckles?" he says, looking deep into my eyes for some form of answer. His bright green irises sparkle at me, and instantly, none of my problems seem to matter. He has always been able to do that.

"Nothing," I lie. I don't want to ruin the moment, and I don't want to admit that I want to leave.

"You've always been a bad liar." His mouth quirks with humor.

"I'm not lying. I've just been busy." I shrug and a grin grows on my face.

Ethan places me on the ground and pulls me into his arms. Slowly, he places a finger under my chin and makes me look up at him. "Remember our freshman year? We were let out of school early because the heat was unbearable, and we walked over to the creek. I decided we should go swimming, and you threw a fit because you had your period and didn't want to tell me that's what was going on. You kept saying *nothing*. And when I wouldn't give up, you picked a fight with me, called me a dumb boy and ran home."

I pout my lips as I remember the day clearly.

"Well, that is the exact same face you have on right now. So, why don't you tell me what's really bothering you."

"My mother," I say as I lean my body on his and rest my head on his chest. "She was up when you dropped me off and we had an argument. It brought up some bad memories."

"Does this argument entail how I ruined everything for you?"

"As a matter of fact, yes." I glance up at Ethan. His green eyes are captivating and the scruff around his chin makes me reach up and run my fingers across it.

"Do you want me to talk to her?"

I shake my head. There isn't anything anyone can say. "It's the past. And like everything else, this too shall pass."

"That still doesn't explain why you were avoiding me."

I sigh and bury my face into his chest. "You make it hard to think straight. So much has happened between us. It's easier to run away."

"I'm not letting you run anymore," he says into the crook of my neck before he wraps his hands around my waist and lifts me off the ground again. I squeal and wrap my arms around his neck. For a moment we stare into each other's eyes. *If we could only live in this bubble.* "No matter how hard you try, I'm not letting you run away. Whatever it is, we will get through this. Together."

His lips capture mine in a kiss, tender at first, nibbling on my lower lip before deepening it. My legs tighten around his hips as I let myself mold into him. Ethan's hands are on my back before moving to the nape of my neck. Holding me close, he walks into the office and kicks the door closed behind him. He sits me on top of the desk and takes a step back. "You know, for as long as I can remember, I've wanted to have sex in this office."

"Really?" Butterflies flap their wings in my belly nervously. I lean back and rest my hands behind me.

"Yes." He takes a step forward. "I think it has to do with the way this thing is skin tight." He runs his hands up my leotard.

"It's supposed to be tight so you can see the movements."

"All I see is the way it hugs your body," Ethan whispers, pulling a strap down from my shoulder. His lips follow along the nylon fabric until my breast is exposed. I whimper when his tongue swirls around my nipple. Hearing me, Ethan yanks down the other strap and cups my breasts.

Unable to take the torture of his lips on my nipples, I reach for his jeans, but he pulls away from my bare skin and grabs my hands. Slowly he shakes his head, and a devilish grin grows on his face. "Oh, no you don't. I'm going to make sure you think twice the next time you consider running away from me." His voice is low and purposely seductive. "Lie back, Freckles. I've been dying to do this for a long time."

I press my back against the cool wood furniture and let Ethan undress me. Exposing myself, I watch as his eyes devour me. Then his hands. And finally, his mouth. Ethan kisses up my legs and inner thighs. When his breath reaches my core, I'm aching.

One lick.

One kiss.

Ever so slowly he teases, bringing me to the edge. His tongue does things to me I have never felt before. Arching my back, I moan out his name.

"Ethan . . . please," I beg.

He grunts in pleasure but continues his slowly-paced licks. Without an ounce of doubt, I give in to him. I give him all of me. He is right there, riding the wave of my orgasm with his tongue. When the trembles cease and I can breathe again, I sit up and lean on my elbows.

"That was—"

"Everything." He wipes the corner of his mouth.

"Can I return the favor?"

Ethan shakes his head and proceeds to unzip his pants. "Another time, Freckles. I need you. Now," he demands. The devil is in his eyes, which only entices me to please him.

"How do you want me?" I ask, hoping my eyes match the carnal want in his.

"Turn around."

I bite my lower lip and hop off the desk. Bending over in front of him, I wait in anticipation. He groans with pleasure as he sinks into me. It's all consuming, all pleasing. I lay my head on the cool wood and enjoy his thrusts. He is tender at first. Slow and steady, and he savors every second, but when my body tightens around him and I beg him to give me more, he does.

Ethan doesn't stop until we are both sated and gasping for air.

One month later

It all seems perfect. Everything seems right in the world and it feels as if nothing ever changed.

We are in love all over again. And this time, I can see a forever for us.

The nights I work late at the studio, he's there to walk me to my car. He takes me out to dinner one night during the week, and we spend countless hours on the phone or making love to each other. We're doing all the things we never got to do, and just like that my life is somewhat normal again. The need to run away is gone.

Darlene and I haven't fought since my walk of shame. She knows Ethan and I are back together and doesn't question it. She spends her days with my dad, who is finally getting better, though I have yet to find the courage to see him. Like I said, everything seems right in the world.

But like so many moons ago, I can't help but feel the world is about to be ripped out from under me one more time.

Chapter Nineteen

PRESENT

Monday morning, I wake up to my mother coughing. This isn't a regular dry cough, but more of a hacking-up-a-lung type of cough. Stumbling out of bed, I walk to her room to check on her.

"Ma?" I tap on the door, but when she doesn't respond, I push it open. The sun hasn't yet risen on the horizon so I turn on her nightstand light. "Mom, are you okay?"

My mother looks over at me and shakes her head. The bags under her eyes and her red, puffy nose are a clear indication of how she feels. I sit on the edge of the bed and place my hand on her head. "You're burning up."

"I think it's the flu," she mutters before coughing again.

"I'll go get you some medicine and bring you some toast with orange juice." I leave her bedroom and rush downstairs. Digging through the medicine cabinet, I locate a cold and flu medication.

With a tray in hand, I walk back into her room and place the tray on her bed. "This should make you feel better." I hand her the pill and OJ.

"Your father is expecting me today," she says before popping a pill into her mouth.

I know what she's hinting at. I haven't seen my father since that night at the hospital. She hasn't pushed the issue, and I know it's because I've been running the studio for her.

"It'll make him happy to see you." She takes a bite of toast and winces as she tries to swallow.

I sigh, knowing there's no way out of this. "I'll go." I force a soft smile onto my face. "Has he finished the last book I sent him?" My mother nods and smiles, and though it's weak, I know she's pleased I'm finally facing my fears.

I grip the steering wheel as I drive toward the rehabilitation center. The school traffic has subsided, making the commute easy. I pull into the parking spot and check myself one last time in the mirror before I get out of the car. Each step feels harder than the last as memories come crashing down on me. Unable to take another step forward, I run back to the car.

Just a few more minutes, I tell myself. *Just a few more minutes to forget this awful place*. Locking myself back in the car, I rest my head on the steering wheel to calm my breaths.

The memories don't just haunt me.

They consume me.

Chapter Twenty

PAST

I couldn't feel my leg.

I couldn't wiggle my toes.

The pain burned as though acid was being poured on my skin, and my vision blurred.

"Leslie?" Ethan brushed my hair. "Oh, my God…" His hands moved from my face to my shoulder as he scanned my body to determine what was hurt.

"My leg," I cried and looked into his eyes. The fear that radiated from them told me to be afraid. "Jerry?" I asked, not knowing exactly what had happened.

Ethan shook his head and his eyes filled with tears. "He was going after you. I had no choice."

"Where were you?" I cried, desperate for answers.

"He made me drive his car to the shop. I ran home, and

when you weren't at the party I rushed here." He cupped my cheeks and kissed my lips. "I saw him touching you. I heard your screams." His voice cracked.

"Is he . . . dead?" I winced as I tried to move.

"I don't know." His voice was so low it caused a chill to run up my spine.

"Ethan . . ." My lips quivered. "I can't feel my leg. We need to call for help."

He nodded and kissed my head. "It will all be okay. I promise."

And just like that he was gone.

When the garage door closed, reality hit me. My leg was broken, and Ethan's father was lying under a shelf with his skull cracked open, the pool of blood only a few feet away.

I screamed.

I screamed until my voice grew hoarse.

I screamed until my throat felt as if it were on fire.

I screamed until it was completely silent and there was nothing left inside of me.

I didn't know that my dream of dancing was over, but I knew whatever I shared with Ethan, the pure innocent love we had, had been tarnished by Jerry.

I lay on the cool cement floor for what felt like hours, sobbing until someone came to get me. When the door swung open, I heard my mother screech. My father rushed to my side.

"Leslie . . . Are you hurt, sweetie? What happened?"

I couldn't answer him. All I could do was cry. My mother kneeled beside me and grabbed my hand. From my peripheral, I could see my entire party had shifted from my house to inside Ethan's garage. My eyes scanned the garage for Ethan. I needed to look at him. I needed to know it would all be okay, like he promised.

But he wasn't there.

Four men counted to three and then lifted the shelf off my body. In unison, everybody gasped when they saw Jerry's motionless body underneath it, a pool of blood surrounding him. My mother quickly turned my head away and that was when I noticed my foot was bent in the opposite direction. I hadn't broken my leg. I had obliterated my ankle.

This had to be a nightmare. This couldn't be happening.

I looked at my parents who were both staring at me with concerned eyes. "I can still dance, right?" I asked past the tears in a hopeful tone.

My mother's lower lip quivered and she nodded. But there was something in her eyes, something I had never seen before, something that caused a shiver to run up my spine. It told me everything I already knew deep in my gut. Dancing was out of the question—permanently. I bit back a sob and allowed her to hold me tight as she shielded me from the pain.

Minutes passed, but it felt like a century before the ambulance arrived. The cops walked in first, surveyed the premises, and asked everyone to leave. That was when I finally spotted Ethan. He stood in the corner with his mother and Charlie. I needed more from Ethan in that second than I ever had in my entire life. I needed him to give me a sign that everything would be okay.

But he never did. He never met my eyes. He refused to look at me.

My parents both walked alongside the stretcher as the officers spoke to the other group of EMTs that were crouched down near Jerry.

It wasn't until I was almost out the door when I heard one say, "He has a pulse. He's unconscious, but he has a pulse."

My heart rate sped up and it felt impossible to breathe. My eyes darted to Ethan, and I watched as his knees hit the ground.

Jerry was still alive.

The world around me passed in a blur. That my ankle was broken didn't matter to me as much as the fact that Jerry was still alive. And for the life of me, I couldn't get the image of Ethan dropping down on his knees out of my mind. I wanted to know what he was thinking, what he was feeling. What the hell was going to happen to us?

When we arrived at the hospital, I was rushed to see an

orthopedic surgeon. Their mouth's moved but I couldn't hear anything. The only thing that reverberated in my head was Ethan was nowhere to be found and Jerry had a pulse. The man who tried to rape me was still alive. My mind raced at high speed but I kept forcing my shattered ankle out of my head. I still refused to believe that to be true.

My skin began to itch and I reached to scratch my cheek. It was then I realized I had been stripped of my clothes and put into a hospital gown. An IV was jammed into my arm and for the life of me I couldn't remember how it got there.

"Leslie, sweetie." My dad gripped my hand. "The doctors say you're in shock." His voice was low, as though he were speaking to a small child. "We all are." He held my hand firmly. "But everything will be okay. They're taking you up to surgery now and we will be right here." Tears welled in his eyes, and his eyebrows pinched together.

"I'm okay, Daddy," I said, not feeling an ounce of pain. "I'm fine." I sat up on the bed. "Really, I'm fine. I just need to find Ethan."

My father's strong hand rested on my shoulder. "Leslie." He said my name in a stern tone. "Listen to me. Your ankle is badly broken. They need to go in there and fix it before you have permanent nerve damage and won't be able to walk."

There had to be a misunderstanding. I wasn't in any pain. I looked at my mother for some kind of reassurance, but her back was pressed against the wall and she was crying.

"But I'm fine. I just need to get to Ethan. I'm fine."

"It's the morphine drip that's making her like this," I heard an unfamiliar man's voice say.

Was he right?

I lay back on the bed and closed my eyes. Tears slowly slid from the corners. "Daddy?" I turned back to face him. My voice broke with each syllable. "I'll be able to dance again, right?"

"Yes, sweetie." He brushed his hand along my hair. "The doctors will do everything they can and you'll be able to dance again." I smiled and closed my eyes once more.

That was the first time my father ever lied to me.

BROKEN DREAMS

When I woke up, my throat hurt and my body felt as if it weighed a ton. Peeling my eyes open, I spied a doctor talking to my parents. My mother still had that look of death in her eyes, and my father's arms were crossed as he listened to every word the doctor spoke.

"Dad," I whispered. They grew silent as everyone turned to face me. "Mom, what is it?" All she could do was shake her head at me.

"Leslie, I'm Doctor Weiss. I performed the surgery on your ankle." He spoke in a calming tone. "You'll be a bit groggy for the next few hours, but that's the anesthesia wearing off. Your surgery went beautifully. You'll be in a cast for the next six weeks, and then we'll start physical therapy right after that. I believe you'll have to do at least three months of physical therapy before you are able to walk without a cane."

I sat up on the bed, wincing at the pain that radiated up my leg. "That's impossible." I shook my head. "I leave for Juilliard in three weeks." I glanced over at my mother. "Mom, tell him!" My mother ran her hands under her eyes and shook her head before turning on her heel and walking out of my room.

The moment I needed my mother the most, she left.

"Dad . . ." I cried. "I can dance, right? I can go to Juilliard? They're expecting me." I couldn't control the tears that dripped down my cheeks. "I got in. Out of thousands, they only picked twelve girls. They picked me!" My hands rushed to shield my face. "Tell him I can't do physical therapy. I have to go to New York."

"Leslie, sweetheart." The somber tone of his voice broke my heart. "Unfortunately, you won't be able to go to Juilliard."

This had to be a nightmare.

Dr. Weiss cleared his throat. "Leslie, when the shelf fell on your ankle, it tore your lateral and medial malleolus. The bones around your talus are being held in place by plates and screws." Dr. Weiss held up the X-ray of my ankle.

I gasped when I looked at the black film. There were six small screws on the inner part of my ankle, and one long screw from the outside into the bone. I would *never* dance again.

"I'm sorry, Leslie. With time, you might be able to dance socially, but you will never be able to dance professionally."

I leaned back on the bed and closed my eyes. "Go away," I muttered under my breath.

"Leslie . . ." My father tried to calm me, but I didn't want anybody's pity.

"Go away. Leave me alone!" I screamed as I covered my face. I heard my father sigh before he and the doctor walked out of my room. I dropped my hands from my face and scanned the empty room. Everyone and everything I had ever loved had vanished from my life.

Every memory tarnished.
Every dream broken.
I was alone.
Completely alone.

It was a week before my eighteenth birthday.

A full month had passed since the day I was supposed to leave for Juilliard. Nearly two since my dreams were shattered, along with my ankle. Ethan and I had planned out this entire day. After we were done with school, we would take a walk through Central Park and head over to Serendipity III. We were going to split a frozen hot chocolate and spend the night at his place.

We had mapped out every single day of our first summer in New York, from our meeting spot in the departure lounge at the Arizona airport to how we would transform ourselves from tourists to New York natives.

Now I sat in the hospital room, by myself, waiting for a nurse to take me to physical therapy. There were no special days planned. There was no hovering mother to watch my every move. There was no loving boyfriend to hold my hand. My days now consisted of waking up, eating breakfast, and participating in physical therapy.

The only person who visited me was my father when he was

done with work, and the detectives who insisted on getting my version of the story over and over again. According to my father, Ethan wouldn't speak to the police. He just sat in an interrogation room completely silent. It was up to me to tell the cops what happened, so I told them the truth—it was self-defense. Jerry was attacking me, and Ethan saved me by hitting him over the head.

Apparently, they weren't happy with my story. The detectives were in my room three times after my initial debriefing, and when they walked in for a fourth time, I reminded them I was a minor, and until I had a legal guardian or a lawyer present, I wouldn't be saying anything else. Having spent well over a month in the hospital watching *Law and Order* on re-runs, I knew my rights.

I arrived back in my room after therapy, exhausted and in pain. They had removed the hard cast but I still wasn't allowed to put weight on my foot. Who knew moving your foot back-and-forth for an hour caused such exhaustion and pure agony? When Megan, my therapist, wheeled me back into my room, I spotted a coat sitting on the table. Instantly, a smile appeared on my face. *Was that Ethan's coat? Had he finally come to visit?* It was wishful thinking, but it was my birthday after all.

As we moved further into the room, I realized it was my father's coat. My smile faltered and I pulled myself onto the bed, shifting until my back rested on the firm mattress.

"There you are, kiddo." My father walked back into the room holding a cup of coffee. "I left work early to spend your special day with you. When I got here they said you were in therapy so I figured I'd go down to grab you a treat. I bought you a glazed donut." He lifted up the white bag.

What was the point of watching my weight now? "Thanks, Dad." I took the bag from him. He leaned forward and kissed the top of my head. "How was therapy?"

"Great," I said with zero enthusiasm.

"Leslie." My father pouted. "You have to give it a try."

"I did. I am." My voice grew angrier.

"Fine." My father sat at the edge of the bed. "What's really going on? You don't seem like yourself."

I scoffed and shook my head. Did he really have the nerve to ask me that question?

"Do you really have to ask?" I didn't wait for him to respond. "Mom is gone. Ethan hasn't called or even come to visit me. I won't ever dance again. I had to call Julliard and tell me them I'm not going. Everything I loved has turned to shit!" My words came out in hysterical, uncontrollable sobs. "You keep me locked in here when all I want to do is go home." I paused and wiped the tears from my cheeks. "Why hasn't he come to visit me? I told the cops it was self-defense. Did they arrest him and you don't want to tell me? Is that it?"

"Easy there, Leslie." He grabbed my hand. "I don't want to see you upset on your birthday."

"Why hasn't he come? Why!"

My father sighed and ran his hands through his peppered hair. "Right now I want you to focus on therapy."

"They arrested him, right?"

"No. There is a lot going on, but there is no charge of attempted murder. It was self-defense and Joyce isn't doing so well, so Ethan has been busy with that. Plus, I asked him to give you some space."

"What? Why!" I slammed my hands against the comforter.

"I want you to rest." My father was flippant as he took another sip of his coffee.

How could he just dismiss me that way? Couldn't he see what this was doing to me? "I don't want to rest, Dad! I want to see him. I need him to know I don't blame him."

My father's eyes bore little compassion. "I'm sorry, but unfortunately you're our number one priority. Getting you healthy is my main concern."

Whether it was a stern act to keep me focused or his true intention, I was full of rage. "I hate you!" I cried. "If you wanted me to get better you wouldn't keep me locked in here." I covered my face with my hands and sobbed. "Get out! Get out! Get out!"

BROKEN DREAMS

I felt the mattress move and I knew he had gotten up. "I know you're mad now. But this is for your own good." He kissed the top of my head when he was finished speaking his clichéd words. Defiantly, I turned away from him. Unless he was allowing Ethan to visit, I didn't want anything from him.

Weeks turned into months. Doctors said I was depressed. Others said I was defiant and throwing tantrums because I didn't get what I wanted. But I simply felt numb. The light inside of me had died. The lotus flower that once bloomed through the muck had withered and wilted away.

When they brought in a therapist to speak to me, my father was worried. I had been in rehab for almost three months. My ankle was healing and I was finally able to walk with the help of a cane.

It dawned on me one morning that no one else *lived* in the hospital like I did. Yes, people stayed for weeks at a time depending on their injury, but I was perfectly healthy and still there was no discharge. I began to ask every day why I was still there and the answer was simple. *Your father has requested this.*

And like that my depression worsened.

"Leslie," My father said in a low tone. I was picking at my lunch when he walked in the room. I didn't pull my gaze from the soft cream wall. "Sweetie, we're all worried about you. Talk to me, Leslie."

I shifted on the pillow and looked over to him. I hated that he kept me in here like a caged animal. I hated that my mother never came to visit me. I hated that Ethan never called.

"I want to leave." I whispered and glanced over at him. "I want to get the hell out of here."

"Okay. We can make arrangements to move you to a different facility."

"No!" I sat up on the bed, fueled with urgency. "I don't want to be in a hospital anymore. I don't know why you've kept me here for so long but I can't do this anymore. Don't you see, Dad? I want out! Out of this hospital, out of this town. Out! I want to go to college like I was supposed to."

"Juilliard—"

"Fuck Juilliard!" I yelled, shaking my head. "I was accepted to other schools, too. Please, Dad. Let me leave this place. Let me go on with my life."

I watched as my father weighed his options. He nodded as he reached out to hold my hand. "Let me make a few phone calls tomorrow and I'll come back."

"Thank you." I whispered as the tears blinded me.

My father returned the following day with a manila folder tucked under his arm.

"I made a few calls." His voice was low and hoarse. "But first I want you to understand a few things." I nodded.

"It was my choice to keep you in here. I didn't understand the type of man Jerry was until you were lying in a hospital bed. He had men follow him and it was my fear that with him being injured they might come after you. I didn't feel you'd be safe at home given your mother is currently unstable. So, I want you to know I'm sorry for keeping you here for the past three months, but I did it to keep you safe."

He reached out and held my hand. "I called the dean at UCLA and explained what happened. Luckily, he was my history professor when I attended and he remembered me. I know it's not Juilliard, but if you want, they will accept you. The fall semester starts next week, but you can do a late registration."

I didn't wait for him to finish. "I'll take it."

"Leslie." He paused and glanced deep into my eyes. "This is your career, your life. Don't make a rash decision just because you don't want to be here anymore."

"Dad, if I can't dance like Mom, then I want to be successful like you are," I admitted.

My father sighed and pulled me into his arms. "I'm so sorry, kiddo. I thought by keeping you here I was keeping you safe."

"It's okay," I cried. "I just want to leave now."

BROKEN DREAMS

My father pulled away and framed my small face with his big hands. "You'll still need to continue with physical therapy. I've talked to Dr. Weiss about a referral."

I nodded. "And Mom?" I couldn't imagine a world where Darlene was unstable.

"She'll be all right. She just needs a little time." I knew it was a lie but it was a lie to protect both of us.

Chapter Twenty One

PAST

I sit inside the car for seconds, minutes, hours. I don't move until the pain in my chest has subsided and my breathing has normalized.

It has been years since I relived that horrific day. I inhale as much air as my lungs can take until I find the courage to step out of the car. Jerry can't harm me anymore. Enough time has passed. The dreams I had eight years ago have changed. *I have built myself back up.*

With my shoulders back, I walk with my head held high. My heart is racing rapidly, and there's a soft humming in my ears when I pull on the glass door. The sterile scent hits me and I'm thrown off my axis.

It's all too familiar.

I spent months here. I was held prisoner. My mother didn't want me home; she was unstable, as my father would say. He felt I was safer here. And the entire time, Jerry was being held only a few rooms away.

Bile rises in my throat and I push past it. I'm three steps through the doorway when my stomach drops completely. My eyes lock on his and I'm rooted to the ground. His eyes are hooded and I can see his hesitation.

Slowly, I shake my head, not believing what I see. Ethan wouldn't come here. He never once visited when I was here. Even when I begged him to come. *Never.*

"Les."

Before he can reach me, I'm out the door, gasping for air.

"Leslie, wait . . ."

My ankle burns as I run to the car. My fidgety hand betrays me and I can't open the car door.

"Leslie, please," he begs. "Talk to me."

"I need to go," I whisper, hoping I can maintain my grace.

"Let me explain."

"Explain?" I snap. "Fuck you and your stupid explanations. You're here to see *him,* your piece of shit father. Not once did you visit when I was trapped in here. Not once did you come to make sure I was okay. Never!" I slam my closed fists on his chest. "I needed you. I needed my boyfriend. I needed my best fucking friend." I cry out the last sentence on a sob, and my knees buckle.

Ethan wraps his arms around my body. "I'm sorry. I'm so fucking sorry." Minutes pass before he lets me go. My cheeks are stained with tears, and I can't find the courage to look up at him. My gaze is glued to the scruff around his jawline. He runs his thumb along my cheek, brushing away a tear.

"He's dying," he says. Stunned, I look up at him. "I've never been here before today. *Never.* I refused to visit him. My mother was checked into a psych ward and I was made responsible for him.

"A part of me is angry he didn't die that day. That he now became an even a bigger burden on my life. I was wrong to never come and see you, but if I hadn't hit Jerry with the crowbar, he would have never pulled down the shelf. It was my fault you broke your ankle and I couldn't find the courage to face you." I shake my head, hating that he has carried this blame for so many years.

"It wasn't your fault," I finally muster the courage to speak. "I should've never gone inside the garage."

Ethan presses his forehead to mine. "He's dying, and as his POA I had to sign the documents for them to turn off his life support. I hope he burns in fucking hell for everything he did."

The anger in Ethan's voice is terrifying, and I realize that Jerry will always be a burden to us. Until we learn to let go, we will never be able to move on. "He's dying?" Ethan nods. "Right now?"

"Soon I guess. Sometime today, I'd assume."

My mind floods with every bit of anger Jerry has caused in my life. There is so much I'm holding on to and I realize until I can face my demons I will never be able to move forward. I chew on the inside of my cheek for a few minutes before I speak again. "Can we go see him?" *I can't believe what I just asked.*

Ethan winces. "Les, I don't think that's a good idea."

"I feel as if he will have this hold on us for the rest of our lives. It's something we will carry with us always." I swallow and contemplate what I'm about to say. "Jerry broke me physically and emotionally, but I think I need to face him in order to move on, and in order to start fresh with you. We say we're starting over, but are we really? I see you in this hospital and I have a panic attack. I need to face Jerry and forgive you." I find the courage to look up at Ethan.

He sighs and kisses my forehead. "They're doing one more test to check his brain wave activity, and then they are turning off his life support." He exhales and brings me closer to him.

"You're not going to stay with him?" I ask. He buries his face in the crook of my neck and shakes his head. In that moment I realize that I'm not the only one who needs to forgive Jerry. I'm not the only one who is holding on to so much anger and resentment. For years, Jerry used Ethan and his mother as punching bags. Ethan's mother was in a mental facility because of all the abuse she received, and Ethan carried the weight of the world on his shoulders.

I wrap my arms around him and whisper, "I think we both need to face our demons."

"Okay." He pulls away and looks deep into my eyes. His emerald irises regard me with hope. Hope of leaving all the bad behind us. It takes everything in me, but I nod.

Ethan shifts and places his muscular arm around my shoulder and brings me to his side. "I love you, Leslie." He kisses the top of my head. "You have always made me strive to be a better person."

Together we walk toward the front door of the rehab facility. Ethan never leaves my side as he leads me to the elevator, up to the third floor and down a long hallway. Jerry's room is the second to last. My heart tightens as we approach.

A nurse walks out of the room as I'm gathering my courage to walk in. "Oh, Mr. Prescott. I thought you weren't staying?" she asks Ethan.

"I'm not," he answers.

The nurse glances over at me and then back at Ethan. She forces a kind smile on her face. "His tests came back the same. There is no sign of brain activity." She pauses, waiting for any kind of emotion from Ethan, but he remains stoic. "I'll notify Dr. Loch so we can proceed with your request."

Ethan simply nods and looks down at me. "Ready?"

Inhaling, I swallow the golf ball sized knot in my throat and nod.

Goosebumps rise all over my body as I step inside the quaint, familiar room. The walls are a dull gray, and there is no sign of life. No flowers, no cards, nothing. Jerry's motionless body lies in the hospital bed in the center on the room. Bile rises up my throat and I force it back down. Ethan and I stand at the foot of the bed looking down at his frail body. He doesn't look like the same Jerry who used to terrify me as a kid, but I don't let it fool me. I know the devil still lives deep inside his soul.

I glance over at Ethan. His fists are balled at his sides, and I know this is harder for him than it is for me. This is his father, the man who was supposed to love him unconditionally, but who never once showed him an ounce of affection.

I move from Ethan's grip and rest both hands on the rail of

the bed. Exhaling, I speak to the man lying there. "I will never forget what you did to me. I'll never be the person I was destined to be because of you, but I learned that doesn't define who I am. Eight years ago you took a piece of me that I'll never get back, but you don't scare me anymore. You broke my dreams, but you didn't break me. I'm still here, standing, and moving on with my life, I'm surrounded by people who love me, while you lay here all alone. I refuse to let you hold any power over me anymore." I exhale the breath I didn't know was stuck in my chest and look over at Ethan. His nostrils are flaring and his breathing is erratic. "Ethan . . ."

Slowly, he shakes his head as he stares at his father. "You should have bled to death that day I hit you with that fucking crow bar," he says through gritted teeth. "I hope you burn in hell. I hope you suffer for eternity. Mom never deserved what you did to her, and Charlie was an innocent child who needed a father."

"Ethan!" I gasp, stunned by the hatred in his voice.

"Fuck him, Leslie," he growls. "He deserves to die alone for all the shit he did to you, to me, my mom, and every other poor soul." He runs his hands through his hair. "Rot in fucking hell, Jerry." He turns on his heel and heads straight out the door.

Stunned by the hatred in his voice, I run after him. "Ethan, wait!" He is halfway down the hallway when I reach him. "Hey." I grab his hand.

"Fuck." I see the tears forming in his eyes. "I'm sorry. I can't. What that piece of shit did to me, to us . . ." His voices cracks and I lace my arms around his body.

"It's okay." I realize Ethan's demons are much bigger than mine.

He coils his arms around my body and cries onto my shoulder. When his body begins to tremble, I can't stop the tears that fall down my cheeks. Nurses, patients, and visitors pass us, but we remain in each other's arms until he pulls away.

Gently, he kisses the tip of my nose. "I'm sorry. I thought I could move past everything, but when I saw him lying there all I could remember was his fists hitting my mother's face, and him kicking me in the gut. I'm sorry, Leslie, but I can't."

With my heart breaking, I catch a tear with my finger. "I know." I rise on my toes and kiss his lips. "You don't have to, and I forgive you. I know that day in the garage you weren't trying to hurt me, but protect me. The shelf falling was an unfortunate event."

"Mr. Prescott." A nurse approaches us. "We are ready to turn off the machines. Would you like to be there with him?" she says when Ethan I look over at her.

Ethan shakes his head. "No. He deserves to die alone." The nurse nods and continues to walk down the hallway. "I need to get some air."

"Want me to come?"

Ethan shakes his head and brushes my hair behind my ears. "I'm assuming you came here to see your father. Why don't you go do that and we'll meet up later?"

"Okay," I say but I can't ignore the pinch in my heart. I know he shouldn't be alone now. "Call me if you need anything."

"Sure thing," he says and kisses my lips.

Ethan steps into the elevator, but instead of going to my father's room, I stand in the hallway and wait for the nurses to exit Jerry's room. I wait to make sure he is actually dead.

Twenty minutes pass before she walks out of the room and discards her gloves. Our eyes meet and she nods letting me know that the devil has finally returned home. A lone tear slips from my eye, and a wave of relief washes over me. I don't know if it's the knowledge that he is finally dead or the fact I have faced him, but I feel lighter.

Turning on my heel, I say good-bye to Jerry and go find my father.

My heart aches as I walk inside my father's room. It's not because I'm sad to see him; my pain is for Ethan. I want to shield him from his anger and his hatred and take his burden as my own. But in that moment I can't do anything but force a smile. My dad is sitting on his bed, his reading glasses on the bridge of his nose as he holds the paper.

"Looking good," I joke, hoping my voice is masked with optimism.

"Kiddo." He puts the paper down.

Walking up to him, I sit on his bed and lean in for a hug. "I'm sorry I haven't been here, Dad," I say as I bury my face in his chest. His familiar scent is gone. The scent of home has been replaced with the sterile scent of the hospital.

"I figured it would be tough for you to come here given everything this place reminds you of." He kisses the top of my head. "Your mom told me what you've done with the studio." I pulled away and looked up at him. "I'm so proud of you, Leslie. You have become a beautiful and talented businesswoman."

I smile widely at him. He has always known what to say to me to make me feel like I matter. "How are you feeling?" I grab his hand.

"Not one hundred percent, but I'm almost there." He shifts on the hard mattress to make room for me to sit with him.

"That's good. I'm happy you're getting better."

"The doctors think I'll be out of here soon, and I'll be able to finish the rest of my therapy at home."

"I know Mom will be thrilled to wait on you hand and foot." I lean my head on his shoulder.

My father clears his throat. "Your mom probably doesn't say this to you, she's stoic that way, but she's proud of you." He looks over at me. "You saved us."

I try to smile but tears betray me. "You saved *me*, Dad. I was drowning with no direction, and you helped me get out of here."

He pulls me closer. "You're my little girl. I would do anything to keep you from suffering."

The room grows silent for a moment and I rest my head on my father's shoulder.

"Ethan just pulled the plug on Jerry," I mutter. "I was coming here to see you, and Ethan was walking out. He had to sign some documents letting them turn off the life-support."

"How's Ethan taking it?"

"Not so good," I sigh. "I wanted to say a few things to Jerry before he died. I wanted to let go of all the anger I had inside. I told Ethan it would be good for us, and it was the only way we could move on from everything that happened." I nervously brush my hair behind my ear. "So, I said my peace. I was willing to stand there and let go and move on. But when it was time for Ethan, he was so angry and hurt."

My father wraps his arms around me. "That boy has been living with that man all his life. We all know what Jerry was capable of, but we never really experienced it. We stood on the sidelines watching, unable to do anything about it. Ethan lived it. I don't blame him."

My father's words resonate deep inside of me. He's right. We were bystanders staring at a horrible car accident, unable to look away. Ethan was stuck in the wreck his entire life, and for the first time, he's finally able to break free.

I spent most of the afternoon with my father, catching him up on everything that had happened in my life. I explained how much I loved Chicago yet it had never really felt like home. I told him about my friends Harry, Emilia and Weston, and how much they had helped me grow over the past few years. Once we moved from the past, we discussed present time. I told him I was concerned about my mother's newfound addiction for sleeping pills, and he shared something I had never known. My mother turns to sleeping medication when she's depressed. It also happened when I broke my ankle and left for Los Angeles. He said she has a shrink who comes to the house once a week while I'm at the studio, and that doctor is the one who prescribes her the pills. I sigh, relieved to know it's one less thing I need to worry about.

When I arrive home, I find my mother in better spirits. She's still in bed, but there's no fever and her cough has subsided. I whip up an early dinner, and we both eat in her bed as we watch the five o'clock news. I keep glancing at my phone waiting for Ethan to call, but the phone never rings. By nine o'clock, I'm crawling into bed with my phone next to me.

BROKEN DREAMS

I won't let him push me away.
Finding the courage, I dial his number.
"Hello?" he answers on the third ring.
"Hey," I say nervously. "I was waiting for you to call."
"Sorry, I just got held up with paperwork. How was the rest of your day with your dad?"
"It was fine. How are you? How's Charlie?" I don't know how to tiptoe around the subject.
Ethan sighs. "We're all okay. If anything, Charlie is relieved as much as I am."
"Do you want me to come over? We can rent a movie or just chill?"
"No, it's okay. I'll be here for a while making funeral arrangements."
"I thought Jerry wasn't getting a funeral."
He sighs again. "If it were up to me, I would dump his body in the desert. I would let his carnage be picked off by the crows. That's how I would want him to rest." I swallow back unable to say anything. The image of crows picking off Jerry's dead skin enters my mind. "But Charlie wants a funeral. He insists we bury him, so that's why I'm doing this."
Instantly, my heart melts. There isn't anything in this world Ethan wouldn't do for his brother. "I understand. Do you need me to help you with anything?"
"No, I'm okay. I have it figured out."
"Okay, well I'm here if you need anything." I can't hide the disappointment in my voice.
"Thank you, Leslie."
"I love you, Ethan."
"I love you, too."
The phone goes silent, slowly sliding for my ear and onto my lap. Ethan seems as fine as one going through what he is going through would be. He is handling it well but the tone of his voice tells me something else.
Putting my hand over my heart, I close my eyes and silently pray that no matter what lies ahead, we can make it in the end.

Chapter Twenty Two

PRESENT

I wait an hour before I head to Ethan's house. He said he had everything under control, but something tells me he has taken on more than he should. Stopping at the bakery, I pick up a few cupcakes before heading his way.

His car is parked in his usual spot, and I walk right up the stairs and down the hallway to his apartment. My fingers gently tap on the door, and when it's pulled ajar, a joyful, boyish grin greets to me.

"Charlie," I sing his name.

"Leslie." He too sings my name, and opens his arms wide. "Ethan's not home," he says after our quick embrace.

"Oh. I saw his car outside. I figured he was home."

"Nope." He shook his head. "He got a call about some issues with one of the supers in the apartment complex across town. But you can hang out with me if you want."

"If you don't mind, I'd love to keep you company." I smile

and close the door behind me.

"I don't mind at all. Besides, no one likes to keep me company." He shrugs.

I follow Charlie into the kitchen, and he pulls out a stool for me. "Don't say that, Charlie. I'm always willing to keep you company. You know I love you."

"Thanks, Leslie." His eyes are glued on the white cardboard box in my hand. "Is that box from the Bavello's Bakery?"

"Yes, it is." I smile at him and flip the box open. "I figured I could bring you guys something sweet to lighten up your day with everything that's going on."

Charlie pulls out a cupcake and runs his pointer along the frosting before putting it in his mouth. "Ethan doesn't want my dad to have a funeral," he says, his gaze locked on the buttercream frosting.

"Oh, Charlie." I reach my hand across and give him a comforting grasp. "How are you feeling? With everything going on with Jerry, and all that has happened with your mom, how are you holding up?"

Charlie peels the wrapper down, then tears off the bottom part of the cake and lays it on the top of the frosting to make a cupcake sandwich. His eyes never pull away from the buttercream filling, and when he speaks his voice is low. "My world isn't black and white like everyone else's. And I'm not stupid. I know my dad was a bad man. I know he used to hit my mother and Ethan, and I know he's the reason you left. Ethan doesn't want to have a funeral for him, but I think the only way we can make sure he's dead is if we put him six feet into the ground."

"Charlie." I grasp his arm. "It's okay to be sad."

"No, I'm not sad. I'm happy because now Ethan doesn't have to worry about taking care of everything. And mom can maybe get better, and we can be a family again."

"I think that'll be very nice," I whisper and can't help the tears that swell in my eyes. The dangling of keys and the door opening startle me. I spin around, and I'm greeted with Ethan. His eyes are darker than I have ever seen them before, and I know he's carrying the weight of the world on his shoulders.

"Hi," I whisper nervously.

Slowly, Ethan closes the door behind him and sighs. Dropping his keys on the console table, he walks straight toward me, the worry lines on his forehead softening with each step. He doesn't utter a word. Instead, his lips land on mine, and he lifts me off the chair. He buries his neck in the crook of my neck and leads us straight to his room. "Goodnight, Charlie," he mumbles, and I giggle at his caveman-like actions. Ethan kicks his bedroom door shut and gently lays me on the bed. Wasting no time, he climbs on top of me and wraps my small frame around his body.

"You're not mad I'm here?" I whisper, and he gently kisses my neck.

"You always know exactly when I need you most." He pulls me even closer.

"I wasn't sure you wanted me here. When we were on the phone, you seemed busy and distracted."

Ethan lifts his head from my neck. "I'm sorry. I have a lot of shit going on, but never think I don't want you here. You're the only thing that keeps me going when all I want to do is tell everybody to go fuck themselves now that Jerry is dead." He closes his eyes and sighs. "I'm so tired of being responsible for everything."

My arms wrap around his neck and I bring him down to my lips. We stay like that for a few minutes, kissing like teenagers unable to pull apart from each other. Ethan finally breaks the kiss and his eyes are filled with hunger. He kneels back and discards his shirt. He yanks my shoes off and lifts me off the bed.

If sex is what helps him clear his mind, I'll gladly give in to him. His thick arms cradle me as he carries me into the bathroom. Lowering me slowly to the floor, he begins to undress me. I don't protest; as a matter of fact, I help him. My hands move to his belt, and we hungrily discard each other's clothing. He kisses me on the lips once more before turning on the massive shower head. The steam quickly fogs up the small bathroom and we step into the shower. We take our time washing each other's body. My hands move over his shoulders, and I gently rub out the tension I feel under his wet skin.

"I love you," I whisper and kiss his cheek. "Don't take on the weight of the world by yourself. Let me help you."

He moves a wet tendril of my hair away and kisses my neck, my cheek, and finally my lips. It's only a gentle, chaste kiss, but I feel an abundance of love. "I love you, too," he says as he presses his forehead to mine. "And I love your body." He grasps my full breasts in his hands and I shiver when his thumbs circle my nipples. "You're beautiful." His voice is raw.

He releases my breasts, grabs the nape of my neck, and his lips come down on mine. We're both panting, desperate for each other. I curl my arms around his neck, and he places his hands under my thighs, lifting me and wrapping my legs around him. My hands tug his hair as his tongue wrestles with mine.

Ravenous . . .

Desperate . . .

Needy . . .

He positions himself at my opening and I slide down his length. Walking backward, he sits on the built-in marble bench and I straddle him and then ride him, up and down, each time bringing him deeper inside of me. I can't control myself. All I know is that I want to please him.

His lips find my nipples as I arch my back and moan his name. He knows me, he knows my body. He knows exactly how to touch me and make me squirm. Riding him, I slam hard until I find my orgasm. He holds on to my hips and drives into me while my body convulses with pleasure.

Holding me firmly with his head pressed to my chest, he finds his own release.

"No, leave me alone. You can't hurt us."

I shift in bed and rub the sleep from my eyes. Slowly, I lift

BROKEN DREAMS

myself and glance over at Ethan. Through the moonlight I see the sweat forming on his forehead.

"No," he says again.

"Hey," I whisper and gently place my hands on his cheeks. "It's a dream."

"No, no, no," he cries out and his eyes flash open.

"It's okay," I say, holding on to him. He seems paralyzed. His eyes scan mine for a few seconds. "It's okay. You're okay. It was only a nightmare."

He sighs and pulls me to him. My head rests on his chest, and I can hear his erratic heartbeat. With a vice grip, he holds me close.

Ethan has been sleeping in my bedroom since I was ten years old, and never once has he had a nightmare.

When his breath has regulated, I look up at him. "Do you want to talk about it?"

"No." His voice is as cold as ice. I don't pry. Instead, I give him his space and hope for sleep to find us both.

The morning sun peers through the bedroom window and warms my skin. I open my eyes and reach for Ethan, but the bed is cold. Wrapping the sheet around my chest, I sit up. There's no sweet aroma of coffee. No savory scent of bacon. The house is completely and utterly quiet.

I get dressed and tiptoe through the house. All is quiet and there isn't a single thing out of place. As I approach the kitchen island, I notice a note with Ethan's handwriting.

Sorry, had to go in early.

I run my fingers across the black ink and feel a tug at my heart. There's so much I want to ask him. So much I know he is going through, and not knowing exactly what he needs from me is driving me mad. *Jerry's death was supposed to be our freedom.*

I tuck the note into my back pocket as I locate my shoes and purse. Everyone grieves differently, and all I can do is offer Ethan the space he needs.

Monsoon season in Arizona is usually between the months of June and September. Throughout most of the year the air is dry, and on the rare occasion during the winter months we will get a few snow showers. The mountains are snowcapped but in the lower elevations of the city, the air is cool with a few flurries.

The mid-March day of Jerry Alexander Prescott's burial isn't forecast for rain, but as we make our way to the cemetery, dark gray clouds take shape above us. It's as if Hell knows the devil is finally returning home.

My black dress hugs my hips as we walk toward the gravesite that was picked as Jerry's final resting place. My heels dig into the grass as I stand next to Ethan. A few others surround the casket: Stephanie, Charlie, Joyce—who was released from the ward for the funeral—and a few co-workers. The casket is bare. In lieu of flowers Ethan requested donations be made to a local charity that helps battered women.

We are all here not to mourn Jerry's death, but to support Ethan and his family through this tough time.

Pastor David says a few kind words, and there isn't a single tear shed as the casket is lowered into the ground. My hand entangles with Ethan's as I observe his every move. He is stoic through it all, never once changing his face. It's traditional for a loved one to throw a rose or toss a handful of dirt in with the casket, but the second the casket stops moving, Ethan turns on his heel and walks straight toward his car.

I hand Stephanie my car keys since I picked her up earlier. "I'll go with him and make sure he's okay." She nods and gives me a kind smile.

My heels poke into the wet grass as I follow behind Ethan. His shoulders are tense and his strides are quick and calculated.

"Ethan, wait!" I shout, afraid he will leave me behind.

He doesn't look back. Instead, he opens the passenger door for me before heading around the car to the driver's side. I climb in just as he slams his door. The force behind his rage makes me tremble with fear, but I don't say anything. There isn't a single word that can make him feel better.

We drive for an hour in complete silence. I watch the miles pass us, the landscape changing from patches of green to rocky mountains. It isn't until we are approaching red rock that I finally find the courage to say something.

"Talk to me. Don't push me away." I look away from the open road and over to him.

His hands grip the steering wheel, and he inhales slowly before exhaling. "I don't feel anything. I don't feel sad. I don't feel happy. I just feel completely numb."

His voice is hoarse and painful. With my hand on his knee, I offer him a kind touch. "Everyone grieves in their own way. Whatever you feel, that's what you're supposed to be feeling. Jerry wasn't a great person, but at the end of the day he was your father. Regardless how much you hate him, you still buried a parent."

He coils one of his hands with mine. "Thank you for standing by me." He brings my hand to his lips and kisses it gently.

"I wouldn't be anywhere else." I smile, hoping I can make him feel better.

Ethan takes a sharp right turn off a dirt road. We have been here many times during our senior year. It was where we would escape our lives and watch the sun set and the moon rise over the crimson rocks. For that year it was our spot.

He shifts the car into park and glances over at me. "I haven't been here since . . ." His words fail him.

I kiss the back of his hand. "Me, neither," I confess and stare deep into his eyes. The last time we were both here was the day before the graduation party. We sat in his car for hours staring up at the twinkling stars. I was pissed that my mother was throwing such an extravagant party, but Ethan reminded me that in three weeks we would get on a plane and never look back. "We can start over, you know. We can pretend what Jerry did after we left here never happened. We can move on now."

In one sweep, Ethan pulls me off my seat and onto his lap. His hands run through my hair as his mouth crashes over mine. His kisses are hungry, desperate, and violent. He moves his hands away from my hair and hikes my dress above my waist.

"Ethan," I say from between our pressed lips and reach for his hands. I scan his face and wonder what's going through his mind. *What does he feel?*

He presses his forehead to my chest and hugs my small frame. "I need this, Leslie. I need you. I need to forget everything that man ever fucking did to me. To us. And you're the only one who can make me forget. You're the only one who can shine light into my darkness."

His voice is broken, like the man he is inside. I can't deny him what he needs. *If being with me can give him one ounce of relief...*

I frame his cheeks with my hands and kiss him softly.

He kisses me back.

Tenderly...

Lovingly...

Desperately...

Without pulling our lips apart, I lift up on my knees as he unzips his pants. Moving my panties to the side, I sit down on him and let his erection fill me. We stay like that for minutes, simply holding on to each other. Two kids petrified of the same demons that haunt us. With him inside of me, our lips joined, we finally break free.

He is slow and gentle at first. I feel the tears drip from his eyes and warm my skin. I don't let go; I take his pain and offer him love. He becomes ravenous, desperate with each thrust. We are panting, hungry, and unable to fill our satisfaction of each other.

I am what he needs, and he is my whole life.

Chapter Twenty Three

PRESENT

Dear Leslie Sutton,
Capital Financial Inc. is pleased to announce it has merged with Credit Constant. This merger will take effect June 1. You must be an active employee when the merger is finalized to obtain the health benefits and 401k plan offered by the company. We understand you are on an approved FMLA leave, but Credit Constant will not be honoring this leave of absence.
If you have any questions, please feel free to call our office.
Your response is required by May 15.
Helen Marsh, HR

I stare at the screen for a good fifteen minutes before I move from my chair. My life and responsibilities in Chicago are calling me home. Unable to sit still, I pace my bedroom, contemplating the steps I should follow next. Surprisingly, life has been great in Prescott. Other than my father's heart attack, it's exactly what

I've wanted my entire life. My gaze lands on the Post-it I have stuck to my desk.
Dad will be released on Monday!
"Fuck." This is the worst time to get this letter from HR. My father will be home Monday morning and he will have to transition from living in a hospital with round-the-clock care to being here. I definitely don't want to leave until he's situated and my mother can hold down the fort on her own.

It has taken some time, but over the past few weeks, my relationship with my mother has blossomed. We've gone from constantly bickering to having a pleasant mother and daughter relationship. Yes, I'll be the first to admit it isn't perfect, but we're working on it.

I'll also have to find someone to help her out in the studio. There's paperwork to be filed and choreography to learn, and my mother doesn't even know any of the students. I massage the side of my head, and sit on the bed feeling exhausted. There's one more reason this letter came at the worst possible time, too.

Ethan.

God, I don't want to leave him—not again. We finally have a chance to make this last a lifetime.

I sigh once more, stand, walk back to my table and open the laptop. I read the letter once more and look up at the calendar. It's already April twenty seventh, which means I have less than three weeks to figure out exactly what I'll do.

I pull out my phone and dial Ethan. I need to know what he thinks. I need to know that he and I are can make it work. If he doesn't feel the same, it means I have three weeks to get my father situated and my mother up to speed.

Biting my nails, I hold the phone to my ear until his voicemail picks up. Quickly, I hang up and dial him again. Still no answer. I can't hide the pain in my chest. *The man I love seems to be drowning inside.*

Just as my mind is about to wander into uncharted territory, my phone buzzes in my hands.

Ethan: *Hey, I'm having a meeting with the guys. Is everything OK?*

I quickly type out a message for him.
Me: Sorry, I just wanted to hear your voice. You didn't stop by after work like you promised.
I hate that I sound like a desperate girlfriend.
Ethan: I'm sorry, babe. I have a ton of paperwork to go through. Can I call you when this meeting is over?
Me: Yes, I'll be up waiting for you.
Ethan: I love you.
Me: I love you more.
With my phone volume on high, I crawl under the covers and wait for his phone call.

The sun is warm on my skin the following morning. I stretch my arms above my head as my body thanks me for another full night's rest, but my eyes shoot open as I realize I missed Ethan's call. Locating my phone underneath my pillow, I press the home button to light up the screen. Ethan hadn't called like he promised.

He completely forgot about me.

I turn over and tuck my hands under the pillow and let the disappointment resonate deep in my bones. I'm in the midst of throwing myself a pity party when my phone rings. Hoping and praying it's Ethan calling, I rush to grab it.

It's not Ethan; it's Stephanie.

I debate whether to answer when my phone stops vibrating in my hands and the voicemail picks up. I decide sitting in bed all day will get me nowhere and I call Stephanie back.

"Morning, sugar," she answers happily. "How's life? How's Ethan?"

"You're chipper this morning," I grunt into the phone with a yawn.

"I just went for a seven-mile run. It's absolutely gorgeous outside. Do you have plans this morning? I wanted to treat myself to a Danish at Bavello's. Want to grab breakfast?"

"No plans. I'm actually off today, so a sugary breakfast

sounds perfect."

"Meet you in thirty?"

My body wants to protest leaving the bed anytime soon, but when I realize it's already nine in the morning I force myself up. "Yeah, that works."

After I hang up the phone, I drag myself into the shower. I don't know why I feel so exhausted; I slept for over eight hours, but still I can't shake the sleep off. My body is aching for a few more minutes in bed. Still, I push through the exhaustion and slide my head under the shower spray. I'm halfway done when my stomach drops and a chill runs up my spine. Shutting the water off, I grab a towel and rush to my room. I kneel on the floor and dump the contents of my purse all around me. When I find the small black packet, I flip it open and pull out the small pills.

"Fuck," I curse and sit back on my feet. My period is four days late. Water drips from my hair to my skin and onto the carpet. "This can't be right." I flip open my agenda, my hands trembling as I count the days. Once. Twice. Three times. "Fuck. Fuck. Fuckity fuck, fuck, fuck."

This is not what I want. Well, at least not this second in my life. Kids seem like a possibility. Eventually. When I'm in my thirties and I have my life figured out. Shoving everything back inside my purse, I decide not to panic until I know for sure. My period has been late before, and I've been under a lot of pressure lately. Aside from being tired, I have no other symptoms, so I choose to ignore this little bump until I'm one hundred percent certain.

When I arrive at Bavello's, Stephanie is waiting outside for me. As always, she looks stunning, her make-up and hair flawless. I yawn as I greet her. "I really hate that your hair is perfect all the time."

"Morning to you too, buttercup." She nudges me with her shoulder. "You look tired. Didn't sleep well?"

I pause as we walk inside and quickly fabricate something to tell Stephanie. "No. I tossed and turned all night," I lie. "I was waiting for Ethan to . . ." My words fail me as I stumble forward from the impact of someone behind me. Looking back, I sigh in annoyance.

"Excuse you," Stephanie says to the back of a platinum blonde's head. She doesn't have to turn around for me to know it's Erica who rudely bumped me.

"Oh, my goodness," she simpers. "I'm so sorry!" She gives me a sly grin.

"Cut the crap, Erica, we know you did that on purpose," Stephanie quips and crosses her arms over her chest.

Erica's mouth opens dramatically as she yawns. "No, seriously. I'm really sorry. I'm so tired this morning." Her gaze cuts directly at me. "Ethan had me up all night."

Instantly, my teeth grind.

"You know how he can be in the sack." She winks at me but then pouts. "Or do you? I mean, he wouldn't be knocking on my door if you did."

My hands ball into tight, white-knuckled fists. I step toward her to strike, but Stephanie moves between us. "Erica, I suggest you leave before I let Leslie whoop your ass first thing in the morning."

Erica takes a step back and laughs. "Bye, Stephy." She blows her a fake kiss and then looks over at me. "Bye, Dance Queen."

"Fuck off!" I shout, and the entire crowd at Bavello's looks over at me. Instantly, I'm embarrassed and I lower my gaze.

"Find us a table and I'll grab our coffee," Stephanie says to me in a softer tone.

A few minutes later, she pulls back the wooden chair across from me and places my cup and a tray of sweet Danishes on the table. Lost in thought, my mind wanders to what Erica said. Had she spent the night with Ethan? Were they seeing each other? And was that why he was pulling away? I lower my head on the cool table, feeling lightheaded.

"Hey, you okay?" Stephanie waves her hand at me and I shake my head, throwing those thoughts out the window.

"Sorry, lost in thought."

"You weren't thinking about what Erica said, were you?"

"Oh, God no." I lie again, choosing to be the bigger person. "She simply wants attention and to get a rise out of me." And I believe the words I say. I know Ethan. I've known him my whole life, and even when he was a teenager the last thing I had to worry about was him being with another girl. He has always loved me. I find myself thinking this and I force myself to believe it, but there is a tiny voice in the back of my mind that reminds me the Ethan I knew and loved, the one I never had to worry about, is not the Ethan who's been present.

"Okay, good. Because I'd have to kick your ass if you believed her for a second." I laugh and take a sweet treat from the basket. "I can't believe you told her to fuck off in front of everyone."

I close my eyes, mortified. "Uh, was it that bad?"

"Let's just say the whole town will be talking about it by lunch."

"Great. Something else I'll have to explain to Ethan."

"What do you mean *something else?*" Stephanie asks.

I chew on the inside of my lip and decide it's better to use Stephanie as a sounding board before telling Ethan. "So, I got an email from my job. They need me back by June first."

"Oh, crap."

"And my period is four days late." Stephanie's eyes widen as she takes a bite of her food. "Yeah, now I have to add this little quarrel with Erica to the list."

"Did you take a test?" Stephanie's voice is an octave louder than before.

"*Shh.*" I kick her under the table and glance around to see if anyone is listening to our conversation. "No, I realized all of this half an hour ago."

"You need to pee on a stick."

"Because me buying a pregnancy test won't get back to Ethan. You know how this town lives for gossip. Besides, it's probably nothing. I'm just stressed with Jerry's death and whatnot. I'm probably just late."

"You know . . ." Stephanie pauses and puckers her lip.

"What?"

"I am married." She lifts her left hand and her emerald cut diamond sparkles up at me. "I can buy the pregnancy test. It's not like Bruce would care what the town says."

"You're a genius." I sigh and I feel a grin grow on my face.

"Carlton's opens at ten. We can finish here and head right over." I nod. "Some people smuggle drugs. We'll be smuggling pregnancy tests."

I chuckle and take another sip of my coffee. There wasn't anything I could say. The possibility of me being pregnant weighed heavily on my chest. It was only a matter of time before I could put this all behind me.

With my heart pounding with each step, Stephanie and I walk over to Carlton's, the town pharmacy. We are halfway there when I spot Ethan getting out of his car. I stop and watch his every move. He walks around the car to pop open the trunk and pulls out a folder.

"Are you just going to stand there?" Stephanie asks.

I shrug. "I don't know if he wants to see me."

Ethan closes the trunk and his gaze lands directly on mine. "I guess you can't hide now." Stephanie nudges me. "Go talk to him while I run inside Carlton's to grab the goods."

I nod and will my feet to walk across the street. Ethan leans on his car and crosses his arms over his chest. His blue jeans hug his waist, and his white T-shirt is tight around his chest.

Nervously, I grip my purse strap. "Hey," I say when I approach him.

When I don't move, he loops his finger in the belt strap of my jeans and pulls me toward him. "Morning, Freckles," he whispers before kissing my lips. "I went by the studio this morning."

"We're closed today, third Saturday of every month." I pull my eyes away from his green orbs.

"What's the matter?" He lifts my chin so I'm forced to look at him.

"You never called last night." I purse my lips.

"I know," he sighs. "I didn't get out of the meeting 'til late and I didn't want to wake you."

I gnaw on the inside of my lip. A part of me wants to say that he never had a problem climbing through my window at two in the morning, but not wanting to sound like an annoying girlfriend, I choose my words carefully. "I ran into Erica at Bavello's." I pause and stare at his face. There isn't a single flinch. "She said she spent the night with you." I swallow and watch his every movement.

Ethan digs his hand in his back pocket and pulls out his phone. He clicks a few buttons and his speaker turns on as his phone begins to ring. He pulls me flush against him, and wraps his free arm around my body.

"Hello?" Erica's voice erupts from the speaker.

"Where were you last night?" His voice is angry.

"Home, why?" Erica's mousy voice has softened.

"Was I with you?" he barks.

"No."

"Then do me a fucking favor," he growls, and a shiver crawls up my spine. "Stop spreading fucking rumors. I hear about you lying one more time, Erica, and I swear to God . . ."

I smack his chest, not wanting to know what he's about to say.

"I'm sorry." Her voice is barely audible before the line goes dead.

"You didn't need to threaten her." I pull away from him.

"I'm tired of her running her mouth."

"Hey, lovebirds." Stephanie's voice interrupts us.

"All set?" I ask, and she nods. I turn to Ethan. "Okay, I'll see you later." Before I can take a step, he yanks me into his arms and his mouth crashes over mine. His hands tangle in my hair as his tongue invades my mouth. When he pulls away, I'm breathless.

"Don't let what Erica said change anything, Freckles. I have—and will always—only love you," he says against my lips. "I'll come by later, okay?"

"Okay." I kiss his lips one last time.

"Bye, E." Stephanie says when he lets me go, and Ethan waves.

We are halfway down the block when Stephanie laces her arm with mine. "Do I want to know what that was about?"

"Me finding out if he was with Erica last night."

"Was he?" Stephanie looks up at me.

"Ethan's eyebrows furrow when he lies." I smile up at her. "He wasn't with her last night."

"Oh, good. That's one thing crossed off your list." Stephanie lifts up the white pharmacy bag. "Now let's see if him not being a Daddy is another."

CALLIE ANDERSON

Chapter Twenty Four

PRESENT

Three minutes feels like an eternity. My hands rest on the bathroom sink as I wait for the buzzer to go off on my phone. With shaky hands and my heart in my throat, I turn over the plastic stick.

"Well?" Stephanie asks from the other side of the bathroom door.

I read the word flashing on the screen. My brain can't comprehend it.

Pregnant.

I read it over and over again.

"Leslie, you're killing me here." Stephanie's voice is impatient as she bangs on the door.

Pregnant. I read it again and this time it all clicks. I'm fucking pregnant.

"Fuck," I say.

"Oh, shit," I hear her whisper.

I glance in the mirror and look down at my belly. How the hell will I explain this one? Gently, my hands rub along my flat tummy. This can't be happening.

I open the door.

Stephanie's wide blue eyes are staring at mine. "Baby?" she asks and bites her lower lip.

I nod and lift the stick for her to see. "Yep." I lean on the doorframe. "What do I do now?" I ask and my eyes well up with tears.

"It's okay. It will be okay." She rests her hands on my shoulders and gives me a reassuring smile. "Sometimes these things are wrong."

"I've heard of false negatives, not false positives."

Stephanie nods and purses her lips. "If you want to know for sure, you'll need to do blood work. You can go to my mom; she's still practicing obstetrics."

"I'm not going to see your Mom!" I complain.

"Think about it. I can call her right now and she'll meet us at the office. They're closed today so no one will be there. We can go through the back entrance and no one in town will find out about it." Her voice trails behind me as I sit on my bed." She can do blood work and you'll know for certain what you're dealing with."

"Fuck it." I throw my hands up in defeat. "Let's yank the Band-Aid."

Within an hour, Stephanie and I are across town walking into her mother's OBGYN medical office. The light green walls and dark green carpet smell of antiseptic and latex gloves. My heart races with each step we take further into the office.

"Mom?" Stephanie calls out when we reach the hallway that has exam rooms on either side.

"In here," she shouts.

Stephanie and I make our way into Dr. Carey's office. "Leslie." She stands and smiles up at me. "It's so nice to see you." She walks around her mahogany table to give me a hug.

"I wish it were under better circumstances," I say when she lets go.

"It's fine." She guides us to sit. "So, Stephanie said you tested positive on an over-the-counter test and you'd like to get blood work done?"

I swallow the golf ball lodged in my throat and nod. "Yes."

"When was your last menstrual cycle?" she asks as she pulls out a circular graph.

My lips pucker as I find the courage to speak. "Um . . . March twenty-fourth, I believe. It was definitely after St. Patrick's Day."

"And have you been sexually active?"

I nod. "I'm on LoEstrin, but I've been busy and I skipped a day or two."

Mrs. Carey sets the graph down and folds her hands. "Unfortunately, LoEstrin is only ninety-one percent effective when taken regularly. The estrogen and progestin, the two hormones that prevent pregnancy, are very low, which means your ovaries can still ovulate."

"Great," I say sarcastically.

"According to my calculation, you're about five weeks. We can do a blood test if you like. The blood does take a few days, but since your urine test was positive we can do an ultrasound to see if I can see anything. It's very early and we probably will not get a heartbeat, but I'll be able to tell exactly how far along you are."

I glance over at Stephanie who is sitting next to me, and then back to Mrs. Carey. "Okay."

"I'll wait for you in here." Stephanie says and gives me a reassuring smile.

Mrs. Carey leads me to the lab room in the back. My feet twitch as I sit on the blue leather chair. Mrs. Carey ties a rubber band around my bicep and instructs me to make a fist. The pinch of the needle is painless and I watch with amazement as the blood seeps out of my body and into the vial.

When she discards the needle and fastens a Band-Aid over the blood dotting my skin, she smiles up at me. "Come on." She places her hand on my shoulder and leads me toward an exam room. "Let's see how far along you are."

She leads me into an exam room, provides me with a gown, and instructs me to undress. Moments later she returns and I'm sitting on the exam table with both of my feet up in the stirrups. She dims the light and explains that she will be doing a transvaginal ultrasound. I lay my head back and close my eyes during entire thing. I don't want to look at the screen. I don't want to see that there is a little tiny baby inside of me.

"There." Mrs. Carey says and I force myself to look up. Her hand is tapping the black screen and I squint to make out what she's pointing at. "This black circle is the gestational sac and this little tiny spot right there." She points to the screen. "That is the embryo."

My eyes well with tears. Tears of happiness, fear, and most of all, love. The little tiny spec on the screen was made by me and Ethan. "Wow." I say and brush my hands under my eyes.

"By the size, it looks like you are just shy of six weeks. Still very, very early. And still hard to detect" Mrs. Carey says and turns on the lights and turns off the ultra sound. "Leslie, the state of Arizona requires a woman must receive state-directed counseling that includes information designed to discourage her from having an abortion, and then you must wait twenty-four hours before the procedure."

"No." I shake my head. "I would never be able to have an abortion. Not when it's something that was made out of love."

"Okay. I just want you to know all your rights before you make any decision."

"Thank you." I sit up and place my hand on my flat belly.

"Now, it's still very early, but I'd like to see you again in two weeks for a full screening. Then we can start your prenatal visits." She hands me a list of foods I should avoid along with a script for prenatal vitamins." I want you to start taking these right away.

I nod, unable to speak as my heart is filled with emotion. "Thank you again, Mrs. Carey. I really appreciate it."

Once she leaves the room, I sit back on the exam chair and hold my stomach. Excitement fills me and I laugh. Instantly, I'm filled with love. I have no idea what this means for me and

BROKEN DREAMS

Ethan, but I know I want this child more than anything.

CALLIE ANDERSON

Chapter Twenty Five

PRESENT

Later that night, I pace my room anxiously not knowing what to do. After I left Mrs. Carey's office, Stephanie sat by side as I had a panic attack in the car. She suggested the best way to figure out what to do next was to make a list. Pros and Cons.

When I first packed my bags to come here I never imagined that staying permanently would be an option or that being a mom was in the cards for me. Now, everything is changed in the blink of an eye. My father is due home Monday, and the studio is up and running smoothly, and for the first time I want to stay in Prescott. I want to see where things with Ethan go. Kids, marriage, and a happily ever after finally seem like an option.

With a shaky hand, I glance down at my list one more time.
Pros: Staying/Baby
Ethan.
Cons: Staying/Baby
Does Ethan want kids?
Does he want me to stay?

Ethan said he would stop by, and I find myself running to the window every time I hear a car drive by.

"Where are you?" I say to my empty room, and I pull out my cell phone. The screen is blank, my finger shakes as I debate calling him, and then I toss my phone on the bed.

"No." I coil my hands under my chin. "I will not push him into coming over."

The last thing I want to do is force him here and then drop the bomb that he is about to be a dad.

I take in a cool calming breath and decide when the time is right, I will tell him.

One week later...

Stephanie says I'm being a coward and prolonging the inevitable, but I'm not avoiding Ethan. I've been so preoccupied with other things that I haven't had the chance to tell him. Besides, it isn't something I want to do over the phone.

My father is finally home and we're adjusting. Andrew, my father's aide, comes to the house for three hours every day to help him with his physical therapy and any other things my father can't do on his own. While Andrew is at the house, my mother and I have been at the studio interviewing potential coaches who can help while I am gone. Though I still haven't completely made up my mind, I figure it's best to be prepared. Not to mention, if I stay in town I won't be able to teach once my belly becomes too big. I find myself smiling every time I think about waddling, and Ethan behind me kissing my neck as he rubs our little bundle of joy.

By Friday afternoon my mother and I have agreed that Lindsey is the best fit for the studio. She has dance experience and picked up the routines quickly. When she handed me back the job application, my stomach dropped as I glanced at the date.

May 5th.

I have ten days to reply to HR.

"Is everything okay?" she asks as I stare down at the date.

"Oh." I snap my head up and smile. "Yes, it's perfect."

"Thanks again for this opportunity, Leslie. I won't let you down." She throws her duffle bag over her shoulder.

I smile and nod, unable to say a word. I needed to make a decision and I needed to do it quickly.

When I arrive home later that night, I decide there is no more hiding and making excuses. I'll tell Ethan about the job offer and the baby. I huff one last time, finding the courage before I pull out my cell phone from my back pocket and shoot him a text message.

Me: Hey, I was wondering if we can get a drink later? I want to talk to you about something.

My decision will be based on Ethan. If he wants me to stay, I will, and together we will raise this child. If he doesn't want this baby, then I will go back to Chicago where I have a great job with great benefits, and I will raise this child on my own.

My phone chirps twenty minutes later.

Ethan: I'll be at the pub later, come by.

I sigh. I wanted to chat somewhere more private, and definitely not a place where Erica was watching us. But being that Ethan hadn't been himself lately, I didn't want to push my luck.

Me: Sure. Be there around 7.

By six thirty I'm dressed and walking out the door. As I slide inside my car I keep reassuring myself that maybe, just maybe, the news of a baby will pull Ethan out of his funk. Before turning the car on I close my eyes and silently pray this conversation goes well.

The Pub is filled on a Friday night. The scent of fried food wafts through the air, and for the first time, the smell of anything fried bothers me. Holding my breath, I scan the crowd. It takes me a few seconds to spot Ethan, but he is sitting at the bar with his back facing the front door. To my luck, Erica is nowhere in sight. Inhaling (and quickly regretting it), I force my feet to move forward.

"Hey," I say, pulling the barstool back. Ethan cocks his head to the side and nods at me. There's no hello, how are you, I miss you, you look nice. Instead, I ignore the feeling in my gut and sit next to him. My gaze lands on the half-empty bottle in front of him. By the looks of it he's been at the bar way longer than I expected him to be. Nervously, I crack my knuckles. Maybe this isn't the best place or time to tell him.

Ethan raises a glass at me, silently, and I know he's asking if I want a drink. "Bourbon is a little strong for me," I answer.

"Chavez." Ethan waves over the bartender. "Get her whatever she wants," Ethan slurs.

Chavez stares at me politely. "I'll have a club soda with a lime please." I glance back at Ethan. His lids are lazy and I can tell he has surpassed his limit. "How long have you been here?" I try to sound optimistic but I know my voice is failing me.

"A few minutes or so," Ethan answers, but we both know he is lying through his teeth.

I wait until Chavez sets my drink in front of me and walks away. Leaning into Ethan, I whisper, "Maybe we can talk somewhere else. Get some fresh air?"

Ethan glances over at me, a devilish grin growing on his face, and for a split second I see Jerry in his eyes. Ignoring my request completely, he holds the glass to his lips and drinks the entire shot. He wipes the back of his mouth with his hand and shifts on his seat to look directly at me. "You said you want to talk, what's up?"

"Doesn't seem like the right time." I shrug, not wanting to say anything that will piss him off even more. I've never seen him in this state before. Talking about having a child and me leaving can set off a chain of events we will both regret.

"Les." He leans forward, and I can smell the liquor permeating from his pores. "You wanted to talk, let's talk. What's going on?" His voice is gentle.

I stare deep into his green eyes. I want to see if my Ethan is still in there, or if the monster who has taken over his soul for the past few weeks is the one present. Gnawing on my lower lip, I contemplate whether I should say anything. Deciding on the lesser of two evils, I slowly say, "My company is merging with another company. When I decided to stay here I took a leave of absence for six months, but because the companies are now merging, I have to make a decision to either resign or go back to work." I pause and wait for a reaction. Ethan doesn't speak but his stare is locked on mine.

"A part of me wants to stay here. I want to see where things with you are going, but I want to make sure you're on the same page."

Ever so slowly, he nods as though he is registering what I'm saying. Each second drags on. He opens his mouth to speak but closes it quickly. I wait on bated breath for an answer. For a simple, yes, of course, stay, but instead, he digs into his pocket and pulls out his cell phone.

Ignoring me completely, he slides his finger across the screen and brings it to his ear. "Hello?" he says, and I'm shocked that his words are clear and no longer slurred with the liquor that courses through his body. "Yeah, give me a second. I can't really hear you." Ethan holds up a finger at me before walking away.

I feel stunned, as if I've been punched in the gut. I asked him here to talk, asked him to give me a reason to stay, and instead he completely dismissed me. Annoyed, I turn back toward the bar and wrap my hand around the cold glass, taking a huge gulp of my drink. *I hate this no alcohol thing.*

Every fiber in my body is telling me this isn't a good idea. I'm debating leaving when I feel a light tap on my shoulder. Startled, I jump up and turn to face the person whose subtle touch scared me. Michael is staring directly at me with a kind smile on his face.

Remembering the last time I saw him, my eyebrows furrow and I pull away. "What do you want?"

He doesn't say anything, just slips onto Ethan's empty stool. "I wanted to apologize," he says running his hands over his fine black hair. "The last time you were here, I said some things to you and that was wrong and childish of me." I watch him carefully, my eyes studying the features on his face. The way his eyes are open wide and rounded I can see a bit of sincerity behind it.

Not wanting to argue with anyone tonight, I sigh and take another sip of my drink. "It's okay, Michael." I shake my head. "It's in the past now."

"Good." A wide grin grows across his face. "So, how does it

feel to be back?"

"It's different, I guess. A lot has happened in the few months that I've been here."

"Yeah, I guess nobody saw Jerry finally kicking it. I could've sworn that man would outlast us all."

"I can't say I'm not happy he's gone." I shrug and Michael chuckles.

"Fuck, yeah! And I know Ethan is over the moon his pops is finally dead. Now he can finally let go of the big ball and chain."

"I don't think he's taking it too well," I admit. I don't know why I say this to Michael. He's probably the last person I should be talking to about Ethan, but not being able to understand what he is going through is making me crazy.

Michael must see the hesitation in my eyes; he gently places a hand on my shoulders. "Ethan is a strong man. The strongest person I know. He'll get through this—"

Ethan's fist collides with his face. I stand from my seat and open my mouth to scream, but it all happens so fast. Ethan is standing beside me, waiting for Michael's retaliating rage when I get stuck in the crossfire and my pelvis crashes into the corner of a wooden table. I wince with pain.

The baby?

Oh, God . . . Please, not the baby.

I force myself to ignore the thought and look back at the two men. Ethan's eyebrow is split, but Michael has blood spurting out of his mouth. Ethan's closed fist meets with his cheekbone, and Michael's head pops back. His defeated body is on the dirty pub floor and Ethan's on top of him.

"Stop!" I manage to scream.

One. Two. Three punches. "You fucking piece of shit!" Ethan shouts.

"Ethan!" I shout, but there is no use.

"I told you to stay away from her!" I am paralyzed, my eyes glued to a monster beating on a poor, helpless man. The scene is all too familiar. Bile rises in my stomach, and I cover my mouth, refusing to let it out.

My vision blurs, and my eyes play tricks on me. First, I see Jerry, then I blink and I see Ethan again. This can't be real.

Ethan is not his father, I remind myself.

Seconds pass as Ethan continues taking his wrath out on Michael before he is finally pulled away. Chavez is on the floor holding Michael up. His face is bloody and almost unrecognizable. My hands rush to my mouth to cover a scream that wants to pour from my lungs.

I'm too scared to look at Ethan but I force myself to anyway. "Get off of me!" he demands of the two men holding him.

In that moment I look at him with every ounce of disgust I have. This isn't the man I love. This isn't the man I want to be the father of my baby.

"What the hell is your fucking problem?" I manage to ask as tears swell in my eyes. "Michael is your friend. Your fucking employee! You just beat him to a pulp for no reason!"

The restaurant is silent as every pair of eyes scrutinizes us.

"No reason?" Ethan steps closer, his mouth mere inches from mine. "I fucking told him not to go anywhere near you, and I walk back in the fucking bar and he has his fucking hands on you!" He growls.

I refuse to let him intimidate me. "He was apologizing." I shake my head, not believing the man before me. The devil is embedded in his soul. "You are no different from your father." The words slip out of my mouth.

Ethan's eyes narrow on mine, and for the first time in my life I'm afraid of him. "This is who I am, Leslie. This is who I've always been." He throws his hands in the air. "I am the devil's spawn. That shouldn't surprise you. "

"I can't believe I ever thought about staying in this fucking town."

"Nobody's asking you to stay." He reaches toward the bar and takes a swig of the bottle.

I hold my head up high and grab my purse. Ignoring the cramping in my abdomen and everyone's eyes on me, I force a smile to my face. "You know what you are, Ethan?" I ask but I don't wait for him to respond. "You're not your father. You're a fucking coward. Instead of facing your issues head-on, you're fucking hiding behind the bottle."

I don't wait for him to answer. I simply walk to the door and never look back.

Once I'm a mile away from the bar, I pull my car to the side of the road. Shifting into park, I rest my head against the steering wheel and cry. I'm angry and hurt, but most of all I'm disappointed. The cramping in my abdomen hasn't passed, and I feel a warm wetness between my legs. Placing my hands inside my pants, I feel the wetness and pull out my fingers. My other hand flicks the car light on and I gasp at the crimson blood that's stained my fingers. Unable to breathe, I wipe my fingers on a napkin and let out a screech from the depths of my soul.

My body trembles, and tears pour down my cheeks and drip down to my chest. I sit there for a few minutes before I reach inside my purse and pull out the business card Mrs. Carey gave me to call her in an emergency.

"Dr. Carey speaking."

"Hi, Mrs. Carey, it's Leslie," I whimper.

"Yes, Leslie, is everything okay?"

"I . . . I was pushed into a table and I hit my abdomen." My voice cracks and I force myself to continue. "I'm bleeding now. I think I'm losing the baby."

"Oh, sweetie . . . It could be the egg implanting. Spotting is normal."

I sniffle back and wipe my nose. "I don't know," I say, feeling like the world is being ripped out from under me.

"Monitor it," she says and I nod. "Come to my office first thing tomorrow morning and I'll check you out. But don't worry, spotting is normal."

"Thank you," I say and hang up the phone. My heart is beating at a rapid speed and never in my life have I been so scared. Covering my mouth, I cry out in pain as I beg God to not take my baby.

Chapter Twenty Six

PRESENT

At some point through the crying and the pain I make it home. I don't say anything as I walk up the stairs and head straight toward the shower. The warm water trickles down my body as my hands curl around my stomach. The spotting is still there but it is less than before. I find myself checking every few minutes. My breath is caught in my chest as I wait for more blood.

When I'm done in the shower I slip on my pajamas and crawl into bed. Images of Ethan beating Michael haunt me as I toss and turn between checking my pad periodically. Never have I seen Ethan like that, so violent, so angry. Even when he spoke to Erica that day, his voice was laced with anger. It's as if Jerry has taken over his spirit. That thought alone causes me to shiver. I turn over on the bed and look out my bedroom window. My eyes are glued to the latch that is now locked so no one can get in.

Checking one last time to see if there is any more bleeding, I force my eyes shut and will sleep to come. The tightness I feel around my abdomen wakes me from my sleep. I wince in bed and my eyes snap open as I realize what's happening.

"*Ow!*" I say and curl up in a ball. Tears fill my eyes as the cool wetness from my pajama bottoms rests on my leg. Petrified, I shove the covers off and turn on the light.

Blood.

Bright crimson blood pools between my legs. My hands cover my mouth as a scream threatens to crawl up my throat.

This isn't spotting.

This is more than a regular period.

Warm tears drip down my cheeks. My heart shatters into a million pieces as it all settles in. I'm losing the baby.

I pull into Mrs. Carey's office at a quarter to nine. In the past hour or so I've grown numb and my body moves on autopilot. She greets me at the door with a kind smile, but it falters when see's my tear-stained cheeks and red, puffy eyes.

My feet drag across the carpeted floor, and I force myself to swallow back the boulder that is lodged in my throat. There is nothing a blood test can tell me that I don't already know. Once again, I sit on the exam room chair and extend my forearm.

"I'm so sorry this is happening to you." Mrs. Carey holds my hand and a new wave of tears wash over me. "We will know more once we get your results." She nods, and gives me the same reassuring grin that Stephanie has.

"I won't need my results," I say and bite back a sob. "The amount of blood that came out makes it impossible to be okay."

Mrs. Carey hands me a tissue and places her hand on my shoulder. "We don't know for certain."

Once she is finished withdrawing another vial, I hold the cotton ball as she opens the Band-Aid.

"Will I need a D&C?" I ask but I don't look up at her, I can't. The second my eyes meets hers I will lose it all. I will break down and I don't want to do that until I'm home.

"No." she says and as she sticks the Band-Aid on. "A D&C is usually performed on miscarriages after ten weeks."

BROKEN DREAMS

I nod as my vision blurs. "Do you think this happened because I was shoved into a table?"

Mrs. Carey takes both of my hands in hers and crouches down until we are face to face.

"Unfortunately, we will never be able to tell if the blunt force impact caused the miscarriage." Her voice is kind, sympathetic, and somewhat comforting all in one. "Sometimes it's your body telling you this wasn't the perfect egg."

My lips quiver as I try my hardest not to cry uncontrollably. "Your pregnancy is, was, still very early on, and most of the time your uterus rejects the egg implantation."

I nod and suck in a breath as a sob escapes me. "Okay," I say only slightly above a whisper. My body is trembling.

Mrs. Carey hugs me. "There is nothing you could have done to change this outcome." Her hands rub up my back.

"I didn't know how much I could love it already," I cry.

"I know, sweetie." She brushes my hair back and I sob.

Minutes pass before my crying has subsided. Wiping the tears away, I clear my throat. "So, what now?" I say as I take in big gulps of air to fill my lungs.

"The bleeding will be heavier than a normal period," she says, and I hold my breath. "Your body will push it all out on its own. You'll have a bit more cramping than usual, but don't be alarmed. If you have a fever, begin to vomit or develop the chills, call me immediately."

I nod, unable to say anything else. I stand from the chair and throw my purse over my shoulder. Mrs. Carey places her hand on the upper part of my back and follows me out of the office.

By the time I reach my car, the decision has been made for me.

When I get home, I'll be emailing HR and telling them I'm returning.

To my surprise, when I arrive home Stephanie's car is in the driveway. I give myself another look in the mirror and decide keeping my sunglasses on is best to hide the puffiness. Inside, I find Stephanie sitting with my parents in the living room.

"There she is," my father says with a wide grin when I step inside.

"I had an appointment this morning." My voice is still hoarse.

"Stephanie here was just telling your father that Bruce will be home next week," My Mom says and adds more tea to Stephanie's cup. "Would you like some tea?" My mother says, holding up the kettle in my direction.

I shake my head and Stephanie stands. "Excuse me for just a quick second. I need to have a little chat with Leslie."

"Certainly," my father agrees.

"We'll go outside." I lead her to the deck.

"Are you okay?" Stephanie says the second the sliding door closes.

The tug at my heart reminds me of my empty uterus and my eyes fill with tears again. "I lost the baby " I cover my face with my hands and sob.

"Oh, Les," Stephanie says before she embraces me. "Did you call my mom?" She asks after a few minutes have passed.

"I just left her office." I pull away from her. Removing my sunglasses, I wipe the tears from my face and walk over to the three steps that lead down into the yard. Stephanie sits next to me and we both look up into the warm, clear sky. "Did you hear about last night?"

"Yeah." She sighs. "I wanted to come by last night but you didn't answer any of my calls. I rushed over first this this morning."

"Sorry." I sniffle back. "I silenced my phone. Who told you about last night? I look over at Stephanie. Tears still drip down my cheeks.

She sighs and rests her elbows on her knees. "I saw the fight on social media."

"What?"

She pouts her lips and nods. "Some idiot at the pub decided to record it and post it on Facebook."

I groan and bury my face between my knees. "It only showed Ethan and Michael fighting. Well, more like Michael on the floor as Ethan beat him. I figured you'd want somebody to talk to." She reaches out and places her hand on my shoulder.

Turning my face, I glance over at her. "I never saw him like that before. It's like Jerry took over his body."

"Why were you guys there to begin with?"

"I asked him to talk. I was going to tell him about the baby and that I wanted to stay." I shake my head remembering all that had happened.

"And what did he say?"

"He told me to go."

"No!" Stephanie shakes head. "You can't go. Look how much you've accomplished here." She points back to the house. "Your parents are so happy to have you home again."

I lift my head and sniffle back before running my fingers under my eyes to wipe away the tears. "I'm going to call the HR department and let them know I'm coming back".

"Are you not going to tell Ethan you were pregnant?"

Slowly, I shake my head. "It wasn't meant to be, you know."

"Don't say that. Ethan loves you. Maybe a child wasn't in the cards for right now. You guys had a fight; maybe he needs time to cool off." Stephanie forces a smile and I know she is trying to be optimistic.

"It's much more than that." I shake my head, knowing it wasn't just a fight. "Ever since his father passed, Ethan has pulled away from me. It's as if a part of him blames me for this. And I guess I deserve that since a part of me blames him for what happened to me. It doesn't matter how many times we try to fix it. We say we forgive each other for what happened in that garage many years ago, but it broke a part of us and neither of us knows how to mend it."

"He's grieving. It's normal to get mad. You're grieving, too. It takes time."

"I know, and I've given him his space and I've tried to be supportive. But he told me to go so I'm not sitting around waiting for him. I've done that to myself one too many times. He pushed me away once and this time I'm not coming back."

"So, you'll just leave?" I can hear the pain in Stephanie's voice. I look over at her and remind myself that though it didn't work out with Ethan, I gained a new friend here that I will forever cherish.

"Yeah, there's nothing here for me anymore."

"You should really sleep on this. Take some time and think about it. Don't make any rash decisions just because you're mad."

"That's it; I'm not mad. I'm disappointed. I expected more from him. And to hurt Michael the way he did . . ." I shake my head, not wanting to believe what I saw. "It was out of character. He hasn't been himself lately, and I can't stick around and wait for him to change. I waited for him last time, for three months, and he watched from afar as I rotted away in that hospital. It's time I put myself first."

"This is good-bye then?" Stephanie leans her head on my shoulder.

"No, not yet." I place my head on hers. "But soon."

Chapter Twenty Seven

PRESENT

The following Saturday, I find myself sitting on the floor of my bedroom. My door is locked and I let the tears pour from my eyes as I look out my window one final time. Though I keep telling myself I will not cry, I allow myself this time to shed my final tears for Ethan. The sun rays coming through the window are warm on my skin, and I feel a lone tear drip down my face as the memory drifts into my brain.

My back rested on the light green leather chairs at terminal A as I waited for the boarding to start. I was about to start a brand new chapter in my life, and I should've been excited. Instead, I dreaded it.

Leaving Prescott and that god-awful hospital was exactly what I needed, but losing Ethan was never something I wanted. Did he even know I was gone? Would he even miss me?

My eyes filled with tears at the thought of never seeing him again. How I would never have him climbing into my bedroom late at night. Needing to say one last final good-bye, I pulled out my phone.

Me: I'm leaving. I'm sorry for the mess I caused you and your family. Take care of yourself. Leslie.

Within seconds of hitting send on the message, my phone vibrated in my hand. Nervously I answered it. "Hello?"

"What do you mean, you're leaving?"

My lower lip quivered at the sound of Ethan's voice, a sound I had craved for months.

"You don't have to worry about me anymore. You can go on with your life and do whatever it is that you're doing."

"Les don't do this."

I laugh, but it doesn't stop the tears from falling. "Seriously. I was locked up in a hospital for three months and you ignored every single one of my calls, and now you're telling me not to do this. You don't have the right anymore."

"I'm trying to make things right."

"I'm going to Los Angeles. I'll be studying at UCLA." I paused for a quick second, not believing what I was saying but my heart refused to stop me. "Come with me. It can be our New York trip but on the other side of the country."

"Leslie . . ." He said my name as if it pained him.

"Please," I begged but there was no answer. "Please, Ethan. Please come with me."

He sighed and I felt my heart shatter into a million pieces. "I can't," he uttered.

Two simple words that destroyed every fiber in my soul.

I mustered the ability to say, "Take care," and then hung up the phone with the last shred of dignity I had left. I was on my own and in that moment I made a promise to myself.

I would never come back to Prescott.

Gasping for air, I press my hands to my chest to calm my rapid heartbeat. When I'm finally ready, I stand up and say good-bye to my room one final time. Shutting the door behind me, I also close the final door to me and Ethan. A chapter that has finished.

My mother is standing at the bottom of the stairs waiting for me. Though she has a grin on her face, I can see the unshed tears in her eyes. "Do you really have to leave so soon?" she asks before giving me a tight hug.

I swallow back and nod. "I have a lot of work to catch up on and I'm assuming the merger there will probably come with some layoffs, too. I need to stay on top of my game."

My mother releases me and I glance over at my father. He is sitting on his recliner with the paper in his hands. Though walking around without assistance is hard for him, he is getting better each day. The sight of him home makes me smile brightly.

I walk over to him and grasp his hand. "Thank you again, Leslie, for everything. We wouldn't have survived these last few months if it weren't for you." His voice cracks on the last word and I lean down into his arms.

"Don't be silly." I try to brush away the tears that threaten to pour again. When I pull away there are tears in his eyes. "I'll see you both soon."

Once I told them both I had to leave and go back to work, I promised I would come back for a week in the summer. But the chances of that happening are slim. I'd much rather they come visit me instead. The faint horn outside the house lets me know my car service is here. Gently, I kiss my father on the cheek and walk over to my Mom to give her one final hug.

"Call me when you land?" she says, cupping my cheek.

"Yes." I smile and nod.

We've grown tremendously over the past few months. For the first time, I feel we have the mother-daughter relationship I have always wanted. If the past few months have taught me anything, it's that you can grow and let go of the past.

I lean in and kiss her on the cheek. "I love you, Mom."

She stares deeply into my eyes. "I'm so proud of you."

I know we will never go back to where we once were.

With my suitcase behind me, I walk to the black sedan and say good-bye one last time to Prescott.

Chapter Twenty Eight

PRESENT

Unlike LAX or O'Hare, there is a calmness in the Phoenix airport. No one seems to be in a rush to get to their destination and it all feels surreal. I tell myself it's the people who are off and acting strange and not the fact my heart is once again shattered into a million pieces as I make the familiar trek. My feet drag against the carpeted floors as I stroll toward the check-in gate. I don't bother moving the sunglasses from my face as I use them to shield my red puffy eyes. When the stewardess speaks to me about my baggage claim I just nod and move in slow motion. I am on autopilot and nothing around me seems to make any type of sense. I go with the motions and wheel my carry-on toward the TSA line. It's odd really, because I can't hear anything, I, myself, can't utter a sound. I just put one foot in front of the other and follow the crowd.

    I manage to make my way through TSA and down toward

the terminal. Unlike times before, I don't pull out my cell phone, I don't check social media; I simply sit there and stare out onto the tarmac filled with airplanes. Minutes pass or maybe it's hours, I'm not sure because I have no sense of time. No sense of emotion.

Nonetheless, boarding for the plane begins and I stand and follow the crowd as they line up to get on.

"Ladies and gentlemen, we are now boarding flight 8743 with a destination of Chicago, Illinois. We will be lining up by boarding group number."

My knee buckles and I stumble back, bumping into the person behind me. "Sorry," I mutter and from the corner of my eye I feel as if I see Ethan in my peripheral vision. Hopeful, I do a quick glance and stare at every person around me. I know that it's my subconscious, my heart begging once again to not leave the only person who can mend it back together. It's sad really when you realize you aren't as important to someone as you thought. You would think that with our history, with the life we lived and the love we shared that nothing would come between us.

I was wrong.

Some wounds don't ever heal. I'll learn to live with them. There are some bumps in the road you can never overcome, so you learn to turn yourself around and find a new road.

I close my eyes for a brief second and allow it all to sink in. One day he will only be a memory. It may not be today or tomorrow. Hell, it may take a year for me to let go. But with time, Ethan and I will be nothing but a memory.

Needing to leave it all behind me, I decide that Arizona is where I leave my heart. It's fitting really for it to stay here along with all my broken dreams.

Unlike every passenger on the plane, I don't unbuckle the seat belt once we taxi into our gate. Instead, I stare out the window and watch the workers unload the baggage off the plane. Everyone is in a rush to get back to their lives or on to the next journey, but I find myself stuck, unable to move. For the past two hours as we flew across the Midwest, my mind replayed the same thing over and over. How did I get here? How did I let myself become so weak? For eight years I took piece by piece and found the strength to move on. But this time I was more damaged than the last time.

"Ma'am," the stewardess says softly.

"Yes?" I pull my gaze away from the window and look over at her.

"We need you to exit the plane now." She glances back at the empty seats behind me.

"Oh, sorry." I say and stand. Nodding at the flight crew, I exit and walk up to the gate, then follow the signs to baggage claim.

My hands hold the railing as I step on the escalator that leads me down to the lower level baggage claim. Drivers and family wait for their families to arrive. I glance around for my car service guy when I spot him.

Ethan.

He has one hand tucked into his pocket and the other is holding up a white paper with Sutton written across it.

Slowly, I shake my head. Stepping off the escalator I walk past him and toward the carousal of luggage.

"Leslie, wait," I hear from behind me.

"No," I say and my voice is shaky. "You don't get to show up here and pretend nothing happened." I never pull my gaze away from the carousel.

"Just give me five minutes." He steps in front of me and I'm forced to stop walking.

"You have thirty seconds." I refuse to allow myself to look into his eyes.

"Do you remember the first night I climbed into your room?" He steps in and I can smell the scent of his cologne wafting in the air around me. Gently, he places his finger under my chin and lifts my face up to his. Our eyes meet and there's a tug at my heart. He looks like the broken Ethan I have always loved. "We had just moved in and my father was using my mother as a punching bag again. What you don't know is that I planned on killing my father that night." I narrow my eyes as he continues. "When we moved into that house my mother promised me that things would be different. She said my father just needed a change in his life and he would get help. But again, that was her defending him." Ethan swallows and lowers himself so we are eye to eye.

"That night as my mother cried and begged him not to hit her again. I walked out into the backyard and pulled out his shotgun that I had hidden under the deck." His words stun me. "Remember, I told you it was almost over." My mind locates the memory and I replay it over in my head. Tears pool in my eyes and I nod. "I figured killing him and going to jail were better than having to live in that house a day longer. I was at the lowest I'd ever been, and then I heard your voice. And that night, Leslie, you showed me something no one had ever shown me before. Kindness and compassion, something I had never experienced in my life. It was like you were my guardian angel." A tear drips down his face and I find myself reaching up to catch it.

"I knew then that as long as I had you in my life, living with Jerry would be bearable. I knew then, when I was ten years old, that I would love you for the rest of my life." His voice cracks and I find my lips quivering as I shake my head. He frames my face with both hands and presses his forehead to mine. "You're the only thing I believe in. You've made my darkest days brighter. Loving you is the only thing I know how to do. It's the only thing that keeps me alive. Please, Leslie. I fucked up. I know that and I will spend the rest of my life making it up to you. But please, don't let me go."

I close my eyes and the pain mixed with the love I have for him courses through my veins as if they are at war with each other. "You've been so distant, so different."

"I'm so sorry. When he finally died all of it hit me. The grief consumed me and I was reminded of the man he was. We always hurt the people we love the most, but I promise you with everything that I am, I will never hurt you again." He pulls me closer and kisses my lips. "Please, Leslie. I can't lose you."

The warm tears drip down my face. I want to forgive him. I

want to leap into his arms and have him kiss the pain away. But two broken souls will never live happily as one.

With everything in me I take a step back. Ethan's eyes widen and I see them fill with tears. "I can't." My voice is shaky. "I can't do this to myself. What we shared many moons ago was perfect. It was beautiful." I pause and bite down a sob that threatens to crawl up my throat. "But we are broken Ethan. And it doesn't matter how much we try to fix it. Our pieces are shattered into a million pieces." Slowly, he shakes his head not believing what I'm saying. I run my fingers under my eyes and inhale. "I will always love you but I can't forgive you."

"Leslie." His voice is hoarse and I know this pains him.

"I'm sorry, Ethan, but you have to let me go." I mutter and walk past him. My legs shake with each step I take, but I force myself to walk toward the carousel and grab my suitcase. I stand there for a few minutes letting the last fragments of my heart break before I look back to where he stood.

He's gone and I know that it's finally over.

The drive from O'Hare to my apartment in Chicago takes over two hours due to traffic. I allow myself to sit in the back seat of the car and stare out at the highway. My heart is aching but I know that I've made the best decision for myself. Being with Ethan is what I've always wanted but there's too much water under the bridge to ever let us have what we both want. Though Jerry is dead and in the past, his memory haunts me. The fear of Ethan turning into him terrifies me to the core. The car pulls up to the sidewalk of my apartment and I slide my credit card through the machine and sign the receipt. My body moves in slow motion as I climb out of the car and around to meet the driver who has my suitcase in his hand. I smile kindly and thank him for his service. Turning toward the sidewalk my hand releases the suitcase handle and I gasp.

Ethan is sitting on the steps on my apartment. His hands rest on his knees as he watches me carefully. My heart tugs in my chest and I feel more tears swell in my eyes.

He stands and walks over to me. I wait in silence for him to speak as I'm afraid I have no strength left in me.

"I can't let you go." His voice is hoarse and I know from years of loving him that it is laced with pain.

"Ethan." I shake my head.

"Don't, Leslie." He steps forward and takes my hands in his. "We aren't broken. On the contrary, what we lived, what we've experienced, it's what makes us whole." I feel my lips quiver and Ethan frames my face. "The best part of me has always been you. I can't lose you again. I refuse to let you go."

I pull away from his hold and look to the ground. "I can't do this again. I'm sorry but I think it's best you go home." I don't look at him as I gather my belongings and head toward my front door.

He doesn't stop me.

He doesn't follow me.

He let's me go inside.

I sit in my house for two days drinking my pain away and eating Ramen. By Monday morning I'm dressed and ready to head to the office. I'm not due back for another few weeks but I figure making an appearance around the new bosses will be a good idea. I grab my keys from the hook near the door and head down the stairs. When I pull the door open, Ethan is sitting on the top step. I gasp when he looks up at me.

"What are you doing?" I can't hide the surprise in my voice.

"I told you, I'm not letting you go." He stand ups and brushes his hands to dust off his jeans.

"So, you've been living on my doorstep like a bum?" I say and close the door behind him.

"I have no choice, it's not that easy to climb into your bedroom." Ethan gives me a boyish grin. "You look nice."

"Thanks." I say nervously and look down to the ground. "I have to head into the office."

"I see." He shoves his hands in his pocket. "I'll be here."

"Ethan." I say and pause before exhaling. "I'm not changing

BROKEN DREAMS

my mind. You should go home, Charlie needs you."

"I need you more. I'm not leaving Leslie, not until you forgive me for being an asshole."

"Don't hold your breath." I pull the straps of my purse higher on my shoulder and head toward the train station.

I arrive in the office at a quarter to eight. Though I should feel excited to be back, I can't shake the knowledge that Ethan spent the night on my steps. The thought is quickly brushed away when Chloe comes out of her office to greet me.

"Oh, thank heavens you're back." She says and gives me a tight embrace. "I have missed the living hell out of you."

I laugh and hug her back. "What's new here?" I ask as I follow her inside her office.

"Girl, it's crazy." Her eyebrows furrow together. "I know you and I don't have anything to be worried about but there will be a big budget cut and a lot of people will be losing their jobs."

"That sucks." I sit back on her chair and sigh in relief that at least I'll have a job.

"I have so much to catch you up on, are you staying for lunch?"

"Yeah I have a meeting with HR in a few. Want to go to River Roast? We can sit outside." I smile remembering the taste of their infamous cocktails.

"Oh, that sounds good, but it's supposed to pour soon. Maybe Marty's?"

I don't answer her question; instead, my mind is invaded with Ethan sitting outside in the rain. "Yeah," I nod uncertainly. "That's fine."

The dark clouds loom over the skies, that warm crisp spring air has vanished and is replaced with a chill. I arrive home by two in the afternoon, though I skipped lunch with Chloe, my meeting with HR ran late. I'm sprinting down my block, my shoes soaked from the torrential down pour as I try to find Ethan.

I tried to force him out of my mind, I tried to get over what we shared but as Lisa, with human resources went over the new company's policy all I could think about was a life with Ethan. A home we could share together and love that we could mend and fix.

My heels splash through the puddles and when I reach my steps I'm gasping for air.

"Do you want kids?" I mutter out desperate for air to fill my lungs.

Ethan, who is soaked even though his body is covered with a plastic poncho looks deep into my eyes. "With you?" I nod before inhaling. "I want a whole team of kids with you."

"Would you mind living in Chicago or do you want to live in Arizona?" I say as my soaked hair sticks to my face.

"Freckles," He stands and takes my hands with his. "It doesn't matter if we live in the desert or the Antarctic. I will follow you to the moon. I will sit out here for the next ten years if I have too. I will do whatever you want until you realize that in this world you were made for me and I'm never letting you go."

I lace my hands around his body and bring my face to his chest. I tremble from the cold but also from the fear that I'm throwing caution to the wind to be with him. "I was pregnant and I lost the baby." I whimper and I feel his hands tighten around my body. "I found out the day you went crazy on Michael."

Ethan pulls away and locks his surprised gaze on mine. "When?"

"That night," I confess on a sob.

Ethan shakes his head and pulls me into his embrace again. This time we stay that way for a few minutes crying over the pain that will forever live inside of us. "I'm sorry, it's all my fault." He whispers and I can feel his body shaking.

This time I pull away and frame his face. "It's not your fault." I say and I can honestly believe it with everything inside of me. I know now that God had a different plan for Ethan and me; that I needed some time to forgive him, and forgive myself before we could move forward. "Sometimes shit happens. Sometimes the universe makes choices for us because it sees the potential we still have. I don't blame you. I don't hate you. Forgiving is what makes us grow. It's what soothes our souls."

"I've never deserved you." He shakes his head.

"And no one has ever loved me like you." I feel a smile grow on my face. "We may not be perfect and it will take some time for us to ever be the way we were, but I'm willing to try."

"Leslie Sutton," he says and frames my face with his hands. "I will spend the rest of my life trying to make it up to you. I promise to love you, and cherish you every single day for as long as you'll let me."

Gently, Ethan leans in and kisses me like he has done a million times before. It's a kiss filled with love, hope and a chance of forever. Sometimes you need to hit rock bottom, shatter your dreams in order to create new ones.

When I first left to go to Arizona, never did I imagine my new dream would be to run a ballet studio or have a family. But now with Ethan in my arms, it's the only dream I wish to have come true.

CALLIE ANDERSON

Epilogue

PRESENT

One year later.

My fingers quickly move against the keyboard as I type out emails to my friends. One to Lyra that's filled with stories about her mother and me in college. The second to Chloe. And the last email is to Stephanie. Though I stayed in Prescott with Ethan, she ventured off with Bruce and they currently resided in Savannah.

Dear Steph,

So, I just left your mother's office. My heart is pounding. I'm both fearful and excited to tell Ethan. I really should learn to take my pills at the same time every day so this doesn't happen. Anyway, how's Georgia? And Bruce? I can't believe you guys spent a weekend in the Bahamas because you were bored. Must be nice! Your mother misses you, of course, and I miss you tremendously. I can't wait to see you at Thanksgiving!

Love, Les.

"Babe?" Ethan's voice bellows through the house.

"Babe?" Charlie repeats after Ethan.

Smiling, I close my laptop and head out to the living room. "Yes?" I say when my eyes land on Ethan.

"Gray or Taupe?" he asks before placing a small kiss on my lips. From the corner of my eyes I see Charlie scrunch his nose and I smile.

"For what?" I rest my hands on my hips. Over the last few months, Ethan and I decided it was time we got a place that wasn't in the center of town. It wasn't that I didn't love his apartment. It made my commute to work a hop and a skip across the street. But living over a restaurant and bar meant that falling asleep at a decent hour was nearly impossible.

"Tiles in the master bathroom." He opens up the cabinet and pulls out three plates.

"Neither. I would like to have an all-white bathroom."

"Told ya," Charlie says, and opens the white paper bag that is sitting in the center of the island. "Leslie said that two weeks ago." I hadn't noticed the food earlier but the second Charlie's hands pull out the tray of food my stomach turns and I'm gagging.

My hands rush to my mouth as I sprint to the bathroom. Once I've emptied out my stomach and rinsed my mouth, I find a concerned Ethan waiting outside the bathroom door. "You okay?"

A grin grows on my face. "I wasn't going to tell you till later."

"Tell me what?"

"I'm pregnant." I watch Ethan's eyes widen.

"Does that mean you're having a baby?" Charlie asks, and I nod.

BROKEN DREAMS

Unable to pull my gaze away from Ethan, I watch his every move. We've talked about having kids. We both want them but we've talked marriage first, a home, and then kids. His Adam's apple bobs and he shakes his head.

"No."

My lips pursed in confusion. "What do you mean, no?"

"No, you can't be pregnant." He walks over to the console table and grabs his keys.

"Are you serious?"

He turns back and a grin grows on his face. "You can't be pregnant unless you're my wife." He drops down on one knee and presents me with a ring.

Butterflies flap their ginormous wings in my belly. Ethan always seems to amaze me. "Leslie Sutton, my best friend, love of my life, mother of my child. Will you do the honor of being my wife?"

With a few short strides I'm standing before him. Tears fill his eyes and I nod. "A million times yes."

Four years later.

Warm water trickles down my leg. The feeling is all too familiar. Standing in Logan's bedroom, I wince from the pain that shoots around my large belly.

"Mommy, Mommy, are you okay?" He looks up at me with his daddy's green eyes.

"Yup, honey, everything is fine. I'm going to need you to be a good boy, okay?" I tell him as pain shoots straight through me. "Can you grab, Mommy's phone?" I ask and point to it on the other side of his carpet.

"Okay." He nods and walks it over to me.

Breathing in slowly, I unlock my phone and call Ethan. "Hello?" I can hear screaming and crazy fans all around him. He's taken Charlie to see the Arizona State Sun Devils play

UCLA.

"Hi. I'm so sorry to bother you." I wince from another contraction. "But it's time."

"*Fuck!*" he screams.

"Ooooh, Daddy said a bad word," Logan says, pointing to the phone.

I quickly smile and take in a deep breath. "Language."

"I told you I shouldn't have come to this game."

"It's okay. I've done this before. I'll call my mom."

"I'll be there as soon as I can." Ethan says and I hang up the phone before he has a chance to argue about me forcing him to take Charlie to the game since I was thirty-nine weeks pregnant.

"Hi, Mom. My water just broke. Do you think maybe you can take me to the hospital, and Lindsey can stay with Logan?"

I feel another contraction coming and slowly let out a breath. Tiny hands find mine. As I open my eyes, I see perfect green eyes staring at me with concern.

"Yes, of course. I'll be right over,"

I thank my lucky stars every day that Ethan took the time to teach her how to drive again.

Tossing my phone to the side, I grasp Logan's hand. "You don't need to be scared. Mommy is okay. It's just your little sister throwing a fit." I kiss his forehead and run my hands through his light ash brown hair.

"Was I throwing a fit when I was in your belly, Mommy?" he asks

"Oh, yes, except you decided to do this to Mommy at two in the morning." I walk over to my bedroom and pull out my hospital bag along with Logan's book bag. It was then reality set in—our little family was gaining one new member.

I make my way up the maternity wing. My mom is at my side as I'm greeted at the nurse's station. They wheel me into my room. Aside from the contractions every once in a while, I feel fine. There is pressure but nothing too painful.

"Are we ready to do this again?" Mrs. Carey says as she walks into the room.

"It was a long summer. I'm so very ready."

Mrs. Carey examines me. "You're about five centimeters. This one might be faster than Logan," she jokes. When I came into the hospital to give birth to Logan my labor from beginning to end lasted eight hours. Ethan and Charlie were two hours away.

"Can we slow it down? Ethan's on his way. He took Charlie to an ASU game."

"That depends on your body," she says before checking my blood pressure. "I'll make my rounds then I'll come back to check on you."

I nod, unable to speak as another contraction curls up my stomach.

At the six-hour mark, I was ten centimeters dilated and ready to push.

"Wait, I'm here!" Ethan runs into the room.

Finally," I say as I gasp for air. "I've been holding this baby in just for you."

Ethan places a sweet, wet kiss on my lips and grabs my hand. "I'm here now. How about we go and have us a little girl?"

It takes five pushes after her father arrives before Loren Joyce Prescott is born.

Like Logan, her name symbolizes the flower we've tattooed on our body along with a grandmother's name. Mrs. Carey places her on my chest and Ethan cries as he kisses me.

She's perfect with ten little toes and ten little fingers, and a full head of chocolate brown hair.

"You did good, Freckles," Ethan says as he brushes my hair back.

When we're ready for visitors, Ethan steps out and brings Logan in to meet his baby sister. I hold her as Ethan sits on the bed with Logan in his arms. "Logan, this is Loren, your baby sister," I say to him.

"Hello, Loren. I'm your big brother," he say and gently touches her hand.

A tear drips from my eye and I'm filled with joy. This is the family I have always dreamed of having.

THE END

ABOUT THE AUTHOR

MORE BOOKS BY CALLIE ANDERSON

TORRID AFFAIR

CALLIE ANDERSON

PART I

My life was a black hole.

Trapped in a loveless marriage, I was empty, numb. Oblivious to it all.

Until him.

He was the spark that brought me back from the abyss. He was my fire.

But our love was forbidden.

Between the lies, that fire began to take over my soul. That need to feel wanted had me escaping my life, running toward him no matter the consequences.

They say you shouldn't play with fire.

But I *needed* to feel the burn.

CHAPTER ONE

Brielle

Present

I sit on my king-size bed and stare at the dull white wall. It's the only surface in my bedroom I haven't decided what to do with. When we moved into this apartment, Julian and I couldn't agree what to put there. At the time, I thought it was a perfect spot for a bassinet. Now I shake my head at the memory. Eight years have passed. Ten since he first knocked on my door.

I draw up my legs and rest my chin on my knee, the empty wine glass held up by my fingertips. My gaze is still glued to the two coats of eggshell paint that cover the drywall. My throat suddenly tightens and I blink as a lone tear falls down my cheek.

He's late.

Again.

The sad part is that I don't have to look at the clock. I know it's past midnight. I feel it deep in my gut. *Something is off.* Something's always wrong when he's late.

My heart races as I contemplate all the places he could be at this very moment, but the fading purple bruises on my arms and the scar on my left cheek remind me why I no longer let my mind go there.

BROKEN DREAMS

I learned not to ask questions.

I glance down at my large diamond engagement ring that sits next to my wedding band and I lower my chin to my chest, swallowing back a sob. How is this a better life?

He came back for me. He was here when I needed him most. And I made a vow. So I look at my blank wall. It's a reminder of what I am. Empty and alone. Perhaps that's the reason I choose not to do anything to it. It's depressing, like my life.

Misery loves company.

My stomach churns. I'm desperate to know the time, so I pull my gaze away from the wall and over to my clock.

It's a quarter to one.

I pour myself another glass of Sauvignon Blanc.

My phone vibrates under the down comforter. The alcohol swooshes through my body and I'm woozy. The bright light blurs my vision and I squint at the screen.

Julian: I'm running late. I'll be home soon.

I scoff and toss my phone. He texts me *now*? It's almost two in the morning. I reach toward my nightstand for the bottle of wine.

I don't cry because I hate my life.

I don't cry because I no longer know the person who stares back at me in the mirror.

I cry because I realize the wine bottle is empty.

I fall to the floor and let out a guttural scream as tears cloud my vision. I don't deserve this. I wanted a different life. I had dreams!

I push myself off the floor and walk through the cold house. Reaching the bar, I open the bottle of Jameson and chug it back, letting the burn soothe my hurt. Anything to escape my reality.

Anything to make me feel numb.

I brush my lips with the back of my hand and focus on the

art supplies I abandoned in the corner. After dinner I played with the canvas I was working on since Julian didn't come home. A faint smirk touches my mouth.

Oh, how different my life was meant to be. I wanted to be an artist. The dream of majoring in art and moving to Europe to intern at the Louvre was also snatched away from me. I wanted to see the world. Instead, I worked at a local paint supply store where I, on occasion, painted wall murals in nurseries.

If I could go back and find that one crack, that first chip, the one that ultimately broke us . . .

Nathaniel.

Not a what, but a who. He shattered my heart and my soul.

He shattered *me*.

This is all *his* fucking fault.

My bare feet slap against the hardwood floor as I march to my paint. Though I feel the effects of the alcohol, I push past it and grab a brush and gallon. Half drunk, half depressed, I stumble back to my bedroom and toward the dull white wall.

Once I finish, I drop the brush and crawl back to bed. My head woozy, I pull the covers over my body. The hallway light flicks on and I know Julian is home. The second he steps into our bedroom I smell cheap perfume. He was with someone tonight. The musky scent of sex wafts through the air. New tears pool in my eyes.

I need to leave. I need to get out of here. But my own demons keep me here.

I keep my eyes closed as he undresses. The endless possibilities of where he has been begin to haunt me. When the shower turns on I go after him. I can't keep living like this.

I kick the door open and my gaze lands on his. I gasp. Not because he is standing over the sink regarding me like a trespasser, but because of the scratches on his back. I know those types of marks. They're the ones you make on a man to let his wife know she's not the only woman he fucks.

My vision blurs. "You bastard." The words slip out of my mouth. "Who is she?" My voice is hoarse.

Julian turns to face me. He's naked and the sight of him

BROKEN DREAMS

makes my stomach turn. "It's not what you think."

"I don't deserve this, you selfish prick! You're a worthless excuse of a man!"

Julian's raises his hand. With one swift motion it collides with my face and tosses my head to the side. My cheek burns, and for a second I can't see.

"I've told you not to ask me anything. The job I have. The things I do, I do them for you."

Exhausted and emotionally drained, I trudge back to my bed. Minutes pass before the comforter on the bed is pulled back. I hold my breath. I can't stay here. I refuse to live like this anymore. I don't want to leave my home, but if Julian is ever to change, I need to face my fears.

I need to see Nathaniel.

The following morning, the sun peers through the window and warms my skin. I squint and notice that my bed is empty. *Of course he's gone.* Wiping the sleep off my face, I look at the wall. It is no longer blank and empty, but vibrant red. I shake my head and immediately regret it as a piercing headache blurs my vision. *Why did I think alcohol would help?*

My body aches as I roll out of bed and spot Julian's clothes from last night piled on the floor. My stomach turns as I'm reminded of his scent. Dashing to the bathroom, I wash my face and pop two Advil into my mouth to soothe my headache.

I emerge from the bathroom dragging my feet, and stop at the wall. This is the moment of clarity. No. I shake my head in disbelief. I can't—no, I *refuse*—to live like this.

For ten years I've avoided my past. For ten years I've given Julian my all. But enough is enough. I'm going back. Though it will kill me and open wounds that have never fully healed, Nate is the only one he will listen to. I inhale all the air my lungs will take. With my head high and my shoulders back, I march into my closet and pull out my suitcase.

CHAPTER TWO

Brielle

11 years ago.
I felt as if I had run a marathon. No, an Iron Man. *Those were more excruciating.* I was exhausted but my roommate, Delaney, insisted we unpack and put away all our stuff before class started. She also convinced me to move into the dorm a week earlier than *she* needed to. Her classes didn't start until the following Monday, so there was no need for her to move in right away. My classes started Day One of the semester, so I'd planned to drive back to campus, leave my crap in boxes, sleep in, and order out.

She was a pain in my ass but I loved her like my sister.

Delaney had been my roommate for the past three years and was a complete neat freak. Which was probably why we got along. I, myself, had a few OCD tendencies but neatness was not one of them.

The alarm on my phone began to ring and I wished I had twenty more minutes, *or a few hours.* I inhaled as I willed my body to wake up.

"For the love of God." Delaney's groggy voice lets me know she was as tired as I was.

"Sorry, Del." I hit the off button on the alarm and stretched my hands over my body. "You're the one who wanted to move in yesterday," I reminded her.

"You're the only person I know who likes morning classes," Delaney complained as she pulled the covers to her chin.

I sat up, wiping the sleep from my eyes. "It's the only time Professor Comeau teaches it."

I heard her breathing slow and I knew she had fallen back asleep. I tiptoed to the dresser and pulled out my clothes before heading to the communal bathroom. It *was* really early for class, but that meant the showers were empty and I was able to stay under the hot water for a few extra minutes.

Once I was dressed, I headed back to my room to drop off my bathroom caddy, double check which side of campus we were meeting on for class, and grab my bag. To my surprise, there was a new email from my mother. Not only was it too early for class but it was definitely too early to read what my mother had to say. She only emailed me with bad news. I moved the mouse past her email and clicked on the one from Professor Comeau that stated our meet location had changed to the Bissell House.

"Bissell House?" I whispered.

"Literally across campus," Delaney huffed.

"Did I wake you again?"

"No, I snoozed for a bit but I can't get comfortable. I probably need to get used to getting up early. I promised my mother that this semester she would see all A's and I really need to get my shit together." She yawned and sat up on her bed. Her raven hair was pin straight so it appeared almost blue, and her dark gray eyes were shaped like almonds, making her look exotic.

"We'll see how long that lasts." I smirked. Every semester she tried to get up early and get ahead of her classes. It usually lasted two weeks before she started waking up ten minutes before class began.

"Whatever. You're the one who'll be late." She stuck her tongue out at me.

"Late?" I looked down at the clock. I still had thirty minutes before class started.

"Bissell is across campus and University City Blvd has a lane closed because they've been doing construction all summer. Now you have to cut through campus with all the new freshman who have no idea where they're going, which means traffic chaos. Hence, you'll be late."

Crap! "Shit!" I slammed my laptop closed, grabbed my stuff, and headed out of the dorm. There were two things I hated in life: lies and tardiness.

The warm Charlotte air still carried a scent of summer. Moving here from Chicago was a drastic weather change. I didn't mind the heat, but I missed the fall months, the cool, crisp morning air that let you know winter was coming. It was the end of August and I was in a T-shirt and shorts due to the eighty-plus-degree weather.

Delaney was dead on about the traffic through campus. My fingers gripped the steering wheel tighter. A seam of sweat began to build down my spine, and my knee bounced up and down as the stress of arriving late started to rear its ugly head.

A few minutes later, I pulled into Bissell House. To my luck, there was a parking spot available. I released my death grip on the steering wheel and activated my blinker. Just as I began to turn the wheel, a Ford Explorer cut in front of me and took my spot.

"Seriously!" I shouted. The jackass hopped out of his car and strode past my car like nothing ever happened. "Are you kidding me! That was my freaking spot!"

"My bad," was all he said and then continued to walk.

It took another ten minutes before I found an open spot and met up with the rest of the class. This was *not* how I wanted to start the semester.

"Every building has a style and its own history," Professor Comeau explained to the class, which gathered around him in a half circle. His back was to the Bissell House as he continued. "Not only will you learn to read buildings, but you'll know why they were built and for whom." I stopped and stood toward the rear. "You." He paused and pointed at me. The entire class followed his finger and I was greeted with their gazes, including the ass who took my parking spot. Of course he was in this class. Why else would anyone be at the Bissell House so early in the morning? "Is eight a.m. too early for you?"

I cleared my throat. "No, sir. It was a parking issue." My gaze pulled away from the older man with the gray hair and a bushy beard and landed on the guy who had taken my parking spot. "It won't happen again." I crossed my arms over my chest.

Professor Comeau continued with the syllabus, but parking spot stealer continued to stare at me. For the first time I stopped mentally cursing him and actually admired him. He was taller than anyone else in the class, lean, dressed in a graphic T-shirt and worn out jeans. His dark hair was trimmed short, and once my gaze focused on his eyes I couldn't stop gawking. They were light green with hazel specks floating in them. *Thank you, God, for blessing me with perfect vision.* His eyes were captivating. The most beautiful things I had ever seen.

He gently licked his lips and smiled.

All the anger I had toward him vanished in thin air. This perfect man could have my parking spot any time he wanted as long as he smiled at me.

People began to move and someone bumped into me, shaking me out of his hold. I blinked and forced my legs to move. Professor Comeau had assigned us to study the Bissell House and four other buildings on campus. *Two hours of staring at buildings and appreciating them?* This would be the easiest class I had ever taken at UNC.

I took out my notepad and began to sketch everything I noticed about the building. Its four white columns, the double chimneys, the perfectly trimmed and manicured garden. I was counting the windows when I felt his presence near me. I swallowed the ball of nerves that had coiled in my throat and looked up at him.

Crap, he was hot. *Very freaking hot.*

"Yes?" I questioned when he didn't speak. I gnawed on the

inner part of my lip as I waited for him to say something.

A grin grew on his face and I squeezed my grip on my pen until my fingernails were digging into my palm. *How had I been on campus for three years and never noticed him?*

"I'm sorry." He shrugged. "If I'd known you would be late for class, I wouldn't have taken your spot." He was apologizing, but all I could focus on was the way his voice made the butterflies in my stomach triple in size. I blamed the dizziness and gawking on the fact I was exhausted.

"It's . . . D-Don't," I stuttered. "No biggie." I inhaled and blinked nervously.

"I'm Nathaniel. Nathaniel Wright."

I felt my cheeks flush. "Is this where you tell me that you're Mr. Wright or Mr. Right Now?" I lifted my chin toward him and grinned. "Please don't tell me that's your pick up line." I giggled.

"No." He chuckled. "My pick up line is more profound."

"Really?" I widened my eyes. "I must hear this." I turned to face him.

He cleared his throat in preparation. "Excuse me. How much does a polar bear weigh?"

"Ahh." I bit my lower lip contemplating my answer. "I don't know."

"Enough to break the ice." He smiled and extended his hand. "I'm Nate."

"Brielle." I couldn't hold back the smile that grew on my face as I reached for his hand.

"Brielle," he repeated my name. "It fits you."

"How so?"

"It's unique and beautiful." He winked. "Just like you."

Guys. Most were cocky, arrogant and over the top. My eyes rolled. "You just can't stop it, can you?"

"Stop what?"

"Your terrible one-liners." I shoved my notepad back in my bag and turned to walk away. "Have a good day, Nathaniel Wright." I did find him charming. *Even if it was only a tad bit.*

"Wait!"

His footfalls grew closer behind me. I turned and was greeted with his tall frame. His hand ran through his low cut hair and he gnawed his lower lip for a few seconds before he spoke again.

"Come on, let me take you out? It's the least I can do since I took your parking spot."

I shifted my weight from one foot to the other. I hadn't been out with someone since I broke up with Trent last semester. "I—I . . . uh . . ." Clearly, I was developing a stutter around this guy.

"Do you have a boyfriend?"

"No. Do you have a girlfriend?" I retorted.

"No." He shook his head in defense. "Just figured you were thinking of a way to let me down easy." Nate stepped closer. He smelled as though he'd just stepped out of the shower, fresh with a hint of cologne. It was manly but not overpowering. "Come on, Brielle. Have dinner with me?"

I sighed. "Fine. I'll go out with you, Wright." *How could I say no?*

He pressed both of his hands under his chin as though he was about to pray. "So, my pick up line worked after all."

"Seriously! You're pushing your luck, buddy." I shook my head, but my cheeks hurt from grinning. "Unreal."

"Does tomorrow work?"

"Yeah. I get off work at seven. Just tell me where to meet you."

"I can pick you up." His tongue slid across his lip, causing my stomach to twist.

"I've seen you drive, so there is no way I'm getting in a car with you." I smiled and patted his chest. "Plus, you could be a stalker. I don't want you to know where I work or live."

"Fair enough." He lifted his hands in defeat. "DefyGravity, eight o'clock." Nate gave me one last boyish smile before he turned and walked away.

I sucked my lower lip between my teeth to hide my

excitement. Maybe this was going to be a good year.

Nathaniel

I walked away from Brielle, knowing this class was now my favorite. There was something about her that piqued my interest. I blamed her short shorts that hugged her small waist.

I'd originally planned to withdraw from the class. I'd already studied every building on this campus when I took a similar class at the community college, so I showed up because I needed a signature from Professor Comeau to drop the class. But after my encounter with Brie, I walked back to my car and headed over to the financial aid office to make sure I was covered for it.

The line was out the door with students who had issues with registration and others who wanted to add or drop classes. I thought I'd beat the rush, but when there were at least twenty people in front of me I knew I'd be here for most of the morning.

Slowly, everyone began to move up the line. I was next to be called when a buddy of mine from high school came by to chat.

"Hey, man." He extended his hand. "I didn't know you were coming here."

"Yeah." I shifted my weight from one foot to the other. "This is my first semester."

"How's Julian?"

"Good. He's around here somewhere." Unlike me who fucked around for a year, Julian had come to UNCC right out of high school.

"I'm having a party at the frat house Thursday night. Come through." Rick had always been known for the craziest house parties. Once he convinced every sorority and fraternity to cancel their parties so no one else would go anywhere but to his home.

"I just made plans." I shrugged. "Maybe next time." I had two years left in college and I refused to fuck it up now.

"Of course you have a date. Still the same Nate who hooks up with all the bitches." That was a lie. I was simply a friendly guy.

"Next!" a female voice shouted from the small office.

"I'll catch you around, Rick." I held my financial aid papers and marched toward the office.

WANT TO READ THE REST?
Download it now!

https://www.amazon.com/Torrid-Affair-Callie-Anderson-ebook/dp/B01LXH328U

Made in the USA
Middletown, DE
26 September 2018